The Wright Kind of Love:

Toby and Niecey

The Wright Kind of Love:
Toby and Niecey

Genesis Woods

www.urbanbooks.net

Urban Books, LLC
300 Farmingdale Road, N.Y.-Route 109
Farmingdale, NY 11735

The Wright Kind of Love: Tobey and Niecey
Copyright © 2019 Genesis Woods

ISBN 13: 978-1-62286-199-6
ISBN 10: 1-62286-199-X

First Trade Paperback Printing September 2019
Printed in the United States of America

10 9 8 7 6 5 4 3 2 1

Distributed by Kensington Publishing Corp.
Submit Orders to:
Customer Service
400 Hahn Road
Westminster, MD 21157-4627
Phone: 1-800-733-3000
Fax: 1-800-659-2436

Tobias

Watching Niecey on the dance floor had me smiling to myself as I sat at our groomsmen table and ran my finger around the rim of my shot glass. My twin brother's wedding reception was beginning to wind down, but there were still people out there partying like the night had just begun. I looked at the watch on my wrist and knew that if I didn't start to clear this place out, I'd be stuck here until five in the morning, counting receipts and making sure everything was locked up and put up in its proper place. It was something I didn't want to do and would more than likely put off, seeing as I had other things on my mind.

My eyes connected to a set of eyes that I would soon be spending the rest of my life with within a few months as I looked back out at the dance floor. Those tawny-colored irises with specks of golden brown held my gaze and made my dick twitch in my pants. Her smooth, walnut-colored skin was calling for my mouth and fingers to caress. She bit her full bottom lip and lowered her eyes when she noticed me uncrossing my legs and adjusting myself underneath the table. I smiled, and she sexily nodded her head while sticking out the tip of her tongue to wet her lips.

I bit the inside of my cheek to stop myself from getting up out of this seat and bending her little ass over the cake table and fucking the shit out of her. My little vixen knew what she was doing and had no shame about it. I watched as she slowly started to move her body to the beat of whatever song was playing. Her hands moved up and down her curvy frame, taunting me to come and take hold of what I had already proclaimed as mine.

My eyes skimmed over the purple lace bridesmaid dress she had on that hugged her figure in all of the right places. Some sort of silky material clinging to her body, hardly leaving anything to the imagination. Every dangerous curve from her round, melonlike breasts to the dip and expansion between her waist and hips were showcased, and I couldn't wait to get my hands on any of it. My sister-in-law, Audrielle, did pick out a beautiful dress for her bridesmaids; too bad that shit was going to be in the trash by the end of the night. Two hundred fifty dollars of my hard-earned money gone to waste.

Loosening the tie from around my neck, I unbuttoned the first three buttons of my dress shirt, swallowed the remaining shot of my drink, then slouched back in my seat. For some reason, my body started to become really hot, and I needed to calm it down.

Just when I was about to throw all caution to the wind and give Niecey what she was clearly asking for, a hand identical to mine, but with a platinum set princess-and-baguette 3.17-carat men's diamond band on the ring finger, stopped me.

"I see Niecey's ass is out there testing your patience."

"Bro!" I wiped my hand down my face, massaging the five o'clock shadow that I had recently started to wear. "She knows how I am. If she doesn't stop, I'm going to give your remaining guests a show they will never forget."

Cairo laughed. "Man, you have an office in the back, a kitchen over there, and a few bathrooms throughout this spot. Surely, you can pick one of those places to give it to your girl, or you can just hold off like I've been trying to do since I laid eyes on my baby."

His gaze drifted over to his bride, Audri, who was dancing with her father in her beautiful Pnina Tornai V-neck princess wedding dress. A small smile played at the corner of his mouth as he marveled at his bride. The look he had on his face right now was the same look I was sure I would have on mine the day that Niecey walked down the aisle to me.

"Man, I don't know if I could make it. Do you see how she's moving her body out there?" I looked back out to where Niecey was last dancing and noticed that she had disappeared.

"Looks like her mind is in the same place as yours," Cai said, nodding in the direction of my office. Niecey's round backside drew all of my attention as I watched her sexily walk down the hallway and out of sight.

"I think I should—"

Cairo held up his hand to cut me off. "You go handle your business. I was just coming over to tell you that Audri and I will be heading out in a few. The twins and Aniya are already asleep, so now will be the perfect time for us to make an escape and handle our business without having any interruptions from them. We're leaving for Jamaica in a week. When we come back, let's sit down and talk about this new business you're trying to open."

I nodded my head, then stood up and gave my twin a brotherly hug. Although he and I had only met for the first time about a year ago, you could not tell that we were ever separated at birth by how close we'd become. That twin connection is crazy. It had gotten so bad that I even felt the symptoms of Audri's last pregnancy when he was feeling them. The throwing up, dry heaving, headaches, and sleepiness . . . Let's just say that whenever I pop one in Niecey, payback will definitely be a bitch for him.

After giving Cai another hug and congratulating him on his nuptials, I walked down from the VIP section of my club, weaved through the few bodies still swaying on the dance floor, then proceeded down the hallway to my office. The Black Opium Yves Saint Laurent perfume that I'd bought for Niecey a few weeks ago lingered in the air and guided my nose in the direction that she had gone.

Walking up to my office door, I could feel the growth of my dick strain against my pants. If I didn't free him sometime soon, I'd have to take these pants to the cleaners to get the zipper repaired before I returned it to the tuxedo place. Slowly turning the knob, I opened the door and walked in but didn't see Niecey anywhere in sight. The only thing that I did get a glimpse of was her purple bridesmaid dress pooled on the floor in front of my desk and her panties and strapless bra hanging from the edge of my computer.

"Niecey," I called out, but there was still no answer. I closed the door behind me and walked farther into my office, removing my tie, shirt, shoes, pants, and socks along the way. By the time I got to the door of the private bedroom I had added on a few years ago, I was completely naked. With my dick standing at full attention, I slid the door open and almost came at the sight before me. Niecey was rocking her hips over the vibrating seven-inch dong attached to the velvety, inflatable cushion hot seat as if she were riding me.

My hand instantly went to my dick and started to stroke it back and forth. Precum sat at the tip of my mushroom head, begging to be licked off by her pretty pink tongue. A soft moan escaped my lips, which had her opening her eyes and looking directly at me. The lust that radiated from those brown irises made me grow another inch in length. As if they had a mind of their own, my bare feet began to saunter over the soft, white carpet and closer to my freaky little wife-to-be.

Niecey reached her hand out and took over the back and forth rhythm of my hand as soon as I got within arm's length of her. Before I could savor the feel of her palm gripping my pulsating dick, her soft lips pulled the head of my shit into her warm mouth and then into the back of her throat.

"Fuuuck, Niecey," I hissed. The vacuum-suction grip she had on me almost made me cum in her mouth. I had to count backward from ten and think about the football game I had watched over the weekend to stop myself from releasing all of my seeds at that moment. "Damn it, baby. Slow down."

She stopped moving her head and just held my cock down her throat as far as she could. The vibration of her vocal cords started to massage my head as she began to hum. My head fell back in total pleasure when she did that. Snaking my right hand into the updo hairstyle, I removed a few bobby pins and grabbed a handful of it. I took my left hand and placed it on her shoulder, trying to steady myself to keep from falling. Using the grip I had on her hair, I slowly pulled myself a few inches from her throat and started to move her head back and forth. When I felt my dick start to tingle, I pulled her up from the squatting position she was in on the hot seat, slammed her against the wall, lifted her in my arms, and slammed into the tight, warm wetness I wanted to cum in.

"Fuck, Toby! That's it, baby. Right there!" Niecey screamed in my ear as she clawed at my back. I told her about doing that shit, but at this moment, I'd just take one for the team. Pushing her legs open a little wider, I sank my full length into her and didn't stop digging until I found gold. Her sweet, creamy essence decorated my stomach, balls, and thighs. My dick twitched, so I knew he was close to cumming too, but I needed to feel her wetness one more time before I would be able to release. Taking her lips into mine, I kissed her with every piece of soul I had within me. This woman right here was the only woman who could ever get this type of reaction from me. The only woman who could make me cum all inside of her and not care if she got pregnant with my seed. The only woman who could turn my world upside down and have me doing things I'd never done in my life.

Before Niecey, I had girlfriends here and there, but none that I moved into my home three months after dating and proposed in six months after having my nose wide open. I know a lot of people questioned how fast we were moving, but I didn't care. I would marry Niecey tomorrow if she wanted to, but for some reason, we hadn't set a date yet. Every time I brought up the subject, she either changed it or talked around it. I knew one thing, though; before this year was up, Niecey would be my wife, and we would live out our happily-ever-after, until death do us part.

ShaNiece

"Damn it, Tobias . . . Right there . . . baby!"

"What I tell you about calling me that?" Toby growled in my ear as he dipped his hips and pushed deeper into me. My eyes rolled to the back of my head the minute I felt his thick mushroom tip hit the back of my cervix.

"You said . . . you love . . . the way . . . I say . . . your naaameeee," I moaned between breaths. Toby pulled his head from the crook of my neck and looked me straight in the face, those greenish-blue irises looking straight through mine as if he were looking into my soul.

"You know I love you, right?"

I nodded my head and bit my bottom lip. Toby had my head high in the clouds just off of his stroke game alone. I could feel his member slowly swelling in size, letting me know that he was about to cum.

"I can't wait until you become my wife." He kissed my lips. "So that I can make love to you anytime I want."

"You already do," I breathlessly replied, wrapping my legs tighter around his waist.

"Not as much as I want to," he grunted, then picked up the pace. "When are you going to move back in with me?"

A few months after Toby and I got together, I moved into his downtown L.A. loft that had an amazing skyline view of the city. It wasn't because he asked me to, but more so because I couldn't stand all of the drama at my mother's house anymore. See, my twin sister LaNiece got pregnant and didn't know who the father of her baby was. At first, she claimed that the baby belonged to her boyfriend, Li'l Ray, but I soon found out that that was a lie. It wasn't until a family dinner we had one night at my mother's house that she revealed two more possibilities of who my niece's father could be. What was supposed to be me introducing Toby to my family for the first time turned into a Jerry Springer segment in a matter of seconds.

We were sitting at the dining room table at my mother's house and had just finished our main course. While we were waiting on her to return with dessert, I took that opportunity to catch up with my sister since we'd been missing each other in passing. When I turned in her direction and looked into her face, my whole body went still. My sister had tears rolling down her cheeks and was looking really upset. Her crying caused me to cry. I guess it was those twin vibes coming in full effect.

"What's wrong, LaLa? Is it the baby? You know you can tell me anything," I said as Toby started to rub my back.

I heard my ex-best friend, Mya, who was also at the dinner, smack her lips, but I paid her no mind. She and I had our own little issues going on. My mom finally returned with the pineapple upside-down cake and started to cut us each a piece.

"Niecey, I don't know how to tell you this, but—"

"Damn it, LaNiece, spit it out already!" our mother snapped.

She swallowed the lump in her throat. "Li'l Ray might not be my baby's father."

I wasn't shocked with that news because I knew my sister got around; yet, I was still confused by all of the tears and stuff. "OK . . . Who else could it be then?"

She hesitated for a second, then replied, "Jerome."

I know the look of confusion came across my face the minute she told me that name. "Jerome, as in your best friend JaNair's boyfriend, Jerome?"

She nodded her head. Toby, who was now on his second piece of cake, just shook his head. He not being as shocked as I was told me that this little bit of information wasn't news to him. Jerome was his boy, and they talked about everything, so I was sure he already knew. I made a mental note to ask him about that later and turned my attention back to my sister.

"Wow, LaLa! Does JaNair know?"

She shook her head, then took a deep breath. It seemed as if she had more to say and was trying to get up the nerve to say it.

"Jerome isn't the only possibility. There's one more person." The room got so quiet, and for some reason, I became nervous. I cut my eyes toward Toby, and he shook his head, silently answering the question that was swarming around in mine.

"Damn it, LaLa, stop beating around the bush and just spit it out already!" my mother snapped again.

"The other possible father is Big Will," LaLa finally blurted out.

My eyes instantly went to Mya, who sat back in her seat, smirking, then to my mother, whose hand was on her chest as she nodded her head.

I smiled and drew my bottom lip into my mouth, something I would do whenever I was trying to wrap my head around something. Did my twin sister just tell me that my on-again, off-again boyfriend since high school was possibly her child's father? I shook my head. I know she didn't just tell me that. Then again, if she could sleep with her best friend's man, why wouldn't she sleep with mine? I blew out a breath, then sat back in my chair. I looked at Toby, who was just sitting there all calm and collected like he didn't just hear what LaLa said. He knew all about my relationship with Big Will and what he and I went through, so he had to know that even though I was seeing him right now, I had to be hurting a little.

"I'm so sorry, Niecey," LaLa cried. "I never meant for that to happen. It was only one time, and if it's any consolation, it was during one of y'all off-again periods."

I threw my head back and started to laugh uncontrollably. This bitch was really and truly delusional. But I couldn't blame anybody but myself. I saw some of the ways LaLa treated her friends over the years and just assumed that she wouldn't do me, her twin sister, the same. I always thought blood was thicker than water, but now I could see that thickness didn't mean shit.

Once I came down from my fit of laughter, I looked at Toby and asked, "Are you ready to go, baby? Because I am."

Without another word, Toby and I got up from our chairs and went over to my mother's side of the table to say our goodbyes. After hugs, kisses, and foil-wrapped plates were given, I finally turned around to face my twin.

"You know, LaLa, I'm not even tripping off of Will possibly being your child's father, because as you can see"—I looked up at Toby lovingly—"I moved on to someone way better; someone who wouldn't even think about putting his dick in your corroded-ass pussy. So for that, you won't have any problem out of me."

Toby grabbed my hand after I finished saying what I needed to say and was leading our way to the door, but he suddenly stopped when I jerked my hand from his hold.

I turned around and walked back to LaLa. "As far as us being sisters, I can forgive you one day, I'm sure. However, the fact that you are my sister and would do something like this to me will never be forgotten."

The comforting smile on her face quickly turned into a look of terror when I charged into her so fast; LaLa never had time to react. I drew back my arm and slapped the shit out of her. I hit her face so hard, I'm pretty sure Toby, Mya, and my mom couldn't do anything but wince in pain and hold their own cheeks.

"Just so you know, that's just a little taste of what's gonna happen to you once you drop that baby," I screamed as Toby pulled me off of a damn near unconscious LaLa.

My attitude was already out of this world, so when I heard laughter coming from the end of the table, I turned my attention toward the source.

"And what the fuck are you laughing at, Mya? I can't wait until JaNair finds out that you fucked Jerome too. You know as well as I do that she's gonna beat the brakes off of both y'all's ass when she does. Hell, she done already kicked your ass outta her house and got you living from post to pillar. When will you ever learn? With friends like you and family like my sister, it's no wonder why bitches stay in and out of jail," I screamed at her dumb ass. "Please know and understand that this friendship—or whatever the fuck it is that we had—is now null and void. Don't call me for shit, don't ask me for shit, and don't even speak to me for shit when you see me in the streets."

My mom looked around the room and shook her head, disappointment etched across her face.

"Toby, can you please take Niecey with you for a few days? She and LaLa do not need to be in the same house right now."

Toby nodded his head, grabbed my hand again, and took me to his loft.

A couple of days later, after calming down a bit, I went back by my mom's house, packed up a few things, and unofficially moved in with Toby. Everything was going good between us . . . until the paternity test for LaLa's baby came back. When I found out that my niece, Aspen, belonged to Will and not the other possible fathers, I was really hurt.

Even though Will and I weren't together at the time, that still didn't take away from the fact that we were high school sweethearts, and he was my first everything. First kiss, first love, first sexual partner, and first heartbreak. And as much as I wanted to say that I hated him for the way that he treated me, I still had love in my heart for Will. Yeah, our relationship was toxic at times, but for some reason, we always found a reason to come back to each other.

I became so closed off to everyone, including Toby, after the results, that I moved out of his loft and got my own apartment a couple of weeks later. For a few months, I didn't talk to anyone or anybody associated with him, my family, or me. I felt so betrayed by the one person I thought would never do me wrong and wouldn't allow myself to trust anybody. It wasn't until Toby came to my new place and damn near busted my door down that I finally told myself to get over whatever it was that I was going through before I lost the one man who loved me unconditionally and accepted me, flaws and all.

The day that Toby came for me and talked me out of the depressed state that I was in was the day that I finally let go of everything my ex, Will, had ever done or would ever mean to me. I threw caution to the wind and opened my heart to the only man who continued to call me every single day, even though I wouldn't answer his calls. The same man who would send me lunch from my favorite restaurant at work every day, even though I wouldn't go out with him on any dates. And the same man who held me in his arms as I cried my eyes out for a couple of weeks over my ex, without feeling some type of way.

I looked into the beautiful eyes of this man as he released his seed into me and fell in love all over again.

I would do anything for Tobias Wright and his love. I would also stop at nothing to make sure that his heart continued to belong and beat for only me.

One year later

"Come on, Niecey, it's been months. You should've made up your mind by now."

"Toby, you act as if I don't spend damn near every night with you as it is."

"But it's not the same, babe."

"How is it not the same, Toby? Don't I have clothes already as well as a couple of toothbrushes there? Stuff for my hair?" I wrapped the spiral cord of the phone around my finger. "I even get a few pieces of mail at the loft. What more do you want?"

Toby blew out a frustrated breath on the other end of the phone. I could tell by the tone of his voice that he was getting tired of us having this conversation. But he had to understand I still enjoyed having my own space, and I just wasn't ready to fully move in with him again.

"I want to wake up to you every morning, knowing that I'll see that same beautiful face before I go to sleep that night. I want to argue about you taking up more than half of my closet space and coming up with some silly idea to make it better. Niecey, I want you and your friends to have girls' nights at our place, just so you can kick me out and tell me to come back in a few hours. I want us to be comfortable living together in our home so that after we get married, neither one of us will have to adjust to anything." Toby paused for a few seconds, his breathing slightly slowing. "Baby, I'm starting to feel like I'm begging my fiancée to be with me. If you think we're moving too fast, then let me know, and I'll fall back a little."

Fall back? My eyes stopped scanning through the worker's compensation forms I'd just received in my email and focused on the picture of Toby and me at his twin brother, Cairo's, wedding that was sitting on my desk. We'd been going strong for a little over two years now, and I most definitely didn't want him to do that. I loved Toby with all of my heart, and I couldn't wait for the day that I became Mrs. Tobias Wright. However, this whole moving in together thing was just a little too much for me, especially after I'd become accustomed to having my own space.

Looking around my office, it was pretty evident that the love I had for Toby ran pretty deep. In some cases, one might even say that I was sprung. I mean, my walls, shelves, and desk were decorated with pictures of him by himself in some sexy-ass or supersilly pose that I loved. Since Toby and I had been together, I had done nothing but continue to fall in love with the caring man that he was now and love the husband he was striving to be in the future.

"Babe, I know this is important to you, but can we talk about this later? I have a ton of work I have to do before I get out of here," I asked, trying to sound as if I wasn't rushing him off of the phone when I really was.

I heard a low groan escape his throat, and my clit began to thump. Not only did Toby hold my heart in one hand, but he also held the rights to my pussy in the other. It was amazing to me how it only took him to do the simplest things to make her jump and yearn for his touch. I closed my thighs and crossed my legs at the ankle to try to suppress the slow but sensual beat my clit began to do.

"Niecey . . ." Toby called my name, his voice a little hoarse. "I know you hear me calling you, sexy . . . Niecey."

I licked my lips and pressed my thighs together a little tighter. I tried to control the way the rest of my body was responding to Toby's phone sex voice, but as always, it quickly betrayed me. I could already feel my nipples pressing against my purple lace bra and my fingers slowly making their way to the inside of the matching panties.

I had to pull this need to please myself as well as my man together. The orgasm I was sure to experience was more than likely going to take my breath away, but I couldn't risk the chance of being caught playing with myself by my coworkers. Today was Monday, which meant everyone was here, including my boss, and I didn't want to have any of those problems. Plus, I forgot to lock my door on the way back from my break, and these assholes liked to walk into my office without knocking sometimes.

"Niecey . . ." Toby called my name again—this time a little louder. When he didn't hear me respond a second time, he laughed. "All right, baby, I'ma let you keep that nut this time, but please believe, you're going to give up what belongs to me next time, regardless of where you are. You understand?"

I nodded my head as if he could see me, but he already knew I was agreeing.

He cleared his throat. "Oh, and, Niecey, the conversation about you moving in still has to be discussed, so don't think you got off from that either."

"I know I haven't, babe." I switched the call from the base to the headset, and then stood up from my desk. Walking over to the small office window, I took in the sweet scent of the lotus plant I placed there a few days ago and then looked down over the parking structure. "As a matter of fact, why don't I pick up some food from that Thai restaurant you like so much, and we can discuss it over dinner."

"I thought you had to pick up your cousin from the airport tonight."

Shit. I forgot all about having to pick up my cousin, Koi, from the airport. Not that I didn't enjoy my cousin's company, but I had a lot of things going on in my life right now. My twin sister and I still weren't on speaking terms behind the shit she did. My mama was mad at me because I wouldn't be the bigger person and reach out to her. I was trying to plan Toby's and my wedding, which was becoming a task in itself. Then there was this whole moving in together situation. Even after calling me last night and reminding me about her flight landing an hour after I got off of work, I had still forgotten.

Koi, who happened to be my first cousin on my mother's side, was moving back to Los Angeles after being gone for the last twenty years. When my aunt Debra died, Koi's father, who was the dean of students at Clark Atlanta College at the time, flew out here after the funeral and took Koi to live with him. She and I had kept in touch over the years but hadn't seen each other since we were thirteen. For some reason, Uncle Travis stopped sending her out here during the summer, and I never understood why.

Now, after obtaining her MBA and becoming fed up with that country living, Koi was on her way back to Cali. The thing was, she wasn't about to have a thing to her name. Uncle Travis took her car, her condo, and closed the little bank account he would deposit money into every month as her allowance. He didn't want her to go to California and thought that by cutting her off, her mind would change. But with Koi being the headstrong person that she was, she saved up her tips from the waitress job she was working at the Waffle House, bought her a one-way ticket to Los Angeles, and would be here in the next few hours.

Originally, she asked my mother if she could stay with her, but I intervened and offered her the second bedroom that was unoccupied in my apartment. Koi would be living with me until she got on her feet, and I was super excited to have my cousin back. Not only was I going to be helping her out, but Koi was going to be helping me, as well. Yeah, I had a few people in my life that I considered to be friends, but as close as we were, I still didn't feel comfortable telling them all of my business. My personal life was something I normally only discussed with my twin, and with us not seeing eye to eye right now, there were a lot of things on my chest that I wanted to get off and hear some honest feedback about. I was hoping Koi would fill that void of not having my twin in my life since I considered her to be like my sister in a way.

A light knock on my door grabbed my attention. "Oh, uh, hold on, babe. Someone's at my door." I went back to my desk and sat down, placing my cell inside of my open top drawer and taking the earpiece out of my ear. "Come in."

"Hey, Niecey, sorry to bother you," my coworker, Brenda, said, walking backward into my office. "But these just came for you."

When she turned to face me, Brenda had the biggest bouquet of white roses in her hands, covering up her cute little round face. I was in awe as my eyes scanned the beautiful arrangement. The soft scent of the beautiful flowers instantly filled my office, and a huge smile spread across my face. . . . Toby. I looked through the large bouquet for a card or note but didn't see anything.

"There wasn't a card?" I asked Brenda, who was having a hard time carrying the large arrangement over to my desk.

She shook her head. "No, just some delivery dude in a white van that brought 'em in and had me sign for them." She smiled and had a dreamy look in her eyes. "That boyfriend of yours sure does know how to woo a lady.

And he has expensive taste too. From The Hart is a very pricey place."

"He's my fiancé," I corrected, flashing my engagement ring to remind her. "And he sure does."

I took a single white rose from the bunch and held it up to my nose. Toby was really making it hard for me to decide on this moving in thing. A girl like me could get used to things like this, and his sexy ass knew it.

After thanking Brenda for bringing me the flowers and making sure she shut my door after she left, I picked my phone up to thank Toby.

"Baaaaby, thank you for the flowers. You sure know how to make a girl's day."

"Flowers?"

"Yes, silly. The bouquet of white roses you just had delivered to my office. I think it's about one . . . two . . . three . . . about four dozen in a beautiful blue, round hat box, which, by the way, matches the new color scheme in my office," I laughed. "Babe, stop playing like you don't know what I'm talking about. They are absolutely beautiful, and I love them."

"Niecey, I didn't send you any flowers today. And you know that if they were from me, I would've sent you way more than four dozen. I know how much you love receiving them."

I stopped laughing and thought for a second. "Well, if you didn't send them, then who did?"

Before Toby could answer the question, my assistant buzzed through on the intercom. "Ms. Davis, you have a phone call on line one."

"Okay, thank you, Lynn."

I switched back over to Toby. "Hey, babe, let me take this call. I'll call you back. Better yet, I'll see you tonight after I get Koi all settled into my apartment."

"Well, that's the reason why I was calling in the first place. Cai and Audri are back from their second honeymoon, and he wanted to go for a round of drinks with the fellas tonight. Since we never had that talk after their first honeymoon, I figured we could do it now. We're going to meet up at that club I'm thinking about buying. Hopefully, my bro likes it enough to invest in it too, since he's rolling in a little bit of money these days."

I rolled my eyes. Funny how this club thing just came up all of a sudden. This was one of the reasons why I didn't want to move in with Toby now. He was hardly ever home. Now that he owned and managed Lotus Bomb full time, it was like I saw less and less of him. If he bought this other club, I didn't know when we'd be able to see each other.

"So what, you don't want me to come over just because you're going out? I mean, that's never been a problem before," I said, feeling a little upset.

"You have a key to both of my places, Niecey, so do what you want. I won't be in until late, though, so if you come, don't wait up for me."

Won't be in until late? Don't wait up for him? I didn't like, nor did I feel, any of the words coming from Toby's mouth. I knew he felt some type of way about me not wanting to move in with him permanently, and now I knew he was probably wondering who sent these flowers, but, shit, I wanted to know too. Toby already knew the answer to that question. I'd have no problem telling him, so I didn't understand the need for this little attitude I could hear all in his voice.

"I guess I'll just see you tomorrow then. You know I hate being at your place when you're not there."

He grunted. "Yeah, OK. Whatever, Niecey. Tend to your call, and I'll talk to you later."

"Toby—"

"I'll talk to you later, all right? I gotta go."

"OK, babe. I love you."

I sat there for a few seconds, waiting on him to tell me that he loved me back. When I didn't hear a response, I took the phone from my ear and looked at the screen.

"Asshole hung up on me without telling me he loved me." Oh, yeah, his ass was really upset about our conversation.

Putting my personal problems to the side and going back into work mode, I picked up my office phone and pressed down on the button that was next to the flashing one.

"Human Resources, this is ShaNiece speaking. How can I help you today?"

"Damn, it took you long enough."

I sat up straight in my chair the second his low voice flowed into my ear.

"What's wrong, baby? Surprised that I'm calling you?" he asked with a laugh.

I swallowed the lump in my throat. "Wha . . . What are you calling me for, Will? Is something wrong with Aspen?" I asked, worried about my niece. Since I wasn't talking to my sister, the only way I could spend some time or talk to my niecey pooh was through my mother.

"Naw, my little princess is good. She's in the back with my mama, so she's okay. I wasn't calling about her, though."

"Then what are you calling for, Will?" Even though I couldn't see it, I knew he had a smirk on that smooth, chocolate face of his. Years ago, that same smirk would make me weak at the knees; however, it's amazing what a little bit of growing up and adding some cream to your coffee would do for you. "Look, man, if this call has nothing to do with Aspen, then you need to be calling them other hoes you love to entertain these days."

"How do you know who I'm entertaining these days? Are you following me on social media, Niecey?" he laughed.

"All right, Will, please don't call my job anymore with this bullshit. Unlike you, I have real work to do." I started to hang up the phone but stopped when he called my name again. "What do you want, Will? I have to go."

"I just want to know one thing. Did you get the flowers that I sent to you?" My eyes went to the large bouquet that Brenda had placed on the edge of my desk.

"You . . . sent these flowers?"

"Yeah. I know how much you love receiving flowers at work. Who else could it have been? I know that white boy ain't doing no 'just because' shit like that, is he?"

I ignored his question about Toby because our relationship wasn't any of his business, but I did want to know his reason behind sending me a gift.

"Why did you send me these flowers, Will? You and I don't even rock like that anymore."

"Hence the reason for the flowers. I sent them as a peace offering. A lot of good things are starting to happen in my life, and I couldn't think of anyone else that I wanted to share it with besides you. Have dinner with me tonight so that I can fill you in."

"Will—"

"Niecey, come on. I promise it will be just a friendly dinner. If it makes it any better, you can pick the restaurant. My number's the same, so just text me the place and time, and I'll be there, okay?"

I sat on my end of the line, quiet as a mouse. Was this *really* happening right now?

"Niecey . . .?"

I didn't give Will a second chance to call my name again. I hung up the phone and sat back in my chair. Will and I hadn't talked since the day my niece was born, and

I didn't plan on doing it anytime soon, either. He made his decision on where he wanted to be when he slept with my sister and got her pregnant with my niece. What could we possibly have to talk about other than Aspen?

I looked down at the three-carat halo diamond band engagement ring on my finger. Although Toby and I had our disagreements on my living situation for the last few weeks, I wouldn't trade him or his love for anything in the world. However, even feeling that way, there was still this small piece of me that wanted to hear what Will had to say.

I pulled my cell phone out of my desk drawer and sent him a quick text to the number I had programmed in my phone just in case of an emergency.

Me: Lawry's downtown . . . I'll text you later with the day and time.

Tobias

Walking into Decadence, I knew I'd come up on a business opportunity that would make Cairo and me a lot of money. All I needed was for him to back me, and we'd take over the gentlemen's club scene. Yeah, I had enough money to buy the club myself, but a smart man never puts all of his money into a business venture. Plus, Cai and I had already talked about going into business together a few times, and I felt that this would be the first of many.

Decadence was an exclusive strip club in a prime location that catered to high-end clientele only. It was like the Black Card of clubs. You couldn't just walk in off the street and expect to see what some of the finest women Los Angeles had to offer. No, at Decadence, it was invite only, and you had to have some serious cash behind your name to get in.

I was in search of Raul, the manager of the club, as soon as I stepped through the doors. I wanted to make sure the VIP section I called and had set up for us guys was good to go.

"Aye, can you call Raul up for me?" I asked the redhead behind the bar. Her eyes scanned me from head to toe in appreciation.

"He'll be back in a minute. He went to go check on something in the kitchen." She licked her lips, then poked them out. I could tell by the look in her eyes that she was flirting with me, but I wasn't about to pay her any attention, so I nodded my head at what she said and sat down on a stool at the bar.

"Do you want me to fix you something while you wait?" She chewed on her gum extra hard this time while she eyed me up and down again with her overly made up face. The black top she had on didn't hide any of her chest, while the short skirt was damn near to her panty line. Not at all turned on by the way her body looked in her outfit, I made a mental note to see about changing the waitresses' dress code as soon as the ink dried on the paper.

"Naw, I'm good. I'm waiting on the rest of my party to get here before I start drinking."

She nodded her head and went to wipe the bar down, but not before she winked her eye and made sure I noticed her adjusting her cleavage.

I looked around and admired the inside of the plush club for a few minutes and really liked the way that it was decorated. The crimson, black, and silver color scheme went well together and was evident throughout the entire club. If it looked this fly down here, I could only imagine the way the High Roller section was going to be decorated.

"Aaaaw, Señor Wright. It's a pleasure to see you again, my friend." Raul spoke into my ear as he came to stand in front of me. He reached his hand out, and I shook it. "To what do I owe this small visit?"

"Raul, you already know why I'm here. Before my meeting starts, I just want to make sure that you send the best of everything in the High Roller suite tonight." I released my hand from his and looked around the club again. "If I want to get my brother to go in with me on this place, I need him to see why he should invest."

Raul smoothed his hand over his dark hair that was in a ponytail hanging to the middle of his back. The big gold ring he had on his pinky finger twinkled whenever one of the strobe lights hit it. The cream-colored linen suit he had on was unbuttoned at the top, displaying the dark, curly hair on his chest. Raul, no doubt, was a smooth dude and ran this place with an iron fist, but his love of fucking the employees was a problem for me. A sexual harassment lawsuit was just waiting to happen.

He walked over to the bar and picked up the glass of brown liquor the redhead had just placed down for him. "Señor Wright, I have everything under control. Believe me, your brother and friends will love every second of it." He looked down at his watch. "When will the rest of your party arrive? I just came from the kitchen checking on the menu you ordered for tonight. Everything smells and looks good so far."

I nodded my head. "I told them to be here at eight, so we have about fifteen minutes. Make sure we have nothing but top-shelf alcohol and some water on hand, just in case."

"Sí, señor. If you want, I can take you to your suite and show you what we've done. If there is something that you do not like, we can change it before your guests arrive."

I stood up from the stool at the bar and allowed Raul to lead the way to our destination. Thinking about the night Cai, the fellas, and I were about to have, I hoped Niecey would be in my bed naked and ready to take all of this dick before the sun came up. She owed me from earlier today, and I intended to take what was mine.

"So, Cai, do you like the club?" I asked my twin brother as he looked around the suite. Plush velvet chairs surrounded a small stage with a stripper pole at the end. Scantily clad women walked around having conversations, while the others were giving lap dances. Waitresses were walking in and out of our suite, bringing back trays full of alcohol and whatever else the party ordered.

"Yo, I think this place is hot. I might bring Audri back one night."

"Bring Audri back? Are you telling me that my new sister-in-law goes both ways?" I held the shot of bourbon I had at my lips, waiting on him to answer.

He smiled. "Hell, naw, I'm not telling you that. Audri all about this dick and only this dick." We shared a laugh. "I said that because I know she'll love this laid-back atmosphere, and the food will really have her coming back. The girl loves Jamaican food more than me now."

"Well, to keep it honest, the Jamaican food was a perk I had added tonight to try to impress you." I gulped down my shot and wiped my mouth with the back of my hand.

Cairo raised his eyebrow and took a sip of his drink. "Impress me for what?"

"Well, I'm thinking about buying this place, and I want you to invest with me."

He looked around the suite, then back at me. "Honestly, I think this place would be a great investment. Add this Jamaican food to the menu and maybe change a little of the decor and waitress dress code, and I wouldn't have a problem with that." My twin looked me in the eyes. "Just run me some numbers and let me talk it over with my wife; then I'll give you an answer."

"Talk it over with your wife?" I joked. "Oh, you really *are* a married man, huh?"

Cai shrugged his shoulders. "A married man and father who has to take every aspect of my life and money into consideration. If this club falls through, it won't just be me losing. I mean, Audri brings in a nice chunk of change with her shoe stores, but I don't want to have to dip into our joint accounts if something were to happen. The money she makes is put aside for our kids' college funds and things like that, while my money pays all of the bills, mortgages, and miscellaneous things. If

I go into this with you, brother or not, hell, yeah, I have to discuss it with my wife. My money is her money and vice versa, and what I own, she owns too." Cai took another sip of his beer. "You don't talk to Niecey about money?"

I opened my mouth to say something and then closed it. My eyes went to my brother's, who was staring right back at me. Identical twins we were, and it felt a little weird at times, looking into a face that looked just like mine. The only thing that set us apart was Cairo's blond dreads that had grown a few inches over the years, and his eyes were bluish green, whereas mine were greenish blue. We had the same sun-kissed skin, same muscular build and height, same strong jawline, and both quite handsome. I often wondered if Cai would ever cut his dreads off, but I doubted it. Audrielle would probably leave his ass if he did.

I wiped my hand down my face, thinking about his questions. "Dude, Niecey and I don't talk about much lately. Ever since your wedding, I've been trying to get her to move back in with me, but she won't."

Cairo watched the stripper on the pole for a few seconds and then turned back to me. "Do you think she has someone else?"

His question caught me off guard and had me downing another shot of bourbon. "No, I don't think it's anything like that. Then again, someone did send her a bouquet of roses to her job today, and she claims that she doesn't know who they were from."

"Hmmm" and a head nod were Cai's only response.

One of the strippers walking around walked up to us and invaded our personal space as well as conversation."Would you like a dance?" she asked me first. When I shook my head no, she turned to Cairo. Grabbing one of his dreads in her hand, she twirled it around her finger and licked her lips.

"Baby girl, if I were you, I'd give this man a few feet. If my sis smells a drop of your perfume on him, you might not live to dance another day," Finesse told the Amber Rose look-alike. "Last girl that touched this man's hair was pushed into the sand so deep, I bet she could see China."

We all shared a laugh as Finesse took a seat next to Cairo and poured himself a drink. The stripper took heed of his warning and let go of Cairo's hair, but not before rolling her eyes and stomping out of the suite.

"Aye, I think you made her mad, Ness," Cairo tried to say through a laugh.

"Naw, I just saved baby girl's life. You know Audri don't play when it comes to you, bro."

"You act like Ariana ain't the same with you."

"Well, they are sisters," I interjected.

Both Cairo and Finesse looked at me.

"You acting like Niecey isn't the same way. If I remember correctly, she went in on Pop's ex-wife at that little family gathering we tried to have a while ago, and let's not forget the dinner Ness and Ari had a couple of months after their new neighbor tried to push up on you," Cairo laughed.

I waved them off. "Man, that was Niecey just being Niecey." Looking at the new stripper on the pole, I swirled around the little bit of liquor in my glass and thought about a few things. "The two of you know how much I love that girl, right?" They nodded their heads. "I swear to God, if she's fucking around with someone else, I don't know what I'd do."

Cairo held his hands up. "Whoa, Toby. Now, I didn't say that she was messing with someone else. I just asked if the thought had ever crossed your mind."

"Wait, Niecey's cheating on you?" Finesse asked.

"Naw, she ain't cheating . . . I mean . . . I don't *think* she is. It's just that she got some flowers today from someone that wasn't me."

Finesse looked at Cai and then at me.

"What?" I asked, pouring me another shot. The look on his face was making me nervous. Did Finesse know something I didn't?

"When's the last time she talked to her ex?"

I reared my head back. "Why would you ask me that?"

Finesse turned his attention to Cai. "Bro, you didn't tell him?"

"Tell me what?"

I looked at my twin, who was grilling Finesse. What could they possibly know about Niecey's ex that I didn't? The fool hadn't disrespected our relationship this far, so why start now? I knew Niecey would someday have to deal with him regarding her niece if ever Ms. Regina wasn't around, but it hadn't happened that way so far. Whenever she spent time with Aspen, it was either at her mother's house or mine, because she would bring the little princess over to my place for the weekend.

Cai blew out a frustrated breath and sat up in his chair. "Look, man, last week I ran into a dude that Ness and I grew up with around the neighborhood . . . Beano Cooper."

My eyes became wide. "Beano Cooper as in wide receiver for the Los Angeles Sabors Beano Cooper?" Dollar signs began to flash before my eyes. If we invited him and some of his teammates to become members of Decadence, we'd for sure turn a profit and make a lot of money. "Yeah, I know who you're talking about. What about him?"

Cairo grabbed a handful of his dreads and put them in a bun at the crown of his head. "Well, he invited us to chill at his new house for a little bit. Wanted us to see his man cave and game room."

I nodded my head for him to go on.

"While we were there, a few of his teammates swung by. We got on the topic of kids and women. Of course, we started showing pictures and whatnot. When this cat named Will started talking about his daughter, someone asked him about his baby moms. He went into some story about messing with these twin sisters and getting the sister that wasn't his girl pregnant."

Cai paused; then Finesse took over the story. "Dude was damn near in tears talking about how he messed up fucking with the sister. Said losing his girl was the worst thing that ever happened to him. After going on and on about his ex and how good she was to him for a few minutes, he started talking about how he couldn't think of anyone else to share his new life with other than her now that he's doing well for himself." Finesse poured a shot of bourbon and gave it to me before pouring another for himself. "Some of the fellas thought that he was lying about taking down twins, so they asked to see a picture of them. He passed his phone around, and that's when we saw her."

"Saw who?" I asked, already knowing the answer to my own question. Hearing the name Will already told me what and who it was.

"It was a picture of Niecey and her sister. What's her name again?"

"LaNiece or LaLa," I answered.

"Yeah, that's her name. Ole boy was saying how it's been two years since the incident, and he was hoping that Niecey would find it in her heart to forgive him for what he'd done."

Cai and Finesse both watched me with curious eyes as I sat in my seat across from them in thought. I pulled at the hem of my gray V-neck sweater and started to pick at the imaginary lint. Was Niecey back in contact with her ex like that? Did *he* send those flowers to her office? I hadn't talked to Niecey since the conversation we'd had earlier that day. She texted me when she was on her way to the airport to pick up her cousin and when she was on her way back, but I hadn't heard from her since then, and that was three hours ago.

"Aye, man," Cai called, interrupting my thoughts. "For what it's worth, I didn't tell you because I didn't feel you had anything to worry about. Niecey's crazy about your ass, and I doubt she'd go back to him even if she did forgive him."

I placed the shot Finesse had poured me on the table and looked at my twin. I understood where he was coming from, but I bet the shit would've been a different story if it were the other way around.

"Let me ask you something, Thaddeus." I called Cairo by his birth name and saw the way his jaw flexed in irritation. He hated to be called anything other than the name his adoptive mother gave him and wouldn't let anyone call him Thaddeus, including his wife. "If the tables were turned and I heard one of Audri's exes going around claiming to come and take her back from you, and I didn't tell you, you wouldn't be mad?"

He stared at me for what felt like twenty minutes before he smiled and replied to my question. "I'm going to let you calling me by that other name slide this time, Tobias, because I know you're in your feelings a little."

I nodded my head and gave him the same smirk he just gave me, acknowledging the fact that he used my whole name, which I hated as well.

"But I wouldn't be worried in the least if one of Audri's exes came into town talking crazy. That shit wouldn't bother me one bit."

"Yeah, and why is that?" I asked.

"Because I know my wife, and I know she'd never do anything to bring me pain or hurt me. Plus, her heart beats only for me, and her pussy . . . Well, let's just say that my name is tattooed on the inside and the outside of that muthafucka literally." He laughed and crossed his leg over his knee. "So to answer your question, I wouldn't be mad at all."

A few things began to run through my head, all of which were questions that only Niecey could answer. And since she wasn't there right now, I didn't want to ruin the night with a conversation that only she and I needed to have. Picking the shot back up, I downed it, then watched the stripper who was twirling around the pole. It was back to business with my brother . . . for the time being.

"So when do you think you'll have a definite answer on buying this club?" I asked Cai, eyes still on the stage, half of my mind still on Niecey while the other half was on this money.

"I told you to give me about a week, and I'll let you know."

"Wait," Finesse yelled. "Y'all trying to buy this club?"

"Yes," Cai and I answered at the same time and looked at each other. This was something that we'd been doing a lot of lately. I guess for all of those years we missed growing up together, twinning was happening now.

"Yo, y'all have to let me get in on this. I was just telling Ari I wanted to invest in something. She wanted to open up an apparel store, but that was a no-go for me. Ari thinks her ass is slick. That apparel store will somehow turn into a boutique before construction even begins."

Cai laughed. "Don't they sell apparel at the shoe stores?"

Finesse nodded his head. "That's why I said Ari thinks she's slick."

For the rest of the night, Cai, Finesse, and I, along with a few other friends that I invited into the suite, enjoyed the male bonding, good food, drinks, and the lovely assortment of women. Around midnight, I received a text from Niecey. When I opened it up, there was a picture of her beautiful face and sexy-ass body lying naked on top of my bed.

Mrs. Wright: I'm here whenever you're ready . . .

I looked at her picture and reread her message one last time before I tucked my phone back into my pocket and got up from my seat. After making sure everyone was good and could make it home on their own, I slipped out the back door and headed home to my woman.

Niecey and I had something to talk about, but not before I made love to what did and always would belong to me.

ShaNiece

"No, you're OK . . . I'll be there in about thirty minutes . . . It's my fault for not giving it to you last night . . . Stop it . . . No, he's right here lying next to me . . . Bye, nosy . . . I'll see you in a few . . . OK. Bye."

I hung up my phone and looked down at Toby's handsome face. I don't know what happened or what had gotten into him last night, but our sex was off the chain. Don't get me wrong; sex with Toby was always amazing. It's just that last night, it was like he was making love to my soul. Normally, he and I indulged in that kinky, erotic-type sex, but last night . . . Last night was different. It reminded me of the time Toby and I had sex after he first told me he loved me. So sweet, so pure, so much passion. Toby was giving his entire being to me in every stroke, and I gladly accepted it.

My eyes scanned his perfectly sculpted body with the colorful tattoos on his arm and chest, and a chill ran down my spine and traveled down to my toes. Goose bumps began to surface on my skin, and my body started to heat up. My puckered lips tattooed on the very spot he said turned him on whenever my tongue found its mark. I bit my bottom lip and tried to suppress the moan that unwillingly escaped. The things this man had taught and did to my body would never get old. I wanted to climb on top and give him what he deemed as the best part of waking up, but the phone call I had just received had me moving in another direction.

Not wanting to disrupt him from his peaceful sleep, I slowly scooted toward the edge of the bed and tried to get up. Before I could place my foot on the floor, Toby's strong arm wrapped around my waist and pulled me back into his chest.

"Where you going this early in the morning?" His raspy voice tickled my neck, causing the hairs to stand up.

"I have to go back by my place to take care of some business," I said, trying to get up, but he pulled me back. He brushed his lips across my bare shoulder and began to caress my belly with small circles. We lay in silence for a few minutes before he spoke again.

"Who were you on the phone with?"

My body tensed up the second the question came out of his mouth, and I knew he felt it. His hands stopped circling my stomach and gripped my hip instead. I closed my eyes and blew out a breath, trying to control the way my response was going to come out if I decided to answer him. This line of questioning was new, and I had a feeling I wouldn't be leaving his loft with a smile on my face this morning like I normally did.

In the two years that we'd been together, Toby had never questioned me about my phone or who I was talking to, so him asking sorta threw me for a loop. As far as I knew, we didn't have the type of relationship where we'd question each other about things as simple as a phone call. To me, when things like that started to happen in a relationship, it was always the guilty conscience of the person who asked that needed to be fed.

"Uhh, that was Koi. She went to get something to eat since I haven't gone grocery shopping yet and she locked herself out. I forgot to give her my spare key last night, so now I gotta go let her in." When I turned to face him, Toby was looking at me with one eye open and the other covered by his arm.

"Are you referring to the spare key that you were supposed to give to me that I never received?"

I stared at him with squinted eyes for a minute, then removed myself from his grasp and out of his bed while mumbling things to myself.

"What was that? I don't think I heard you."

I rolled my eyes at his sarcastic tone and began to look around for my things.

"You act like I haven't given you a key to my place on purpose. The damn thing is on my key ring like it's always been since I had it made. But I'm over here so much that it just slipped my mind to give it to you." I picked up my yoga pants that were on the floor halfway under the bed and pulled them on. "What's up with all of these questions anyway? You've never asked me about who's calling my phone or where I was going."

Toby rose up from his relaxed posture on the bed and sat up against the headboard. The ivory sheet that was covering the rest of his body sat pooled at his waist, showing off that sexy chest and abbed-out stomach of his. I licked my lips as my eyes couldn't help but enjoy the view in front of me. Because Toby usually wore suits or long-sleeve shirts while he was working, no one really knew the number of tattoos he had covering his body. Aside from my lips on his neck, Toby had some sort of colorful tribal art that started from the middle of his arm and extended up to his broad shoulder. The more detailed parts of the piece covered his left pectoral and stopped just before his upper abdomen. The *Famous Nobody* tattoo started at his waist on the right side of his body and ended a little under his armpit. On some nights, after we'd come down from our sexual high, I would trace the beautifully scripted letters covering half of his rib cage with my fingertips until he fell asleep.

It was mornings like this when the sun would shine through the window above his bed and illuminate this man's beautiful body and his handsome features that made me fall in love with him more and more. I loved the short, dark blond hair on the top of his head to those greenish-blue irises that could bring me to my knees with one look. Toby and his love for me were all I needed, and I prayed that he wasn't out there doing me wrong.

Toby wiped his hand down his face and kept his eyes on me as I continued to get dressed. "So, you're not going to answer me?"

"Answer you about what, Toby?" I slipped on my bra and then tank top. "I already told you who was on the phone and where I'm about to go."

"I'm talking about my copy of the key to your place. Since it's just idly hanging on your key ring, can I have it now?" He stretched his open palm out.

I shook my head. "No."

"No?" he questioned, eyes fully open and boring into me.

I stopped what I was doing and sat on the edge of the bed, eyes looking directly into his. "You don't need the key anymore. Well, not right now anyways. With my cousin living there, what would be the point? If I'm not there, you don't need to be there chilling with her, waiting for me. I can just meet you here if you want to see me or if we have plans to go out or something."

What I said sounded logical to me, but with the expression on Toby's face, I could tell it sounded far from logical to him.

He pinched the bridge of his nose and shut his eyes tight. "So, let me get this straight. Now that your cousin is living with you, not only can't I have the key you just said was made for me, but I can't even go over to your place to spend time with you or stay the night?"

I blew out a frustrated breath because his line of questioning was starting to irritate the hell out of me. "No, Toby, that's not what I'm saying."

"Then what *are* you saying, Niecey?" His voice rose slightly. "Because I'm having a very hard time understanding why I can't have my key or the fact that I can't step foot into my own fiancée's house."

I got up from the bed and walked into Toby's bathroom without responding to his question. What were we doing? What was *he* doing? Arguing wasn't us, and I wanted it to stay that way. Grabbing our toothbrushes out of the toothbrush holder, I placed my brand of toothpaste on my side and the one he preferred on his. Normally, Toby would join me in the bathroom, and we'd brush our teeth together while I fought him off of me, but today, he never joined me. I rinsed my mouth out and then gargled. When I walked back into the bedroom, Toby was nowhere in sight. I picked his clothes up and the rest of my things off of the floor and stuffed them into my overnight bag. After making the bed, gathering up the dirty dishes I left on the dresser last night, and resetting the alarm clock, I went to look for my baby. I didn't want to leave his place today with us angry at each other. I needed to rectify the situation.

I searched the large loft for a few before I finally found Toby in his office, looking over a small pile of papers.

"You didn't hear me calling you?" I asked, walking into the neatly decorated room and leaning against the bookshelf. Toby looked up at me and then back down at his papers without a word. "Really, Toby?"

"Really, Toby, what? I can't do any work in *my* own house now?"

"Wow." I reared my head back. "What happened to this being *our* house? I'm supposed to be moving in, right?"

He smacked his lips and shuffled through the papers, still not looking at me. "Don't you have your own place you claim you need to occupy now? Maybe us moving in together before the wedding wasn't such a good idea. You were right. We need to enjoy our own space while we still have it."

My entire soul left my body the minute the words left his mouth. Then the fact that he wouldn't even look at me was making me feel some other type of way too. I needed to fix this situation, and I needed to fix it now. I took my keys out of my purse and slipped off the key I had made for him.

"Look, Toby, if it really means that much to you, here is your key. Just . . . just . . . Call me before you decide to come over there to make sure I'm home. I don't want there to be any misunderstandings between you and Koi if you ever walk in on her . . . doing whatever it is she does when she's home alone and I'm not there."

He stopped going through the papers, smiled, and shook his head. "Oh, so now I understand where this is all coming from." Toby's eyes connected to mine this time, but the love I normally saw in them when he looked at me wasn't there. He sat back in his chair and crossed his arms over his chest. "This is all about that asshole ex of yours and what he and your sister did to you, isn't it? What, you think I can't control myself around other women when you're not around?"

I returned his glare but didn't answer, and he laughed. "It's a little too late for you to be questioning my self-control isn't it? You *do* know that the business I'm in has me around beautiful women all the time? Hell, I employee about seven or eight of them at the Lotus Bomb. And it will probably be double that number if we buy Decadence. In the two years that we've been together, Niecey, I've never given you any reason to doubt the love and respect that I have for you. So, that makes me ask myself"—he placed his finger on his chin and looked up into the air as if he were thinking—"what or who would have her insecurities coming up out of nowhere? Do you know whose name popped into my head?"

My shoulders dropped. "Toby—"

"Toby, *what?*" he spat, attitude laced in his words. "It took me months to get you to break down the wall that loser caused you to place around your heart. When I finally broke through that muthafucka, do you know how happy I was? Do you know how it felt being in love with someone who you didn't know if they felt the same way about you as you did about them?"

My eyes became misty. "I'm sorry, babe."

"Sorry?" He stood up from behind his desk, dressed in a pair of tan cargo shorts and nothing else. "Sorry for what? Being weak?"

"Weak?" I cried. "You and I both know I'm far from weak."

He sat on the edge of the desk, swirling the platinum stress balls in his hand and looking down at the floor. "I say weak because, for some reason, you keep letting this loser into our relationship. Do I *look* like him? Do I look like I want another woman other than the one I practically beg to sleep in my bed every night?" The balls in his hand started to swirl faster. "At the beginning of our relationship, I expected the little fight you put up because I understand what you went through, but even after proposing to you, giving you the keys to my lofts, and asking you to move in with me, you *still* have the audacity to think I'd cheat on you."

Toby was right. My insecurity about being cheated on was starting to rear its ugly head. But it wasn't because Koi moved in with me. I knew my cousin, and she would never betray me like my sister did. And to be honest, I believed that Toby would never do anything to hurt me intentionally. But after receiving those flowers from Will at work, something inside of me clicked. Maybe the fact that flowers were what he normally sent me to apologize for his philandering ways triggered it, but reason or not, I needed to get over it before I lost the best thing that ever happened to me.

I walked over to Toby and placed the key in his free hand. He held it between his thumb and index finger for a minute and then placed it down on his cherry desk.

"Toby, I apologize if I made you feel some type of way. Maybe I did start to feel a little insecure about Koi, seeing as my own twin sister fucked my last boyfriend and had a baby by him. But I honestly know and believe that neither you nor my cousin would ever do anything to me like that." My phone vibrated in my pocket. When I fished it out and looked at the screen, I ignored the call because I didn't recognize the number.

Toby's eyebrow rose in regards to what I just did. "So, you're not answering phone calls anymore?"

"It was a number I didn't recognize."

"Since when has that stopped you from talking on your phone?"

I blinked my eyes a few times as the tears that were just in them began to dry up. "Wait a minute. Where is all this coming from, Toby? Why are you suddenly questioning me about every little thing I do?" My attitude had changed in one point two seconds flat. I crossed my arms over my chest, poked my hip out, and cocked my head to the side. "Are you fucking somebody else or something? Muthafuckas who normally don't ask questions start playing twenty-one questions when they've been doing shit they shouldn't be doing."

Toby laughed a hearty laugh. "Says the woman receiving flowers from someone other than her man."

"You act as if I told Will to send those muthafuckas. I told his ass when he—" I stopped talking the minute Toby's frame towered over mine, damn near making me stumble in the process.

"*Who* sent you those flowers?" His face was tight and his voice low.

The greenish-blue eyes I couldn't live without were darker and blazing with fire. I opened my mouth to say something but couldn't get a word out at all. Those tears that evaporated a few minutes ago were back and running down my cheeks like they never left. I've never seen the look Toby had on his face before. He looked sexy as hell, but his stare was blank as fuck, like I wasn't standing in front of him at all. He was pissed beyond belief, and my heart was breaking every time his jaw flexed and his nostrils flared, waiting for my answer. I tried to place my hands on his chest to calm him down, but Toby stepped away from my touch.

"Why is he sending you flowers?" he asked through gritted teeth.

"Babe . . . I don't—"

He cut me off. "You *don't know?* How don't you know, Niecey? And why would he think it's OK for him to send you some flowers after all this time? You told me the only contact you have with him is if it's about your niece when your mother isn't around. According to you, your mother has been home, so you shouldn't be in contact with the asshole, right?"

I shook my head but then nodded it when Toby's eyes opened in shock. My mind was going crazy with so many thoughts on what just happened that I was hardly listening to what he was saying. Toby backed away from me, talking to himself and looking like he had just been shot in the heart.

"I think you need to go, Niecey. I got some paperwork for this new club I need to go over, and you have to go let Koi"—he used air quotes—"into your place. I'll get up with you later or whenever you want to talk about why your ex is sending you flowers." He walked back around his desk, sat down, and picked up the pile of papers he was looking at when I walked in. Picking up a pen, he signed what I assumed was his signature to a few sheets, then laid the pen back down on his desk and looked up at me. "You're still here? Please, don't let me hold you up on what you need to do. You jumped out of bed so fast this morning to get going. Don't slow down because of me now."

"Toby . . ." I called.

He opened his desk drawer and pulled out a few folders and began to go through them. "I'll see you when I see you, Niecey."

The tears silently fell down my face as I began to back up toward the door. Both Toby and I were high off of our emotions and would probably say some shit we'd regret later if I didn't leave right now. I'd just try to have this conversation later on when I came back that night. Toby was going to hear me out on this whole Will and sending me flowers thing. I grabbed my keys and bag off the floor and turned to walk out of his office.

I heard the shattering of the crystal globe that sat on the corner of his desk hitting the wall and breaking into a million pieces the second I closed his door. Covering my mouth to hide the loud cry that escaped my throat, I placed my forehead against the heavy oak and prayed that this little hiccup in our relationship could be worked out much sooner rather than later. More so for my sake than Toby's. I didn't think I could go on if Toby really decided to leave me behind some nigga I hated with every fiber inside of me.

Tobias

It had been a couple of weeks since Niecey and I had spent any real time together, let alone had sex. The night after she and I had that big blowup in my office, she came back trying to talk about the whole thing, but I didn't want to hear it. I ate the dinner she cooked that night and even watched a few hours of television with her. Whenever Niecey would try to start up some kind of conversation about what happened, I would simply tell her that we would talk about it later. Safe to say, we never talked about the situation that night after the shows went off and ended up going to bed with her sleeping on her side and me sleeping on mine. At some point in the middle of the night, I felt Niecey scoot over to my side and hug me from behind. I felt her wet face on my back, as well as her lips moving about something, but I never asked her what she was saying. I lay there in my own thoughts until I dozed off and woke up the next morning with her nowhere in sight. She left a note saying that she had to go into work early and that she left my breakfast in the oven, but I just tossed that shit into the trash can on my way into the bathroom.

To say that I was OK without seeing or talking to Niecey like I normally did would be a lie. A few of the days where we didn't communicate at all, I became sick to my stomach. I couldn't focus at work or home in my office like I was now. Thoughts of her smooth, brown legs wrapped around my head invaded every minute of my day. I missed the cute way she would laugh at all of my jokes, or the way she would kiss me all over my face until I paid attention to whatever it was she was talking about. I even missed the way her soft fingers would trace the tattoo on the side of my rib cage after we came down from having some of the most incredible sex. I shook my head. Maybe I was overreacting too much about who sent her those flowers. Then again, if the tables were turned, Niecey would more than likely be the same way.

Picking up my phone, I scrolled down my call log until I got to her name. I just needed to hear her voice for a brief second, and then I'd be okay with focusing on the opening of the new and improved Decadence Gentlemen's Club. Partnering up with Cairo, Finesse, and their boy, Beano Cooper, turned out to be a much better investment than I could ever imagine. The grand reopening for Decadence was going to go down in the next few weeks, and we had a lot of things to do before we opened the doors back up to the who's who in the entertainment, sports, and business world. With Beano's connections to the players in the NFL and NBA and my connections with the CEOs, CFOs, and owners of some Fortune 500 companies, the VIP list and the suites at the club were all filled up and booked for the two-night extravaganza.

The staff was already picked out, and everyone knew what they needed to do on the night of the reopening. Of course, I kept Raul's slick ass on as manager, because, to be honest, the dude knew how to keep the club packed. However, he did have a ninety-day probation period he had to pass in order to be on. And if I heard one word of him messing with any of the new strippers or employees, he was out of there, because I couldn't be at this club 24/7. I hired someone as an assistant manager that I knew would have no problem keeping Raul in line or informing me of whether he was insubordinate.

Instead of calling Niecey's phone, I scrolled past her name and called the new addition to my Club Decadence crew.

"Hey, Toby. What's going on?"

"What's up, Koi? How's it going down at the club?"

She said something to someone in the background, then came back to the phone. "It's going good. The new main stage is being installed as we speak. The new chairs have been delivered and are waiting to be placed. I had to fire one of the new busboys this morning, but I have a few interviews for a new one set up for today and tomorrow. The AC was acting up for a minute, but we got someone out here to fix it, and the chef had a problem with the new additions to the menu. But after I told him that he could easily be replaced just like his son this morning, he shut his ass up."

I laughed and shook my head. I know you're probably wondering why I hired her as the assistant manager of Decadence, but it was a favor for someone I would do anything for. Don't get me wrong; at first, I was totally against it when Niecey asked me if I could find something for her cousin to do since she'd just moved out here with basically nothing. Just two weeks ago, we were arguing about me not having a key to Niecey's place because of her. But after Niecey asking and asking and asking me for a couple of days, I finally gave in. At first, I had Koi hired on as a server, but once I saw on her résumé that she had a degree in business with several years of experience working in restaurants and club scenes, I bumped her up to assistant manager. It was a win-win for me. She could watch Raul when I couldn't, as well as make enough money within a matter of months to get on her feet and move out of Niecey's place.

After getting to know Koi in the weeks that she'd been there, I could honestly say that she was a great woman. Was I attracted to her? No. Did I find her attractive? Yes, or else she wouldn't be working for me. Would I ever cross the line with her if we were ever left alone? Hell nah. Niecey was really tripping when that thought ran through her head. Although I thought Koi was a beautiful individual, I was not attracted to her in any way. I actually saw her as my little cousin too. The friendship we'd formed since I hired her was strictly platonic and nothing more.

"That's great. Make sure he does a taste run on the menu too. Gather up a few of the workers and let them do a tasting or something like that. We want the food and drinks to be on point. Especially the Jamaican dishes we added. I'll have Cairo taste those since they are some of his mother's recipes."

"OK. I'll get right on that. Is there anything else?"

"Will everything be done by the time the reopening rolls around?" I asked, deciding to text Niecey while talking to Koi.

Me: I miss you!

Koi giggled at something, then answered my question. "Yes, Toby, everything will be together and on time. If not, you already know I have no problem firing and hiring someone who will get it done."

I nodded my head. "That's what I like to hear." I looked at my phone to see if Niecey had responded to my text, but there was nothing, so I sent another.

Me: We need to talk. Come over later. You have your key.

I heard Koi giggling again and talking to someone in the background.

"What's so funny?" I asked, wanting to laugh too.

Koi coughed, then cleared her throat. "Uh, nothing, Toby. Nothing's funny at all. Let me get off this phone, though, and make sure everyone is doing their job. If anything needs your attention, bossman, I'll be sure to call you, all right?"

Before I could even respond, Koi released the call, giggling again, and hung up in my face.

Something is seriously wrong with that girl, I thought as I began to go through my emails on my computer. One email I was looking for in particular was from my friend who worked for the California ABC. We had to file for a new liquor license after we took over new ownership of the club. A process that would normally take between fifty-five to sixty-five days for the average person was only going to take seven to fourteen for us. During my weed-selling days in college, I came in contact with and across a few prominent people in the city of Los Angeles. The fact that my father was also part of the top elite in the city helped as well. The last name Wright held a lot of clout in some places and gave me an excuse to exercise my birthright when I needed to.

My mood dampened a bit when I didn't find the email that I was looking for. But I wasn't worried too much. As long as the license was approved by the end of the week, we'd be good. I had a shipment of alcohol coming in sometime next week, and I wanted the bars stocked with nothing but top-shelf spirits for the event.

I checked my phone to see if Niecey had responded to my second text, and just like the first time, my notification bar was empty. I thought about calling her this time rather than texting again but nixed the whole idea instead. If she wasn't responding to my text, she most definitely wouldn't answer my phone calls.

Turning my chair away from my desk, I was now facing my floor-to-ceiling windows and was greeted with the most breathtaking, panoramic view of downtown Los Angeles. One of the reasons why I bought this loft, as well as the one next door, was because of this view. The wood flooring, high ceilings, beautiful crown molding, chef's kitchen clad in marble, spalike baths, and library were just added bonuses.

"Yeah," I spoke into the earpiece in my ear after accepting the call that had just come in.

"Your ass still moping around wishing Niecey would come back?" Cai laughed on the other end. "You and I definitely were raised differently because had that been Audri, she would've been back home already."

I chuckled. "What does my upbringing have to do with the way my woman acts?"

"All of that money you grew up with didn't get you the pair of balls you would need to handle a woman like her."

"And yours did?" I asked, getting up from my desk and grabbing a beer out of the small fridge I had built into the bookcase wall.

"Well, yeah. That and I'm not too proud to beg. I don't know how you went this long without Niecey lying in your bed every night. I get sick when Audri stays the weekend at her parents' house."

"I bet you end up staying there too."

Cai laughed. "I sure do. One night I can tolerate a little, but when the sun starts to rise in the morning, I'm up and driving that hour and a half to be with my baby. You need to be the same way if you want to work out whatever this thing is between you and Niecey."

Wiping my hand over my face, I pulled at the beard on my chin and then took a sip of my beer. Cai was right. If I wanted to work out this small argument with Niecey, I needed to be the one to make the first move, since technically, it was me who pushed her away. Propping my feet up on the edge of my desk, I leaned back in my chair and continued to talk to my twin.

"Enough of the relationship advice, bro. What's the reason for the call?"

"I just wanted to know if you received the paperwork for the club. Chasin's secretary was supposed to fax it over a couple of days ago."

I picked up the thick manila envelope that had the contracts of ownership for the club inside. "Yeah, I got 'em. I guess congratulations are in order for you, Ness, Beano, and me. We are now all the proud owners of Decadence."

"*That's* what's up. How is everything going for the reopening?"

"So far, so good," I said, taking another sip of my beer and leaning farther back in my chair.

I went over a few details about the party and the VIP list with Cai before I got off the phone and went to make myself something to eat. I could have easily had my butler do it, but I didn't feel like waiting for him to come from next door. While I was fixing my sandwich and snacking on some chips, my phone vibrated on the marble counter. Picking it up, I smiled immediately when I noticed that the text message I had just received was from Niecey.

Mrs. Wright: Fuck off.

I laughed at my baby's crazy ass. It wasn't the type of response I wanted to read from her, but it was something. At least I knew her anger toward me was calming down a little bit; hence, the *Fuck off* text. But I could get with that. All I had to do now was figure out a way to get her to come over that night. I had no doubt that I would be able to get us back on the right track again once I fucked all of that unnecessary anger out of her and apologized.

ShaNiece

"Niecey, you better stop doing my boy like that." Koi laughed as she swatted my arm with her clipboard.

"Do him like what? *He's* the reason why our relationship is in this funk—not me."

"Yeah, but he's been apologizing to you for the last couple of weeks. How many times does he have to tell you he's sorry before you take your ass back over to his place?"

"Uh, for someone who hasn't paid me a month's worth of rent yet, you sure have been trying to kick me out of my own shit since I've been back."

Koi rolled her eyes. "It's not even like that, Niecey. I just don't want you to fuck around and end up *really* pushing Toby away by being stubborn."

"Stubborn? Girl, bye."

Ignoring her questioning eyes, I walked from where we were standing in the main room and headed toward the bar area. Taking a seat on one of the stools, I looked over Club Decadence in amazement. Everything was starting to come together, and I was happy for Toby. The interior decorator Koi hired did a wonderful job with the ruby and gold color scheme. Even the reupholstering of the chairs, stools, and couches took my breath away. Expensive crystal chandeliers followed you throughout the whole place while the aroma of Jamaica's sweet and savory spices lingered in the air from the kitchen. The bar shelves weren't stocked with alcohol yet, but I was pretty sure that top-shelf, wallet-breaking liquor would be in place by the time the grand opening party went down. I marveled at the beautiful artwork that decorated the velvet walls, the Swarovski crystals hanging from everywhere, and the fancy ostrich feather centerpieces that sat in the middle of every VIP suite.

Although Toby was on my last nerve right now, I was proud of him. He told me that he was going to make this place L.A.'s next hottest spot, and I believed that he would. I smiled, thinking about my baby. Although I hadn't seen him in a minute because of my own *trying to prove a point* reasons, I did miss him. Taking my phone out of my pocket, I sent him another text message that I was sure would get a response from him this time. The *fuck off* one I sent a few seconds ago didn't do the damage I needed it to do, but I was pretty sure this next one would.

"What are you shaking your head for?" I asked Koi as she walked up next to me and tried to look over my shoulder at my phone screen. Her short ass had to stand on her tippy toes because she was so petite.

"You and these games you keep playing with that man is why I'm shaking my head."

"Since when did you become so #teamtoby?"

"Since #teamtoby hired my black ass. I told you the first thing I wanted to do was find a job when I got here, and that's what I did, thanks to your man."

I playfully rolled my eyes and sucked my teeth. "Family ain't shit, man. You are such a traitor."

"In no way, shape, form, or fashion am I a traitor. You know it's me and you until the day I die, Niecey, but . . ." Koi shook her head and blew out a short breath. "Never thought I would say this, because you know I'm all about black love and shit." She held her fist up in the air and bowed her head. "But he's a good look for you, Niecey, and I can tell that he loves you. Regardless of his color. Whatever it is y'all beefing about can get worked out. You just gotta be willing to do the work."

I heard everything she was saying, but I wasn't trying to hear that right now. Toby and I were going to be fine. He just needed to realize that I loved him just as much as he loved me, and there wasn't anyone in this world who could ever stop that. I looked down at my phone screen, kind of upset that Toby had not responded to my last text. Maybe he hadn't seen it yet. I continued to play with my phone as I sort of turned my attention back to Koi. I could feel her eyes on me.

"What? I hear you talking, Koi, and I'm taking everything you just said into consideration."

"You hear me talking, but do you really *hear* me?" she asked, causing me to look up from my phone. Something about the way the tone in her voice changed caught my attention. My eyes traveled in the direction of hers, which was toward the back of the club.

"Who are they?" I wondered when my sight landed on the ebony and ivory beauties that just walked through the double doors.

Koi looked down at her clipboard and flipped through a few papers. "The black chick is Halo, and her sidekick is Storm. Some tag team stripper dancing duo from Atlanta that one of Beano's people recommended."

"Okay. So what are they doing here now? The club isn't open yet."

"They're here to audition for the last two slots open for dancers. We were supposed to hire ten last week but only ended up hiring eight. Beano's homeboy was here and said that he knew the perfect two dancers to fill those spots."

"Is Beano's homeboy an investor? Since when do outsiders recommend the help?"

Koi turned to me and laughed. "The help? Ooooh . . .
I see what this is. I think someone's a little intimidated
by Yin and Yang over there. What's up, Niecey? You
think one of these chicks might try to step to Toby or
something?"

I was never one of those girls who got jealous of another female because I wasn't a bad looking one myself, but
these two . . . They had me ready to go to the gym and
put in some extra workout hours or go see Dr. Miami for
a few sessions. Both of their bodies were banging. The
dark-skinned one was what some would consider slim-
thick, with a flat-ass stomach and hips and ass for days,
but she had some broad-ass shoulders. Her homegirl,
who reminded me of Ice T's wife Coco, obviously had
some work done, but she was still one of the baddest
white girls I'd seen in a long time. The name Storm was
very becoming to her. And I could tell that the color of
her hair was no doubt the reason why she went by that
name. Her makeup was flawless, and her whole style
caught your attention at first glance. A little thicker than
the chocolate girl, Storm would be any man's fantasy up
in here and would make a lot of money from the horny-
ass rich men who were going to be in attendance.

I waved Koi's comment off. "Girl, I ain't worried
'bout nobody takin' my place with Toby." I flashed my
engagement ring. "My position in his life is solidified.
Neither one of them bitches compare to me." Looking
down at the spaghetti strap one-piece cotton jumpsuit
I had on, I smoothed my hands down my waistline and
over my hips. I'd gained a few pounds since Toby and I
got together, but not noticeable enough to where my rolls
would show through whatever tight-fitting outfit I had on.
Luckily for me, I got my mama's genes when it came to
my body. Every pound I gained either went to my titties,
thighs, or ass. I had some small love handles, but Toby

loved them, so the thought of toning up never crossed my mind.

"Okay, then, Ms. Solidified, since you're here, why don't you be the third judge for me. Cai and Ness couldn't make it, and Toby said he had something to do. So that just leaves me, you, and Beano up to the task of giving them the yay or nay to work here."

Judging these two chicks sliding down the pole wasn't how I wanted to spend my day, but since I was already here . . . "I'm in. Where's Beano?"

As soon as the words left my mouth, the double doors at the back of the club opened again and in walked Beano, followed by two of his friends. You could tell by the way they were dressed and the expensive-ass sunglasses on their faces and the chains hanging from around their necks that they had money. Their broad shoulders, tall frames, and athletic bodies told you that the money in their pockets came from some professional sports contract. Since Beano was one of the NFL's fastest and best running backs, I assumed his friends were in the same profession.

Koi smacking her lips made me turn toward her. "This nigga here." She shook her head. "He always gotta make some kind of entrance wherever he goes. That shit gets on my nerves." Although her lips were talking shit, I couldn't help but notice the tint of red that covered her face. Was she blushing? Her dark eyes stayed trained on Beano as he and his crew got closer to us. She even crossed her legs a little tighter when his cologne surrounded the whole little area we were standing in.

"What's good, ladies?" Beano asked as he took off his glasses and gave what had to be the prettiest smile I ever saw. Well, next to Toby, of course. He pulled us both into a hug but released his grip around me first. With his chocolate arm still wrapped around Koi's waist, he whispered something in her ear that caused her to smack him in his chest and then turn to me.

"Now that he's here, we can get this show going. Halo! Storm!" she yelled at the two friends who were drooling at the sight of Beano. "Y'all follow us to the smaller stage. The main one isn't ready yet." Koi looked at Beano and rolled her eyes. "We'll have them dance to one song each and then together. All I need is a yes or no from you. No one from the peanut gallery behind you."

Beano smirked. "You got that, little mama. You won't hear a peep from Armell or my partner, Big Will."

The second Beano said Big Will, my eyes went over his shoulder to the man behind him—and I damn near had a heart attack. "What the fuck are you doing here?" I asked, pushing past Koi and Beano, standing directly in front of my ex-boyfriend. Me talking to him didn't register because he was so busy looking at Halo and Storm. It wasn't until I pushed his shoulder that his eyes landed on me.

"Niecey?" His eyebrows furrowed. "What the fuck are you doing here? Better yet, why the hell did you stand me up a few weeks ago? You had me looking stupid as fuck, sitting by myself at Lawry's waiting on you to never show up."

He was right. I did stand him up. After I sent him that text about meeting him at the restaurant in downtown L.A., I ended up going straight to Toby's loft and forgetting all about Will. Especially after Toby basically ripped off all of my clothes the second I walked into the door and wouldn't come up for air until my pussy was literally dry. I didn't think meeting up with Will was a good idea. Not without talking to Toby about it first.

"Will, you know I'm engaged now. Us meeting up for drinks or whatever would not have been cool with my fiancé."

His eyes lustfully scanned my body from head to toe.

I'm not gonna lie, whatever Will has been up to since the last time I saw him had been doing him good. I mean, he'd always been a handsome man, but something about his whole getup was different. Gone was the broken, mad-at-the-world, don't-give-a-fuck-about-how-I-look boy who had a baby by my twin sister. What stood in front of me now was a grown-ass man. A grown-ass *sexy* man at that.

LaLa and I were still not on speaking terms, so I had no idea what had been going on in his life. This new job he had must have made him a lot of money, because the chains around his neck looked just as expensive as the ones Beano had on.

"Your fiancé must be an insecure muthafucka if you can't go to dinner with an old friend." He grabbed my wrist and pulled me closer to him. "I gotta give it to the fake-ass Calvin Klein model. He's taking good care of you, because you look good. Your hair still fly as always. Not a fan of the bob, but it looks good on you. Your body still thick and tight. I'm surprised he let you come outside dressed in this thin-ass shit."

When his fingers caressed the top of my cleavage, I smacked his hand away, and he laughed.

"And you still feisty as hell." He licked his lips. "I've always loved that about you."

"Yo, Will, who is this?" their other friend asked, finally taking his attention from Halo and Storm.

Will bit his bottom lip. "This is the twin that should've been my baby mama."

"Ooooh, shit. This the other twin? This Niecey?"

Will smirked and nodded his head.

"Man, you said she was fine as fuck, and you wasn't lying." He stuck his hand out to me. "I'm Armell Bullock. Tight end for the Los Angeles Sabors."

Will smacked his hand from in front of me. "My guy, fall back with that weak-ass game. This one is already spoken for."

"You still tapping that, Will?" Armell asked, his eyes going from my lips to my chest and then back to Will.

"He isn't tapping shit over here and hasn't in a long time," I answered for him after Will took too long to respond, attitude all in my tone and body language. "My fiancé, who owns part of this club with Beano, however, is. Now, if you don't mind, Koi, Beano, and I need to get to these auditions. You two can wait here or outside somewhere."

Armell smacked his lips. "It's like that, shorty? Yo, Bean . . . I thought you said we could help with the auditions, bro. I could've stayed in bed with that Latina cutie I met last night if I would've known this."

Beano, whose attention was still on Koi, addressed both Will and Armell with his back turned to them. "You heard the lady. Maybe next time."

"Man, this is some bullshit," Armell fussed.

"Nah. We good. Let's go down the street and grab something to eat from that soul food spot at the corner. You're more than welcome to join us, Niecey," Will offered.

The *I see you checking me out* smirk on his face broke me from the small trance that I got caught up in and had me turning away from him and walking toward the second room with the smaller stage. Grabbing my purse off of one of the tables, I ignored Koi calling my name and Will's boisterous laugh. I'd never do anything to hurt Toby and mess up what we had, but being around my ex and seeing him in person after all of this time had me feeling some type of way. I didn't know what was going on, so I had to get as far away from Will as I could before that "solidified position" I was just bragging about to Koi became null and void.

So lost in my thoughts about everything that just happened, I wasn't surprised when I ran into a hard body that was standing in the doorway of the smaller VIP room. I stumbled back a bit but was caught by a pair of familiar arms before I completely fell on my ass. The second my body was pulled into his, I instantly melted into him. Any thought of Will and his lustful looks were gone, and the only thing I could do was inhale the scent of the one man who set my soul on fire with a single touch.

Instinctively, I buried my face in his chest and wrapped my arms around his waist. His soft lips kissed the top of my head and then traced a blazing trail down my face and to my neck.

"I'm sorry," we both said at the same time, and a wave of relief washed over me. Not sure what he was apologizing for, seeing as it was me that refused to answer any of his calls or texts, I would accept anything to get us back in order.

"What are you doing here?" I asked Toby as I looked up into his face. "Koi said you were busy and couldn't make it." Those beautiful eyes of his looked down at me, expressing any and everything he felt for me. The beard on his chin had grown out and made him look kind of rugged, but I liked it. His caramel-blond hair was now a little past his shoulders and in one of those man buns at the crown of his head. The white, V-neck shirt he had on smelled like it was fresh out of the laundry and hugged every muscle across his chest, stomach, and arms. His colorful tattoos were on full display and looking sexy as ever.

When I looked down at the blue sweats he had on, I couldn't help but notice the print of his curved dick that was semihard. My pussy began to thump just thinking about the trouble she was going to get into that night when we made up.

"You send me a picture of you lying in bed naked, playing with yourself, and you didn't expect me to come find you?" he asked, licking his bottom lip and pulling it into his mouth.

"But how did you know I was here? I never told you, and Koi didn't say anything when she was on the phone with you earlier."

He pointed up at the security cameras. "You know I have eyes everywhere." Bending his head down, Toby kissed me and then rubbed his nose against mine. "I got your message. I came to get you. Now let's go home so that I can fuck you so good that you won't ever have to use those pretty little fingers to please my pussy again."

My body reacted to Toby's words, and I could feel that slow burn starting at the tip of my toes and traveling to my core. "Babe, we still need to talk about why I've been ignoring you and staying at my place."

His lips brushed past my ear. "We will. But right now, my dick needs to talk to his best friend and go for a little swim."

I moaned and pulled Toby's hard body closer to mine. Our lips connected, and the kiss we shared was filled with so much passion, promise, and lust, I could feel my panties becoming more soaked by the second.

"Uuuuuuuh," Koi cleared her throat. "Can y'all move that shit somewhere else? We got an audition to see to."

I pecked Toby's lips one more time before we finally broke apart. Then I turned around, still wrapped in his arms. Koi had a goofy smile on her face. Beano was nodding his head, and those two bitches, Halo and Storm, were eye-fucking the shit out of my baby. My body tensed, and I could feel Toby's hold on me tighten. He kissed my neck and then stuck his free hand out to dap Beano. When he turned his attention to Halo and Storm to introduce himself, I gladly took over the honors.

"Halo and Storm, this is my fiancé and your boss, Tobias Wright, but everyone calls him Toby."

Halo was the first to speak. "Nice to meet you, Toby. This place is hot. A real different look from the clubs we used to dance at in Atlanta, but I'm not mad at it."

"A different look? Is that a good or bad thing?" he asked.

Storm stepped her ass up this time and stuck her hand out as if Toby was supposed to raise it to his lips and kiss it. I took it and shook it for him. I could already tell by her body language that this bitch was probably going to be a problem. She smiled at me and then turned her focus back to Toby, her Southern accent super sugary when she spoke.

"Oh, it's a good thing, Tobias. Halo and I can already see that this isn't going to be no hood establishment and all the men with fat pockets will be here. You put us on the team, and there's no doubt that you'll be making racks on top of racks on top of racks."

She licked her lips and winked at Toby. Before I could even step to the bitch, Koi positioned herself between us, and Toby pulled me back. His beard tickled my skin when he nuzzled his face into my neck and sucked on his favorite spot. I smirked at the look on Storm's face and dared that bitch to come out of pocket again with my eyes.

"Look, since you're here already, Toby, you might as well stay for the audition," Beano said. "I think we need another male's perspective since my partnas couldn't come."

"Who? Ness and Cai?" Toby asked.

"Naw. A couple of my teammates. Armell Bullock and Will Davis."

As if they heard their names being mentioned, Armell and Will came around the corner with bags filled with Styrofoam takeout plates and cans of soda.

"Yo, Beano, they didn't have any greens ready at that joint, so I got you some fried cabbage instead," Armell yelled as they walked up closer to us.

"Aye, Niecey, I got you your favorite." Will held a bag out to me, but I didn't accept it. "Catfish nuggets, mac & cheese, yams, and that nasty-ass corn bread dressing. Gravy on the side."

Toby stepped in front of me, and I could feel the tension rising in the room. "I'll take that." He grabbed the bag from Will. "Me and my girl thank you for the lunch, but I'm more than capable of filling her belly up. Good looking, though." Toby handed the bag to one of the construction workers walking by. "By the way, who are you, bro? I don't remember putting a delivery boy on my payroll."

"Um, Beano, can you get your boys and make them leave? I already told you they couldn't come back here," Koi turned to Beano and said.

"He ain't gotta get shit. We heard you the first time, so we leaving," Will responded to Koi but had his eyes still trained on Toby. "And to answer your question, bro, I'm the nigga that bust that pussy open way before you even knew she existed." He pointed to me. "I literally and figuratively hit that sweet spot first. Surprised you don't feel my name carved all up in that shit when you stroking." Will laughed.

Before he could even turn around to make his dramatic exit, Toby pushed past Halo and Storm and socked Will dead in his jaw.

Tobias

The only thing on my mind at this exact moment was to beat the shit out of this asshole in front of me. Fuck all of the hard work Koi and the rest of the team put in to get my club up to where it was at now. The second I saw this loser on the security cameras, I knew who he was. Hence, my reason for being up here right now. Well, that and the picture Niecey sent to my phone of her being extra nasty with those fingers of hers. After I hung up the phone with Koi earlier, I had already planned on coming up here to grab Niecey and bring her ass back home, but seeing him walk his sleazy ass into my establishment just made the need for me to come up here greater.

My knuckles were throbbing from the blow I'd just landed to the side of Will's face, but I didn't care. I hadn't had a physical altercation with anyone since my years in college, but it was all coming back to me now. Especially the few techniques I learned when I took up cage fighting. If Niecey's ex thought he was about to beat my ass, he had another think coming. Stepping back, I allowed him to gain his bearings before I went after him again. I didn't want it to be said that I caught him off guard when I didn't. He flexed his jaw a few times, then balled up his fists and started swinging at me. I dodged a couple of his first tries, but when I stumbled over Niecey, he was able to sock me a few times in my ribs and then on my back as I turned over.

I could hear Koi screaming at Beano to stop what was going on, but he knew better than to get involved. His ass was just added to the closing deal for Decadence, and it would take nothing for me to buy him out and have Chasin change some shit around. Their other buddy Armell tried to jump in and sneak me from the side, but Niecey stopped his ass dead in his tracks when she swung that big-ass purse of hers and hit him in the head. That shit was extra heavy with the weight of the .45 she kept in there, so I knew he was seeing stars right about now.

"Baby . . . Please stop . . . You're messing the club up," Niecey cried as my fists continued to plow into her ex-lover.

I didn't have to do him the way I was, but I kept replaying the way Niecey's body reacted to his touch when he caressed his fingers down the top part of her breasts. Although I couldn't see her facial expression from the angle that the camera was in, I knew my woman's body like the back of my hand. She was turned on for a second, but something snapped her out of whatever was going through her mind, and she pushed his hand away. If Will still had even an ounce of control over the way her body reacted, that meant that she wasn't completely over this fool as much as she claimed to be. Those weeks of crying on my shoulder and me comforting her after she found out that her twin sister was having his baby was basically for nothing if it could be that easy for him to have her feeling some type of way—especially when she was engaged to be married to me. My mind went back to the conversation Cai, Ness, and I had the night I had them come up to the club. Was Niecey cheating on me? And was she cheating on me with Will?

"Tobias!" Niecey yelled, throwing her body in front of me, causing me to stop swinging and break out of the reverie I was in. "Tobias . . . babe . . . Listen to me." Her hand cupped my face. "Baby, you're going to beat him to death if you don't stop. Wh-wh-where did you learn to fight like that?" Niecey's questioning eyes looked over my face. When she saw the small cut I could feel above my eyebrow, she touched it with her finger, and I flinched. "We need to go put some ice on that, Toby, before it starts to swell. Are you okay?"

"I'm good," I grumbled, looking over at Will, who was staring back at me. His face was much worse off than mine, and I hoped I broke something. With the amount of blood leaking from his nose, I was pretty sure I had.

"This isn't over, you white muthafucka. I'ma catch you slipping one day, and when I do, I'ma take your girl and whatever else I can get my hands on," Will yelled as his friend and a few of my security guards, who must've just walked in, carried him out. I went to charge at him again, but Beano stepped in front of me this time.

"Toby, man, I apologize about that. I had no idea Will and your girl had a history. I mean, he showed us pictures of her, but they were old, so I didn't know. My bad, man. And I'll pay for everything that was damaged out of my own pocket." He stuck his hand out, and I took it. Pulling me into a brotherly hug, Beano whispered into my ear. "I never really liked that nigga anyway. But Coach wanted me to hang out with him a bit now that he's been picked up. Just say the word, and I'll drop his ass like a bad habit."

"Nah . . . We good. I don't think he'll come at me like that again anyway." My eyes went to Niecey, who was standing behind me, talking in hushed tones with Koi. When our eyes connected, that crazy feeling I got whenever I was near her started to shift around in my stomach. Just like magnets, we started for each other but stopped when the girl who I know now as Storm stepped in front of me and placed her hands on my chest.

"Oh, Tobias, are you okay?" She tried to reach up and touch the cut above my eye, but I stepped back from her touch altogether.

Niecey's eyes narrowed, and I could tell she was about to jump on the poor girl, but we didn't need both of us getting into fights today.

"First of all, my name is not Tobias. . . . It's Toby, and only my family and close friends call me that. Since you don't hold either of those titles, you can address me as Mr. Wright."

"I . . . I-I'm sorry. The girl over there said your name was Tobias, so I thought that's what I could call you." She stepped back into my personal space but was pulled back by her friend, who was standing next to her.

"Storm," she hissed through gritted teeth with a fake smile on her face when she looked up at me. "Bitch, stop flirting with this man before his fiancée stops our chances from getting hired here. Do you want to go back to Atlanta?"

Storm looked at her friend, then back at me and shook her head.

"Then get your shit together and stop thinking with your pussy for a minute."

Halo turned to me after whispering something in Storm's ear that had her stepping farther back from me and looking at the stage, irritation and attitude all over her face.

"I'm sorry about that, Mr. Wright. I'm Halo, as you already know, and Storm is my partner in crime, and we're here to audition for the open dancer spots. If you don't mind, we would like to go get ready so that we can dance for whoever will be handling the audition today." She smiled and stuck out her hand.

Something about Halo was calming but struck me as odd. I don't know if it was how broad her shoulders were or the fact that she was almost as tall as me without heels on. I shook her hand and excused them to get ready for their performance.

After speaking with Beano, Koi, and a few of the workers who were going to clean up the mess Will and I made, I grabbed Niecey's hand and took her into the small office I had added for Raul. It wasn't fully furnished yet, but it did have an oak desk and a small refrigerator in it. I grabbed the bowl of ice out of the freezer and placed a cube above my eyebrow. Sitting down in the leather reclining chair, I leaned back as far as I could go and closed my eyes, trying to control the headache that was slowly starting to come on. When I felt Niecey push between my legs, I opened them wider to allow her in and placed my free hand on her hip.

"Do you feel better now?" she asked, taking the single ice cube from my hand and adding it to the pile she had in the scarf she must've pulled from her purse, making me a small ice bag.

"I feel great. It's not every day I get to beat the shit out of my fiancée's ex-boyfriend." I opened one eye. "You mad I kicked his ass?"

Placing the ice on my forehead, Niecey smacked her teeth and sat down on my lap. "Why would I be mad? Will's ass deserved that beat-down. It was long overdue. I was more concerned about you. I didn't want you to end up in jail for killing his ass. The way your eyes turned dark kind of had me scared for a minute. It was like you blacked out."

In all truth . . . I actually did black out. It was one of the reasons why I stopped cage fighting back then and caught my first case when I was sixteen. Of course, that part never made it to my records because my father knew somebody that owed him a favor; but still, I knew it happened.

"Nah. I was good. I just didn't like what dude said." I shook my head and winced, deciding to change the subject. "The question I need to be asking is, are *we* okay? You still hiding from me, or are you going to come home where you belong?" I made my dick move on her ass. "You know we've been missing you and our favorite girl."

Niecey's head fell back as she began to laugh. The small vein popping out of her neck caught my attention and drew me directly to it. Like a vampire getting ready to feed, I sank my teeth into that soft spot and started to suck. The moan that escaped her lips had my dick jumping on its own this time and coming fully to life.

"Toby . . ." she moaned in my ear as she lifted her leg over my head and straddled my lap. "I missed you so much, baby."

"I missed you too." Pulling down the thin straps of the bodysuit she wore, I freed her breasts and took one in my mouth while both of our hands played with each other. The warmth and wetness forming between her legs could be felt through the sweats I had on and on my thighs. I tried to place my fingers on her clit but was having a hard time. "Get up so I can pull your pants off," I mumbled against her chocolate nipple.

Her fingers that were massaging my scalp gripped the back of my head and pulled me deeper into her breast, stuffing more of that luscious tittie into my mouth.

"You take them off," she breathlessly said against my ear.

The chill that vibrated down my spine caused the adrenaline in my blood to pump a little harder. Grabbing the thin material of the suit she had on at the seam, I started to rip the thing off of the rest of her body. When the tear reached the crotch area of her jumpsuit, I had a little resistance. My hands started to burn from me pulling so hard and my hands slipping from the sweat on my palms. Instead of damaging my shit further, I blindly felt around the desk for the pair of scissors I saw when I walked in and picked them up as soon as I touched them.

"You better not cut me either," Niecey said, still enjoying the feel of my tongue circling her nipple.

"You know me better than that. But just in case I do nip it a little bit, I'll make sure to kiss it until it feels better. Deal?"

"Deal," she murmured, her lips now attacking my neck.

With swift and careful precision, I placed the scissors at the space between us and cut the rest of her jumpsuit. Her legs were still covered with the stretchy black material, but everything else on her body was exposed.

"Where your panties at, ShaNiece?" I asked, dipping my fingers into that golden goodness between her thighs. The scent of her sex wafted into my nose and drove me crazy. If I could bottle this shit and drink it all night, I would.

"I . . . I . . . I . . . couldn't . . . wear . . . an . . . any . . . with this . . . outfit . . . Aaaaaaaaah, Toby."

I stuck my finger in again; this time, I swirled it around a bit and hooked it to her G-spot. When her body started to shake, I lifted her off my lap just enough to pull my dick out of my pants and then slammed her down on it. The feel of her soft walls contracting around my sensitive head and hard shaft caused me to squeal like a bitch. I could feel my face turning red but didn't give a fuck about being embarrassed at the moment. Right now, I needed to feel my woman's love. I needed to feel my woman's essence. I needed to feel my woman's soul. We'd been disconnected for a couple of weeks, and we had a lot of making up to do.

"Toooooby . . . Baby . . . Fuck, I missed you."

"I, I-I missed you too, baby." I was stuttering and shit. But I didn't care. Niecey always pulled this crazy behavior out of me, and I loved it.

Smacking her on her ass, she began to move her hips and rock into me. She had a death grip on my dick at the same time a moistness that was more heavenly than a cake fresh out of the oven soothed my shit every time she moved. I felt my nut building up, but I refused to cum before she did. Although I was pretty sure we would continue making up after we left here and made it back to my place, I needed to feel that quake between her legs that had me falling in love the very first time she and I had sex.

"Ride that shit, Niecey," I gritted through my teeth, smacking her on her ass again. When I grabbed her hips and started to pound into her shit from beneath, I had to capture her lips into mine to stop the loud noises she was making.

Pressing her hands to my chest, Niecey pushed me farther back into the chair, placing her feet on the arms, and started squatting on my shit. I knew the position was a bad idea in this chair when she first got into it, but if she didn't care about the chair breaking, neither did I.

"Toby . . . baby . . . I'm about to cum," she screamed out as her bouncing became quicker and faster. I heard the first creak in the chair when she doubled down and rolled her hips. When she did that little trick again, I wasn't surprised when the base holding us up finally gave out, causing the chair to fall to the floor. And just like the champ that she was, Niecey continued to ride the hell out of my dick until she came, and I filled her love hole up with all of my cum shortly after her.

We stayed on the floor, broken chair and all, until we both had gained some of our strength back and were able to stand to our feet without falling back down.

"So, how am I supposed to get to my car and into the apartment like this?" Niecey held up both sides of the ripped up jumpsuit that was hanging off of her body.

"You told me to take it off, and I did. You think some flimsy material was gon' keep me from that pussy?" I said, walking up to her and cupping what would always be mine with my hand. "It's been weeks since I had some, and you know I was horny as fuck. I thought I was the Incredible Hulk at first and tried to rip the shit off of you."

She laughed and picked up the scarf that had the ice cubes in it and placed it on my forehead again. "Yeah, I saw that. Now, what are we gonna do?"

I looked around the room for some jacket, sheet, or something but didn't see anything. "Call Koi and tell her to run to that little shopping center up the street and get you something. They should be done with the auditions now."

Niecey pulled her phone out of her purse. "And what are we going to do until she comes back?"

I laid her across the top of the desk and opened her legs, looking at her plump lower lips and the evidence of what we just did glistening on her lips. "I'm pretty sure we can think of a few things to occupy our time."

I didn't even wait for her to finish the phone call to Koi. My lips and tongue were getting reacquainted with every inch of her pussy from the inside out. Will's ass sure had another think coming if he ever thought he'd get close enough even to sniff Niecey's sweetness. I made a mental note to make sure his ass never stepped foot in the club again and nowhere near my woman as long as I was around.

Koiya

"All right, I'm back. Now, let's get this little audition over with," I yelled toward the stage where Beano, Storm, and Halo were having an amusing conversation. The big-ass smile on Halo's face was fake as hell, and Storm's irritating laugh echoed throughout the room. "Looney," I yelled to the DJ, "spin the first track. I'm not about to wait for these heffas."

I sat down at the booth closest to the stage and started going through my checklist of things I still needed to get done before the grand opening of the club. I wasn't lying to Niecey when I told her that I was thankful to Toby for giving me this opportunity. Although I had never run a club before, I could see myself easily getting used to it.

"Girl, take it off for me. You know just what I want
It's always hard to leave this private show . . ."

Chris Brown's opening verse for the song he did with T.I. boomed through the speakers. Placing my pen on top of the paper I just signed, I looked up at the stage and waited on Halo to audition. Moving her body to the beat, she danced around the stage and did the little stripper walk that most strippers do. Her red bikini left little to the imagination and had all kinds of shiny shit glued to it. The matching sky-high stilettos she had on were a little too small for her feet. Hopefully, the dimmed lighting would hide the way her toes were spilling out of the front if she couldn't find a size bigger.

Her dance moves were pretty basic, so I wondered why she came so highly recommended. A few climbs up the pole and some slides down were her most difficult tricks. Aside from the neck snapping, hair shaking, and groping of her titties and ass, I was still lost on what made her so special. Holding my hand up in the air, Looney recognized my signal to stop the music and began to turn the volume down slowly.

"Okay, next," I yelled, still looking down at my to-do list.

"So, what did you think?" Halo walked to the edge of the stage and asked, voice chipper and high pitched as hell, her arm shielding her fake triple-D breasts. Her dark skin was covered in that cheap-ass glitter shit she probably got from the Dollar Store, and the Victoria's Secret body spray she drenched her body in started fucking with my sinuses.

"If you want, I can dance to another song," she managed to say through labored breaths.

"I've seen enough," I answered, still looking down at my papers. "Tell Storm she's up next, and then y'all can do the tag team duo thing you guys are supposedly famous for."

I didn't have to look up to know that she had a stank look on her face at my response, because I could feel it. I didn't give a damn, though. So far, I wasn't impressed with what one half of the team had to offer. Pretty sure I would feel the same way with her sidekick, I pulled out my phone from my pocket and sent Niecey a text, asking if she knew of any other dancers that would love to try out for the two slots and seeing if her and Toby's freaky asses had made it home. I was pretty sure she'd probably jump at the chance to replace Halo and Storm, seeing as she didn't care too much for the two birds in the first place. *Solidified, my ass,* I thought and cracked a smile. I liked the fact that they caused Niecey to feel some type of way with their presence here. That way, she'd stay on her toes and stop pushing Toby away by playing these childish-ass games.

"Looney," I yelled for the DJ again, "play the next track."

Getting up from my seat, I walked to the small bar at the back of the room and grabbed a bottle of water from the fridge while making sure that the shipment of juices we received for the mixed drinks were stacked in their proper place. After wiping the already-clean bar top down, I made it back to my seat, only to become highly annoyed when I saw Beano sitting his ass in my vacated spot. I rolled my eyes and snatched my clipboard from out of his hands.

"Aye, you mean as fuck, yo," he licked his lips and said. "But I like that shit. Turns a nigga on like a muthafucka."

I cleared my throat and shook my head. "Can you please move out of my seat? I'm trying to work here."

"I am too, fun size. Did you or did you not invite me here to help with these auditions?"

"I did. But that was *before* you almost caused me to get fired by inviting your little entourage with you."

He shrugged his shoulders. "I didn't know Toby's girl was Will's ex. I mean, he showed me a picture of her before, but that was it. I didn't recognize her face when I walked in. She wasn't one of mine to remember anyway."

"One of yours to remember, huh? So you got 'em lined up like that?"

He flashed the sexiest smile at me, his smooth chocolate skin shining underneath the tinted red light. Beano was fine as hell, but I'd never tell his ho ass that. Gripping the bill of his fitted hat, he twisted his hat to the side, giving me a clear view of his face. Long lashes lined his slanted eyes. His dark orbs were a chestnut brown. The facial hair surrounding his full lips and jawline was neatly trimmed and lined up to perfection. Even the two iced-out studs in his ears caught my attention—not because they were so big, but because they were shining like diamonds in the dim light. My eyes traveled down to his arms, chest, and the rest of his body. Him being the NFL's leading wide receiver, I could only imagine what his body looked like.

My cheeks heating up broke me from my nasty thoughts and had me looking away and shaking my head. Beano's cocky laugh caused me to look back in his direction.

"Would me having a line of females make your thoughts about fucking me any different?"

"Who said anything about fucking you?"

He stared at me for a minute before he smirked and looked toward the stage, totally ignoring my question. Ludacris and Nicki Minaj's "My Chick Bad" started to flow through the speakers, telling me that Storm was about to get up there and probably bore me just like her homegirl.

"My chick bad, my chick hood, my chick do stuff that ya chick wish she could. . . . My chick bad, bad, badder than yours."

When she stepped out in a silver bodysuit that resembled a disco ball, I couldn't stop the laugh that escaped my lips.

As she was walking over to the pole, I was expecting Storm to walk around it a few times and then twirl, but I got the shock of my life when her ass damn near ran up the pole, placed her heels on the ceiling of the room and started twerking her ass around in a circle. If that wasn't enough, she started sliding down the pole upside down, without her ass missing a beat. Once she was close enough to the stage, she slid one leg down the pole, and the other leg up, landing in a split. I thought the trick was over until she started to spin around the pole again, legs still split and in place. Storm was doing some real-life Cirque du Soleil shit without all of the costumes and props.

"Yo, shorty is bad. You gotta hire her," Beano said, his eyes trained on Storm as she snaked her body across the stage and dropped to her knees to twerk again, ass jiggling to the beat and everything.

Beano was right about one thing. Storm was bad and would make us a boatload of money with her talents. The only thing I was worried about was if she would accept my offer to dance here when she found out I wasn't going to offer Halo that other slot. As if she knew I was already on the fence about her, Halo walked out on stage, dressed in the same outfit as Storm, but purple. Her body didn't fill the outfit out like Storm's did, but she had a nice silhouette from where I was sitting.

The music switched up to some song I had never heard before, but the beat was still knocking through the club. I watched as Halo turned into a totally different person once she and Storm began to dance together. Their interaction with each other was borderline porno style but would have all kinds of bills flying in the air once they started their routine. When Storm wrapped her thighs around the pole and lay straight back, I was wondering what the hell she was doing. But when Halo hopped on top of her stomach, stilettos and all, and started twerking her ass off like she was on a surfboard, I had already seen enough. I raised my hand, and Looney stopped the music. I walked up toward the stage. Both of them were trying to catch their breath as they met me at the edge.

"I'm not gonna lie," I started, looking down at my clipboard. "I was ready just to offer Storm one of these slots, but after seeing you guys dance together, I can see why y'all were recommended." I bit my lip and looked at them, still debating on whether I should offer them the positions. I thought about running it past Niecey first, but this was an executive decision I needed to make on my own.

Before I could say anything else, Beano walked up behind me with two bottles of water and handed them to the dynamic duo. "I don't know what Koi just said to you two, but you're hired."

"They're *what?*" I reared my head back, not liking the way he just did my job.

"You heard me. *They* are hired. My dick hard as fuck right now watching that last show y'all just did. I know if I was turned on, all the other muthafuckas will be too. Turned on men with money in their pockets means . . ."

"Money in ours," all three of them said at the same time.

"Hold up. How can you make a decision like that without talking to me first?" I rolled my eyes and turned my body toward him. "*I'm* the manager, which means *I* have a say in who we hire around here. And although I think their performance was great, I think I need to run this by a couple of other people before we can give them a definite answer."

Storm snorted. "A couple of other people like who? Ole girl that was here earlier hating on me? She doesn't own this place. Her man does."

"And I do too," Beano said, smiling up at Storm and taking her empty water bottle. "And I say that you guys are hired. Go change in the dressing room, and I'll meet y'all back there. I'm hungry as hell and want to take y'all to In-N-Out since y'all never been there."

Storm was all smiles as she turned her fake ass around and rushed off the stage. Halo nodded at both Beano and me before she made her exit.

I waited until Looney grabbed his shit and left the room before I turned my rage toward Beano. "Nigga, don't you *ever* do no shit like that again. I don't care if you own all or a small part of this club. Toby left *me* in charge of entertainment, and *I* have the last say, regardless of whose name is on the deed."

"Are you done?"

"Am I done? What the hell does that mean?"

Ignoring my question again, Beano pulled me by my shirt into his chest and pressed his lips against mine. At first, I fought against his kiss but got in sync with it once his tongue invaded my mouth. Stars, moons, and rainbows were the only things I could see as we stood there, locking lips in our own world. When he finally pulled his face from mine, I was weak at the knees and almost lost my balance. If it weren't for his quick reflexes, I would've easily hit the ground.

"We're ready, Beano," Storm cooed as she walked up behind us. I knew she probably saw us kissing but didn't care either way.

"Do you wanna join us?" Beano asked, looking at me and smirking, evidence of our kiss still on his lips.

I placed my hands on his chest and pushed myself away, giving a good amount of distance between us. I opened my mouth to answer his question but closed it shut when my mind went blank.

"I guess that's a no for the manager, huh?" Storm sarcastically said as she placed her hand on Beano's forearm and pulled him toward the exit. "You think we can get that tour of your house after we eat? We've always heard about the mansions you professional athletes have in The Hills. It would be so cool to see one in real life." Her voice was very suggestive of what she really wanted to do, and for some reason, I started to get a little jealous.

Beano looked back at me one last time with questioning eyes, silently offering me a spot again, but this time I shook my head no. Even though his kiss just knocked me off of my feet, I wasn't about to be another one of these females he had waiting in line for him to settle down. Besides, I just moved to Los Angeles, and there were plenty of men out there for me to meet once I was ready to start dating. I was sure Toby, Cai, or Finesse had more friends to choose from. Hopefully, they looked, tasted, and smelled as good as Beano's ass, though.

"Yeah," I answered my ringing phone, walking out of the small VIP room and back into the main one.

"Aye, Koi, my partner just called. We got approved for the liquor license, so call up Raymond and put in the order for everything I had on the list. Make sure you get more than enough for the opening. I don't wanna run out of any liquor on the first night. Oh, and make sure you have the waitress cross-selling that Decadence 24K Gold. I already put in an order for fifteen cases of it. At 15K a pop, they would be crazy not to get their 5 percent," Toby said into the phone as I scribbled down everything he was saying. "How did the auditions go?"

"Uhhh . . . They were cool. I wanted to run it past you and the rest of the fellas before I offered them the position, but Beano already gave it to them."

Toby laughed. "They must've really put an impression on him, huh?"

"Something like that," I responded, sending an email for the order of alcohol to Raymond.

"All right, then, Koi, keep up the good work, and I'll see you in a few days."

"Okay . . . Toby?"

"What's up?"

"Can I speak to Niecey real quick?"

"Uuuuum, she busy right now. Was it something important?"

I shook my head as if he could see me. "No. I'll talk to her the next time I see her."

"All right, then, Koi, later."

"Later."

Hanging up the phone, I made a mental note to let Niecey know that Storm and Halo would be working for her man now. Yeah, they left with Beano, but the look in Storm's eyes when she first saw Toby told me that she would try her hand at him one day. Niecey's position may have been solidified now, but if she didn't get her shit together, she might just make room for the next bitch to swoop in on what she claimed as hers.

ShaNiece

A soft moan escaped from my mouth as Toby pressed his lips to the arch of my foot and then lightly ran his fingers from the tip of my toes, up to my ankle, and then back down to my toes again. We had just gotten through with our fourth round of makeup sex since we made it home a few hours ago, and my kitty kat was in dire need of some rest. From the second we stepped into his loft, we had been going at it like two dogs in heat. Never mind the quick fuck we had in his office or the *hot ten* we couldn't pass up in the car before we pulled out of the parking lot. My lower lips were so sore right now that I couldn't close my legs if I tried. The pressure from my thighs pressing against my shit was so uncomfortable that all I could do was lay spread out in the middle of Toby's king-size bed with nothing but his scrunchie hanging from my wrist and getting expertly rubbed down. Green silk sheets still damp from our sweat and sex, empty bottles of water thrown on the abandoned side of the bed and floor while my fine-ass fiancé, in all his naked glory, was lying on his stomach, playing with my feet and reading the subtitles at the bottom of the muted TV screen. All I needed now was a cigarette and a glass of wine to complete the relaxed state that I was in.

Lazily grabbing my phone from the nightstand next to me, I browsed through my Google playlist until I found something I wanted to listen to and pressed *play*. Toby's grip tightened on my thigh, and my eyes went down to him.

"It don't get no better, and my tongue writing your leathers . . ."

He sang along with R. Kelly as the beginning of "Drown in It" by Chris Brown began to play. Toby's slick ass knew what he was doing singing this song to me and touching all over my body. His voice was like a natural aphrodisiac for me, and he knew it. But as much as my core was starting to heat up and my clit was starting to thump, my pussy was still on time-out. Playfully snatching my leg from up under his arm, I rolled over to my side of the bed and grabbed another bottle of water.

"Why did you move?" Toby asked, that sexy, boyish grin on his face. His hair, which I loosened from the man bun he had earlier, was messy and hanging in his face. The caramel-blond strands that were a little past his shoulders now complemented his sun-kissed skin and gave him that dirty-but-sexy bad boy look. I had my own personal "Jax" Teller from *SOA*, and I loved every minute of it. He smirked when he caught my lustful glare. "What you over there smiling about?"

I licked my lips. "I'm loving how much you look like that dude from *Sons of Anarchy* now with your hair being longer and your facial hair growing in."

He pulled at his beard. "Oh, yeah? Well, why don't you come hop on this dick and take me for a little ride then?"

"Haven't you had enough already, boy?"

"Not really. Niecey, you know I could fuck you all night long and never get tired. That pretty thang between those thighs of yours is golden and has me completely infatuated."

The blush that covered my body caused a few goose bumps to decorate my arms and chest. "As much as I appreciate your infatuation with my private part, unfortunately, she's out of commission until further notice." I tried to get up from the bed to go to the bathroom but fell back down from my legs still being a little weak.

"You need some help?"

Waving him off, I got up from the bed successfully this time and walked into the bathroom. I was in desperate need of a good soaking. Sitting in the tub for an hour or two would be the best thing for me to do before I even thought about letting Toby or his dick near me again.

After the bathtub was full enough to cover my body from the neck down, I eased my frame into the hot water and laid my head back on the tiled wall. Looking out of the large bay window, I got so lost in the view of downtown Los Angeles and the millions of lights that served as its background that I fell asleep within minutes. I didn't know how long I was knocked out, but it wasn't until Toby's strong arms wrapped around my body and lifted me out of the tub that I woke up.

"How long was I asleep?" I asked as he walked us back into his bedroom and placed my feet on the soft faux fur rug. Toby grabbed the white plush towel on his now-made-up bed and began to dry my body off from head to toe. After I was completely free of any remaining droplets of water, I was gently laid back across the bed and treated to one of the most relaxing full-body massages ever. The sweet almond oil he used to release the built-up tension in my shoulders, back, and thighs had me feeling like I was on cloud nine.

"Damn, baby. What I do to deserve all of this?"

Toby, who was now straddling my back and kneading the fuck out of my shoulders, leaned over, pressing his chest to me and kissed my neck. *"I just wanna be your favorite,"* he sang into my ear.

I couldn't help but laugh at his corny ass. See, it was shit like this that had me falling more and more in love with Toby every second of the day. Not only did he treat me like a queen, but he catered to me like one too, regardless of my attitude or how stubborn I was about

certain things. Thinking about it now, I was really tripping not giving him a key to my apartment, because he
didn't hesitate to give me keys to both of his. Hell, I was
even tripping about this whole moving in officially with
him thing. Who wouldn't want to come home to stuff like
this just because?

My mind went to my cousin Koi. With the money she
would be making at the club now, she most definitely
could afford to take over the rent for my place and pay
the bills by herself. If not, I was sure the complex had
a one-bedroom she could easily move into if she didn't
want to stay in the two-bedroom.

Toby was still singing in my ear about him being my
favorite when his cell phone started to ring. Not missing
a note, he picked his phone up from the nightstand
and looked at the caller ID before answering. "Hey,
everything good?" he said into the speaker, removing his
weight from my back and sitting on the side of the bed.

I rolled over from my lax position on my stomach and
got up on my knees. Wrapping my arms around Toby's
neck from behind, I laid my cheek on the top of his head
as he continued with his conversation. Reaching his free
hand behind his back, Toby pulled me closer into his
body and squeezed my ass. I could tell by his responses
that he was talking to Koi about club business, but I
couldn't hear what she was saying on the other end. They
stayed on the line for about ten more minutes before he
released the call and turned his attention back to me.

"What did Koi want?" I asked, inhaling the scent of the
Axe shampoo he used in his hair. Toby must've taken a
shower while I was sleeping in the tub earlier, because
his blond locks were still a little damp, and he had on his
pajama bottoms now.

He shrugged his shoulders and started flipping through
the TV channels. "Nothing. Just wanted to run a few
things past me."

"A few things like what?"

"Damn," he chuckled. "Just a few things about the club, nosy. It wasn't anything really important."

"Not important, huh?" I squinted my eyes. "Did it have anything to do with Ebony and Ivory, and if they were hired or not?" I don't know why those two bitches from earlier were on my mind. There was something about the white chick that I didn't like. And the black girl . . . There was something off about her. I just couldn't pinpoint what it was yet.

"Ebony and Ivory?"

I smacked Toby in the back of the head. "Stop acting like you don't know who I'm talking about."

"I don't, Niecey."

"You don't, huh?" He shook his head no, but I knew he was lying when he smiled. "I know you remember that snow bunny I almost had to slap the fuck out of and her chocolate buddy."

"You mean Storm and Halo?" He laughed.

"Oh, you don't remember *them,* but you remember the hoes' names?" I asked, removing myself from the bed and standing directly in front of Toby. With my arms crossed over my bare breasts and my hip poked out, I waited for his response. I knew his ass had to remember Storm, because she damn near pushed me out of the way trying to stand next to him when he walked in the club.

Toby's eyes roamed my body from head to toe and back again. The minute his eyelids dropped into that sexy bedroom look and he drew his bottom lip into his mouth, I knew he had mentally checked out of this conversation. My gaze went down to his dick print that was starting to become more visible through his pajama pants. It was only going to be a matter of time before he threw me onto the bed and took what he desired from me again.

"I hope you don't think I'm about to give you some. I already told you . . . She"—I pointed to my kat—"needs some rest. Now tell me what Koi wanted before I call her back and ask her myself." I tried to snatch his phone out of his hand, but he moved it out of the way and tossed it across the room, on top of the pile of dirty clothes he was going to take to the cleaners.

"You threw that as if I wouldn't walk over there and get it."

"That was the whole point of me throwing it. I love to watch your ass jiggle as much as I love staring at that beautiful smile on your face."

I couldn't help the blush that rose on my cheeks. "I swear you get on my nerves."

"But you love me."

"That I do," I returned, walking over to the pile of clothes with a little extra sway in my hips to give Toby the show that he wanted. Bending over slowly, I tooted my ass a little higher in the air and picked up his phone. As soon as I gripped the iPhone in my hand, it began to vibrate.

"Hey, babe, someone's calling you."

Toby darted his eyes from the TV screen and then back to me. "If it's vibrating, it's a text. Who is it?"

"You want me to check your messages?" I asked, walking back over to my side of the bed. This was new for us. Instead of lying back down, I sat Indian style on top of the sheets and pulled a pillow into my lap.

He shrugged his shoulders. "Why not? It's not like I have anything to hide."

"But it's not about you having anything to hide, Toby."

"Then what is it about?" He chuckled. "I don't have a problem with you answering my phone or reading my text messages, Niecey. Never have. Now, you, on the other hand, might."

I sighed because I could already tell and feel where this conversation was about to go just by that last comment.

Maybe I should've left that whole phone call thing with Koi alone, especially if it was going to bring us to where we were headed now.

Toby and I hadn't discussed in full detail the last little fight we had about Will, so it was only a matter of time before it was brought up again. The thing was, I didn't know how I would explain to my fiancé why my ex was sending me flowers, or why I was ignoring his phone calls. If the shoe were on the other foot, I would indeed feel some type of way, but as I said before, Toby didn't have anything to worry about when it came to Will and me. Besides, after the ass whipping Toby just handed out to him, I doubted he would be contacting me anytime soon.

"What do you mean, me, on the other hand? What are you trying to say, Toby?"

"If you don't know, I guess I'm not trying to say anything, Niecey," Toby said, getting up from his side of the bed. After stretching his arms and back, he ran his fingers through his hair and put it in a bun at the top of his head. "I'm about to go into the kitchen to find me something to eat. Do you want something?"

"I can't come with you?"

"Not if you're not ready to tell me why Will's been calling you."

"Toby—" I started, but he raised his hand and cut me off.

"If it's not the answer to the question that I just asked, then I don't want to hear it. Now, do you want me to bring you a sandwich, or I can get us something from that Mexican spot down the street? Matter of fact . . ." He pulled his pajama pants off and slipped into some gray sweats and a black tank top. Going into his drawer, he grabbed a pair of white socks and put them on his feet before sliding them into the Ferragamo Groove Slides he bought a couple of months ago. "I got a taste for a burrito. I'll grab you a dinner plate and a few horchatas and be right back."

I jumped off the bed and searched around the room for a T-shirt and a pair of his basketball shorts. "Wait. I wanna go with you."

"Nah. You stay here, Niecey. I need a minute to myself."

Toby didn't even give me a chance to object to him going to the little Mexican joint without me. Before I could even make it around the bed, he was gone down the hallway and out the front door, the soothing tea tree scent from his shampoo lingering in the air. Just that fast, our fun, sex-filled night went from sugar to shit just at the mention of Will's name.

I pouted all the way back to the bedroom and threw my body over the bed in a big flop, knocking over a few of the books and picture frames that sat on the floating shelves above the headboard. Toby's room had a very masculine feel to it, but the small details like the black-and-white architectural paintings on the wall and the gray-and cream-colored scheme with the rose-red accents gave it a modern but soft feel.

I glanced toward the TV that was mounted on the wall above the electric fireplace that was illuminating the room in a soft blue glow and tried to keep up with the subtitles but was failing horribly. Some accident on the 405 freeway was the story that the anchor was reporting about, but I didn't care either way. My mind was still going over this whole Will thing and trying to figure out the best way to make Toby understand and feel as solidified in his position with me as I did with him.

The silence in the room was killing me, and when I couldn't find the remote to change the channel and turn up the TV, I reached for my phone, which had stopped playing music before Toby left. Picking it up off the nightstand, I walked over to the small crimson couch that sat in front of the floor-to-ceiling windows and scrolled through the calls and text messages I'd missed while listening to the Donell Jones station on Pandora.

"What the hell does she want?" I asked myself when I saw that my twin had called me a couple of times. I made a mental note to text her sometime tomorrow to see what she wanted and called my mother back next.

"Hey, Ma, what's up?"

"ShaNiece, why haven't you been answering your phone? I've been calling you all day."

"I was busy."

"Hmmm. Busy doing what is the question I should be asking."

I laughed. "What do you want, Mom?"

She cleared her throat. "Well, I know you took the week off to help Toby with the opening of his club, but I need you to do me a favor." When I didn't say anything, she continued talking. "I'm going to Jamaica with Cliff for a couple of weeks, and I need you to help with watching Aspen until I get back."

"Where is her mother at?" I asked, wondering if that was the reason why LaLa had called me. She and I were still not on speaking terms, but we sometimes communicated when it came to my niece.

"Well, you know her and Ray are taking a break from each other. And now with William hardly being home, she depends on me to look after Aspen when she's out doing whatever it is that she does. But Mama needs a life too. Shit, I'm done with raising my kids. Grandma doesn't mean *drop your baby off anytime*. Now, don't get me wrong, I love my grandbaby to pieces and don't have a problem spending time with her, but Granny got places to go and people to see, and I'm not about to stop living my life because LaLa all of a sudden wants to live hers now that she's a single woman."

LaLa and Ray breaking up was news to me. Then again, it really wasn't, because she didn't know how to treat the man who stepped up and took responsibility for Aspen when Will's trifling ass didn't. The same man who stayed with her even after finding out all of the shit she did behind his back. I always thought that Ray was a good dude for LaLa, but I guess she was too busy fucking her ex-best friend's man and mine to see it.

My line double beeped, alerting me to a new text.

My Love: Chicken or carne asada?

Me: Carne asada

Me: And tell them to put the pico de gallo on the side.

"Niecey, do you hear me talking to you?"

I placed the phone back up to my ear. "Yeah, Mom. I'm just texting Toby what I want to eat."

"And how is my future son-in-law?" I could hear the smile in her voice.

"He's good."

"Have you set a date yet for the wedding?"

"Mom, you will be the first to know when I do."

"I don't see what you're waiting for. Anyone with eyes can see how in love that boy is with you."

"Yeah, but he's mad at me right now. So I don't think he's that in love."

"Oh, Lord. What the hell done happened now?"

I told my mom everything that went down from Will sending me the flowers to the fight that he and Toby had at the club. I thought she would be on my side about me keeping my distance from Will, but she was on the complete opposite side.

"I think you should talk to him, ShaNiece. At least let the boy get some closure. Let him apologize for the shit that happened between him and LaNiece and go from there. You may not know this, but he's changed a lot in the last couple of years. I don't know if it's because of Aspen, but the boy has finally gotten his shit together. I never was a fan of his little nappy-headed ass, especially with all that fighting and fussing y'all used to do when y'all was younger, but I honestly believe that he's finally become a man."

My Love: I'm pulling in. Open the door in two minutes. My hands are full.

I read Toby's message and got up from the couch to find a shirt to throw on, just in case I had to step out into the hallway to help him with the food.

"All right, Mom, I hear everything you're saying, but I gotta go. Toby needs my help with the bags. I'll *think* about talking to Will. But honestly, I doubt us having a conversation like that will ever happen. Like I said, if it's not about Aspen, then he and I don't need to have any communication."

"For someone who claims to be over everything he's done to you, it sure doesn't seem like it. Only a woman who is still harboring some type of feelings can't talk to a man she used to share her life with."

"Mom—" I whined, and she cut me off.

"Okay, okay . . . Okay . . . I won't say anything else about the situation. Just think about it. Now, will you do your mama this favor and watch your niece for me? You know she ask about her TeeTee all of the time. Oh, and honestly, you probably won't even see Will when she goes over there because he's gone a lot during this time of the year. When I drop her off at his house on Fridays and pick her up on Sunday afternoons, it's usually his mother who I deal with."

"How long will you be gone again?" I asked, opening the door for Toby, grabbing the drinks out of his hand and heading into the kitchen. The tantalizing smell of marinated steak, bell peppers, onions, and Mexican seasoning caused my stomach to growl. I couldn't wait to smash this food. Dipping my hand into the greasy brown paper bag Toby was still holding, I pulled out a tortilla chip that I could tell was fresh out of the fryer and stuffed it in my mouth.

"I'll be gone no longer than two weeks, Niecey. Your sister will call in a day or two to talk to her baby, so just let her do that for me, okay?"

I nodded my head and took a sip of my horchata. "All right, Ma, I got you. We about to eat, though, so I'll call you tomorrow if I need any more details, okay? Remember to bring me back something, and I love you."

"Love you too, baby, and tell my fine-ass son-in-law I said hey."

"Bye, Mom." I laughed and released the call, placing my phone on the bar stool next to me.

Toby was already digging into his surf and turf burrito when he looked over at me and chucked his head up, chewing on his food. "Everything cool with Moms?"

"Yeah, she good. Just wants me to watch Aspen for a couple of days."

"Oh, yeah?" He smiled, his cheek still stuffed with food. "Little cutie is coming to spend some time with Uncle Toby and TeeTee, huh?"

Unwrapping my taco from the foil it was in, I damn near stuffed the whole thing in my mouth, dropping pieces of meat on top of the marble counter. "Yeah. I mean, if it's cool with you."

After taking a few more bites of his burrito, Toby wiped his hands on one of the brown napkins that were in the bag and walked around the island to where I was standing, his eyes never leaving mine. Lifting me by my arms, he placed my ass on the cool marble counter and nestled himself between my thighs.

"When are you going to accept this place as your home, Niecey?" He brushed his nose across mine and then kissed the tip of it. "You don't ever have to ask me if I'm cool with anything you do here. You know that, right?"

"I know, baby," I replied wrapping my arms around his neck and kissing his lips. "And I'm sorry about earlier. I didn't mean to make you mad. So to answer your question—"

He shut me up by tonguing me down. "Don't . . . You good. I'm not going anywhere, and neither are you, so there's no need to explain shit."

"You sure, baby? Because I'm ready to."

Toby shook his head and started to grind his dick against my kat. "I'm sure. We good. Now hurry up and finish your food because I want some more of that golden pussy before we go back to sleep."

"Baby, I already told you that she can't take any more tonight."

"She can, and she will. Now eat up so you can get all your strength back. It's your turn to put in all the work."

Needless to say, I finished my food and gave my man what he wanted . . . sore kitty kat and all. Within the week, while running some errands for Toby and getting some last-minute things for the club done, I managed to move all of my things back into his loft and officially signed my lease for the old apartment over to Koi. A few dates for the wedding had been thrown around, but not set in stone yet. We both decided that our focus would be to make it through this grand opening for Decadence and then start on the wedding. Hopefully, everything would go according to plan and without a hitch, but with the way that my life was set up, I was sure something—or someone—was about to disrupt my peaceful bliss.

William

I stared at my reflection in the mirror after splashing some water on my face, trying to wake myself up. This last week had been tiring. With all of the practices, meetings, training, weight lifting schedules, and games I had, I was exhausted. And then having Aspen Fridays, Saturdays, and Sundays on top of that, I didn't have any time to rest. Yeah, my moms was here to help out from time to time, but I prided myself on being an active father in my child's life, and I intended it to stay like that. The way Aspen was brought into this world would be something I would hate myself for until the day that I died, but I didn't regret my baby being here at all. It was like my whole outlook on life changed the second I laid eyes on her, and I'd been grinding ever since.

The last two years had been good to me, and I couldn't complain. I had a nice car, a fly-ass crib, investments with a few companies, and some money in my pocket. I wasn't an A-list athlete yet, but people in L.A. knew my name and who I was. Being the golden child of my high school football team allowed me to be a local celebrity, so you know that they were checking for the kid, on and off the field.

After I fucked up my ACL a few years back, I thought I was done for in the football world. Nigga even went into a deep depression, drinking, smoking weed, and fucking everything moving, including LaLa's trifling ass. Worst mistake of my life. But after going through some extensive physical therapy and having a praying mama behind me, your boy was back on the field and doing what I did best—knocking niggas on their asses. Hadn't touched a drink in almost two years. Hadn't smoked weed since before I tried out for the football team, and I only had a couple of chicks that I called on when I needed to get my dick wet. Although I wasn't at the top of the roster for the Los Angeles Sabors, I had my foot somewhere in the franchise and wasn't no way for me to go but up. Being on the practice squad right now was cool, but I had a feeling that my time to shine was coming soon, and I would be ready for it when it did.

I washed my hands one more time before I left the bathroom and headed back into my living room where I had a few of my teammates chilling and just shooting the shit. Armell, Reggie, and Markus were somewhat like brothers to me. We all grew up around the way but on different sides of the city. Even played against each other during our high school and college days. It was crazy to me how we all played for the same team now. Any past beefs or rivalries were a thing of the past.

Going into the kitchen, I grabbed a trash bag and a Gatorade out of the fridge. While circling my shoulders to release some of the stiffness between them, I opened my drink and took a few sips before placing the top back on and cracking my neck. We had just come from practice a couple of hours ago, and I was still feeling the after effects of going so hard on the field. Although I was only a part of the practice squad, I needed the coaches and owners to see that I could—and would—be an asset to the fifty-three-man roster if a spot ever became available.

Instead of staying for the media session and the dinner that was catered for players, we decided to grab a few boxes of Church's chicken, some sides, a few brews, and just chill at my house. We were scheduled to play the Cincinnati Bengals on Sunday, and we just wanted to have some chill time before game day. Walking back to where my teammates were posted up, I wasn't surprised to see a few new faces as I rounded the corner and walked fully into the living room.

"I hope you don't mind, Will, man," Reggie spoke up. "But I called my girl and a few of her friends over."

My eyes wandered across and over to the four shades of melanin beauties that were now smiling and having a good time in my home, drinks in one hand, with a plate full of chicken and biscuits in the other. I'm not gonna lie; all four of them had bodies stacked nice, tight, and right, with long weaves in their heads either in curls or bone straight, and clothes on that barely covered any of their private parts. Had this been some other night, I wouldn't have minded them being here, but since my daughter would be arriving in about an hour from now, it was time for them and my boys to wrap this little party up and head on out.

"Man, you know I ain't tripping. It's cool that you invited them over and everything. But on some real shit, it was a wasted trip for them," I replied as I began to pick up the empty plates and beer bottles spread over my glass coffee table. Bending over to grab a few napkins that had fallen on the floor, I bit my bottom lip in frustration when I noticed a wet spot and an open honey pack on my beige sheepskin rug. Anyone who knew me knew that I had a mild case of OCD.

"What's going on? Her man at the door or something?" Reggie raised his chin, the team's snapback sitting low on his head, covering his eyes. The gray basketball shorts he had on were raised halfway up his thigh, a clear sign that the girl on his lap was copping a feel of his mans before we interrupted them.

"If her man was at the door, what were you going to do?" Reggie's girl laughed and asked. She was a dark-skinned gem with the sexiest slanted brown eyes and pouty lips I'd ever seen. You could easily tell that she ran their little clique because all eyes went to her before either of her girls spoke.

"I don't have a man, baby. She's just joking around," Armell's friend cooed.

"Whether she has a man isn't even relevant right now. What in the hell did you spill on my rug, and why the fuck you ain't pick up this honey pack?" It was going to cost a few bills to get this thing cleaned, and his ass was going to pay for it.

Armell licked his lips and rubbed his hand across ole girl's damn near exposed ass. "Aaaaw, my bad, Will. Real shit, I was just about to pick it up, but then the girls came in. And can you blame me . . ." He lifted his friend from off of his lap and spun her around. "For getting sidetracked? Do you see the body on this one here?" His voice was now a higher pitch than before.

"Yeah, I see it. And shorty body is bad, but that still doesn't give you a pass to be disrespectful to my shit. You, of all people, should know better, seeing as my couch is like a second bed for you every other day when your girl puts your ass out."

"You got a girl?" Caramel asked with her voice slightly raised. She rolled her eyes and removed herself from Armell's grip. "I should've known. You niggas ain't shit." Her eye went to Reggie's girl. "Twyla, I'm ready to go. I told you we should've tried to get into the grand opening of Decadence tonight, or at least sat out in the parking lot until we snagged us a few ballers."

Twyla got up from Reggie's lap to his dismay and pulled at the hem of her green bodycon dress. The shit hugged every inch of her curvy frame and had my dick twitching against my thigh. Females like her were bad news for recovering addicts like me. And the way she kept eyeing me and licking her lips wasn't helping shit.

"The grand opening for Decadence is invite only, Patrice, and I don't remember you getting an invitation," Twyla sassed. "The only way that we could probably get in tonight is if we posed as some of the dancers and slipped through the back door. But you know I don't get down like that."

"Get down like that? Bitch, please. The only reason you ain't sliding down one of those poles tonight is because they rejected your ass at the auditions last week, so don't act like you didn't try," one of the other friends said before giggling and looking at the caramel beauty I now knew as Patrice.

"Fuck you, bitches," Twyla snapped and turned to Reggie, her long weave slapping Markus in the face. "Baby, let's get out of here and go have some fun some-where else. I feel like getting into some trouble tonight, and I know how much you like when I'm a naughty girl."

Reggie, who was looking at something in his phone, waved her off. "I'm good on all that shit you talking. I'll catch up with you some other night. I got somewhere else to be."

Twyla snaked her neck and placed her hand on her wide hip. "And *where* the hell are you going?"

"Shit." Reggie rubbed his hands together with a big smile on his face. "We just got invited to Decadence."

"Decadence? How the hell you get invited? You ain't rolling in dough like that. From what I hear, you gotta have hella money to get up in there. Decadence is sorta like the Black Card of clubs. You gotta be at a certain status, with a certain amount of money, before *they* even *think* about inviting you to be a member. Where do *you* fit in with any of that? Last I checked, the practice squad don't make shit."

"We don't make shit, but you sucking and fucking me every chance you get to have me lace you with a few dollars, though," Reggie returned. The whole room, including me, erupted in laughter.

The thing was, Twyla had it all wrong. Just because we weren't on the same level as some of the players who signed multimillion-dollar contracts didn't mean that we weren't getting a nice piece of change for our positions. Matter of fact, we got paid rather well. For instance, with my contract, I made the rookie minimum salary because I was just that good, and the Sabors didn't want me to sign with anyone else. That $450,000 salary broken down into payments was around $26,000-plus a week for a seventeen-week season. Plus an additional $26,000 a week if the team went to the playoffs. We weren't rolling in millions, but our cards wouldn't get declined at the Louboutin store if we decided to ball out.

"Yo, Beano just hit me and said he added our names to the VIP list tonight. I think we all should roll," Markus announced, standing up from his seat on the couch and scrolling through his phone.

"Did you just say Beano? As in all-star wide receiver Beano Cooper?" the friend who looked like Meagan Good asked.

"Chyna, shut your thirsty ass up. That nigga curved your ass at In-N-Out the other day, and he'll probably do it if he sees you tonight. You already know he's into white bitches anyway. You saw the way he was hugged up on that mechanically altered Barbie he had hanging from his arm."

"You're such a hater, Twyla."

"Naw, sweetheart, I'm not a hater. I just try to keep it one hunnid with my friends." She turned toward me. "So, are we going to the club or not? Your boy just said we on the VIP list."

"I didn't say *we* were on shit," Markus interjected. "Armell, Reggie, Will, and me"—he pointed—"are the *only* ones whose names were added to VIP. Y'all on y'all own."

"You might as well let one of them roll since we all know that Will's ass ain't coming," Armell chimed in as he grabbed some of the trash by him and stuffed it into the black bag I was holding. "After that white boy whipped his ass the last time we were there, I don't think he wants to show his face again."

"Man, fuck you, Armell. Your ass always talking shit. You know as well as I do that don't nobody pump fear into my heart. Yeah, ole boy got off on me the last time we ran into each other, but that wouldn't stop me from ever going there again."

"What were y'all fighting about anyway?" Reggie asked. "I never got the full story. All I remember is you showing up to practice with a busted lip and a knot on your forehead." He laughed, his big body slamming down into my chair, making the wood underneath the fabric crack. I don't know how this big Jamal Woolard-looking-ass nigga and I became friends, seeing as we used to be enemies in high school.

"Boooooooooooy, let me tell you," Armell hollered. "One minute shit was cool. We were getting ready to watch these two bad-ass chicks audition for one of the stripper spots. The next thing you know, some fine-ass bi—" I cut my eyes at him. "My bad, homie. I mean, Will's ex came up in there looking sexy as fuck."

"Who, the twin?"

"Yeah, man. But not the baby mama. The one he was actually with. She had on this black tank top, one-piece thing that outlined every one of her lips, dips, tits, and hips. Yo, I don't know how that white boy can handle all of that ass if Will couldn't."

"Nigga, I could handle every part of Niecey and did for years. I was her first everything. The reason her hips spread the way that they do now is because of the way I used to beat that pussy from the back and have her riding this dick."

"Shiiiiiiiid. I've seen those old pictures you like to show. She was a little thick back then. But now, I think she might have that white boy to thank for causing her body to spread like that." He waved his hand, making a Coke-bottle shape.

I don't know why I started seeing red hearing Armell talk about Niecey that way. The fact that he was checking her out that hard to have the way her body was shaped embedded in his mind didn't sit right with me. Before I knew it, the trash bag in my hand dropped to the floor, and I charged toward him full speed, knocking him over the chair he was just sitting in. Lamps, curtains, and the TV came crashing down to the ground. Twyla and her girls stood in the middle of the living room, screaming for me to stop, while Reggie and Markus tried to pull me off of him.

"You a bitch for that, my dude," Armell screamed, spitting blood from his mouth after we were finally pulled apart. The collar of his shirt was hanging loosely around his neck, and his hat was now off of his head. "You mad at me for saying how fine your ex-bitch is but didn't get this mad when the muthafucka that's fucking her beat your ass."

"Watch your mouth, nigga. You gon' stop disrespecting my girl."

"*Your* girl?" Armell shook his head and laughed. "Will, she stopped being your girl the minute you fucked her sister and had a baby by her. Man, I wish I knew you like that back then, because I would've scooped her broken heart up just like the white boy did."

I tried to free myself from Markus and Reggie's hold but had no such luck. While the girls began to whisper among themselves and Armell and I stared each other down, I couldn't help but think about everything he had just said. Yeah, it was my fault that Niecey and I weren't together anymore, but I needed her to understand that I was going through some things back then. She knew that I had started to drink and cheat on her, but she didn't know the reason why. Every time she tried to talk to me or help me, I just blew her off and would ignore her for a few days or until I was tired of fucking the different women I was dealing with and wanted to be up under her.

For the past three years, I'd tried to apologize to Niecey for the way I treated her, but she wasn't trying to hear it. Of course, we would still have sex from time to time, but it was never anything more than that. After all of the shit came out about LaLa, that's when she was really done with me. I tried to call, stop by her mama's house at all times of the day and night, but I could never seem to run into her. I later found out that she was dating Toby's ass and was living with him. There were many times that I tried to use Aspen for us to have a conversation, but she never fell for it. On the days when LaLa would disappear, knowing she had to pick our baby up, I would call Niecey to see if she would get her, but every time, she would send a text telling me to call her mama and to leave her the fuck alone.

Shaking my head, I smiled at the memory of some of the good times Niecey and I had. If only she could remember those days and see the type of man that I was now, maybe she would give me another chance. The only thing standing in the way of that, though, was Toby's bitch ass. If I got rid of him some way, I knew without a doubt that Niecey would take me back. We had too much history to let a low point in my life tear us apart.

When I asked her out for dinner a while back, that was what I was going to try to tell her. That and the new things that had been going on in my life. But she stood me up and didn't even apologize for that shit. Hopefully, one of these days, she'd have a change of heart and take me up on the offer again. With Toby opening this new club Decadence, it was going to be too much temptation walking around for him not to slip up at least just once. And when he did, I was going to make sure that I was there to comfort Niecey and, hopefully, get her back with me.

I looked down at my watch to check the time. It was ten after four, and Ms. Regina would be there with Aspen in twenty minutes.

"Y'all know what? Everybody just get the fuck out. Get y'all shit and get out of my house now." Snatching my arms from Reggie and Markus, I picked up the black trash bag I'd dropped in the middle of the floor and started to clean up the remaining trash. I wanted to hop in the shower before my baby got there and change into a beater and some basketball shorts since we didn't have any real plans for the rest of the day. We were staying in tonight, and I wanted to be comfortable. The workout clothes that I threw on after I got out of practice earlier were cool, but I still wanted to change.

"How rude are you to just throw us out!" Patrice said, picking up her coat and purse. "I told y'all we should've went somewhere else. Had me wasting my gas to drive all the way out here for nothing." She cut her eyes at Armell when she said that last part. "Twyla, you better get a couple of dollars out of Reggie's ass to put in my gas tank, or you need to find another ride."

Twyla rolled her eyes at her friend, but then turned around to Reggie with one of those begging, gold digger *baby, please give me some money* smiles on her face.

Before the words could even come out of her mouth, Reggie slipped his hand into his pocket and pulled out a wad of cash and handed it to her. Twyla grabbed the money, squealing, kissed Reggie on his cheek, and then hightailed it out of the house with her three friends following right behind her.

"I take it we have to stop by the ATM before we make it to the club, huh?" Markus asked, smoothing his hand down his shirt and pulling his Beats buds out of his ears.

"Hell naw. The *real* cash is in here." Reggie patted his other pocket. "I just handed her one of those dummy knots. A crisp fifty on the top, but forty dollars' worth of ones underneath. Once she gives ole girl some gas money and buys herself something to eat, she'll be broke again." He laughed. "I was tired of her stuck-up ass anyway. Pussy was all right, but head was mediocre. All of that fineness and girlie ain't worth shit."

"But those are the type of chicks you love, though."

"Yeah. You ain't lying." Reggie laughed. "So, you sure you don't want to join us tonight? That shit that just happened between you and Melle Mel is in the past. Both you niggas was wrong. Him for talking about your girl like that, and you for damn near taking his jaw off."

I chuckled. "Naw, I'm good. You know I get my baby on the weekends anyway, so I gotta get ready for her right now."

"Aw, shit. I forgot all about little mama. Tell her Uncle Reg said what's up, and I'll make sure to smack a few asses for you tonight."

After dapping each of my boys up and apologizing to Armell, they all left my home with promises of seeing me at the game on Sunday. Once I finished cleaning up the living room and washing the few dishes that I had in the sink, I took those last five minutes before Ms. Regina got there and hopped into the shower. Once

I washed away the germs of the day and dressed in some clean clothes, I made my way to the kitchen to pop some popcorn, grab some candy, and get a few juice boxes out of the fridge. My DVD guy had the new Smurfs picture on deck, and today was going to be movie night for me and my baby.

As soon as I had everything situated and set up, the doorbell went off, and I made my way to the front. Opening the door, I wasn't expecting to see the person who stood before me with my daughter's arms wrapped tightly around her neck while she slept on her shoulder. My eyes went from Aspen's face, back up to the one I'd been dreaming about since she left my ass high and dry.

"Niecey—" I opened my mouth and closed it right back.

She held up her hand to cut me off. "I'm not here to talk to you or anything. My mother is out of town, and LaLa is wherever she is." She tried to lift Aspen's hold on her neck but was met with some resistance. "TT, baby," Niecey cooed. "TT, baby, you gotta go to your daddy now. I'll come back to get you in a couple of days."

My baby's smooth brown face wrinkled a bit before she began to stir out of her sleep. Her Shirley Temple–curled pigtails hung a little past her ear with two big red bows tied at the top to match her red dress. When I went to reach my hands out for her, Aspen turned away from me and nuzzled her nose deeper into Niecey's neck.

"Maybe you should just come in and lay her down on the couch. I can deal with her after that."

Niecey looked at me hesitantly before she finally nodded her head and stepped into my home. When she passed me, I couldn't help the way my dick started throbbing at her scent alone. That jasmine and vanilla was doing something crazy to me, but I liked it. Closing the door behind us, I watched as Niecey's eyes moved from left to right as she took in my decor and the inside of my shit. I could tell by the faint dip her eyebrows did as she continued to examine the pictures hanging on the wall and the modern furniture that she was impressed. I'd come a long way from the sofa bed, mini fridge, hotplate, and shower-only studio apartment I had when we were together.

Lightly touching the small of her back, I guided her into the family room, where I removed a few pillows from the couch so that she could lay my baby down. Cradling her head first, Niecey was able to remove Aspen's tight grip from around her neck with a few light tugs. She almost had her laid completely down when Aspen's eyes popped open and she realized what was going on. Before Niecey or I could shush her back to sleep, Aspen started screaming at the top of her lungs and reaching for Niecey's neck.

"Just go. I'm sure I can get her to calm down," I offered, not really meaning that shit. Niecey leaving my house was the last thing I wanted her to do, but I did not want to pressure her into talking to me if she wasn't ready to at the moment.

Dropping her purse down on my coffee table and then looking down at her watch, Niecey rolled her eyes and shook her head. "I have a few minutes to spare before I have to go get ready for Toby's grand opening tonight." She pointed her fingers in my face. "I'm going to put her back to sleep this time. But after that, you're on your own."

Holding my hands up in surrender, I stepped back and gave her enough room to pick Aspen up again and sit down on my couch. Niecey was a natural when it came to this mothering thing. The way she had my baby wrapped up in her arms and rocking her back and forth made my heart flutter a little. This should have been us. Aspen should've been the daughter that she and I shared.

Niecey had always been fine as hell to me, but, right there at this moment, the way that her face was glowing and her eyes twinkled as she stared down into my baby's face, she was breathtaking. Even in the white V-neck shirt and yoga pants, she was beautiful.

So lost in the moment, I didn't even hear Niecey talking to me until she threw one of the pillows off of the couch at me and hit me in the chest.

"I'm sorry . . . What did you say? I didn't hear you."

She whispered, "I said I think she's out. I'ma try to lay her down again and then get out of here."

I nodded my head and watched as Niecey stood up and bent over the couch, gently laying Aspen down next to a pile of bunched-up pillows. Seeing her ass spread the way it did caused my dick to jump again, this time becoming very visible in my basketball shorts. Taking the pillow she threw at me earlier, I covered myself up just before she turned back to me. Her eyes immediately cast down to what I was trying to hide, and she shook her head.

"Okay, Will. I'll be back on Sunday evening to get her. Just text me when you have all of her things packed up and ready to go." She handed me Aspen's Paw Patrol backpack.

"You're coming to get her? Where's Ms. Regina?"

Niecey placed her purse on her shoulder, kissed Aspen on her forehead, and then headed for the door. "My mom is gone on a little vacation and won't be back until the week after next."

"So you'll be the one picking her up?"

"Is that a problem?" she asked, attitude all in her tone. I shook my head no. "She'll also be staying with me during the week since it's been impossible to get in touch with your baby mama."

"You've tried to contact LaLa?"

"I haven't, but my mama has, and she isn't answering her calls."

"She hasn't been answering mine either."

"That sounds like a personal problem to me. I assumed you two had the perfect coparenting arrangement thing going on."

"We did. I mean . . . We do. Ever since we got the courts involved, it's been that way. Friday to Sunday for me and Sunday to Thursday for her. We have joint custody."

"Oh, good for y'all. All right, Will." She grabbed the door handle and turned it. "See you on Sunday."

"Wait, Niecey." I could tell by the look on her face that she was already irritated just being in my presence. The last time we met up didn't turn out the way that I wanted it to, and I wanted to make up for that. "Can you stay for a few more minutes? I got some things I want to talk to you about. It won't take long at all."

Niecey looked at her watch and sighed. "I don't think that's a good idea, Will. The last time we—"

I cut her off. "The last time was some bullshit on my part, and I apologize for that. But, please, just give me ten minutes, and then you can leave. Never talk to me again if that makes you feel better."

She drew her bottom lip into her mouth and bit down on it, obviously thinking about my offer. Her eyes stayed connected to mine as a slew of emotions played on her face. I watched as her breathing began to pick up but then slow down as something—or someone—crossed her mind. When she released her grip from the doorknob and pushed the door back closed, I knew she was going to allow me those ten minutes I asked for. A small smile played on my face, and I walked closer to her and locked the door.

"You got ten minutes. Say what you have to say so I can go on about my business."

I nodded my head. "Come with me, and I'll tell you everything I've wanted to say to you for the last three years."

Her eyebrows furrowed. "What can you possibly say in ten minutes to sum up what you've been holding on to for the last three years?"

I stopped in my tracks and turned around to her, our eyes connecting once again, but this time with emotion crossing over both of our faces. Licking my lips, I reached for Niecey's hand and was surprised when she let me grab it. "Two words . . . I'm sorry."

ShaNiece

As Will held my hand, leading me back into the den of his house, his last statement kept playing over and over in my head. *Two words . . . I'm sorry.* In all of the years that Will and I had been together, he'd never come out and apologized for anything he'd ever done to me. We'd break up for a little bit and then fall right back in line like we were never apart. Not once had he ever apologized for the different women he'd cheated with or the way he used to lash out at me whenever he would think about his failed football career. Then there was that one time in my life when I needed him the most.

The day that my father passed was the worst day of my life. Not only did I lose my best friend, but I lost the first man I ever loved. You would've thought that Will would've been there to comfort me and hold me as I mourned my father's death, but I didn't lay eyes on his ass until the day of my father's funeral. And do you know what his excuse was when I asked him where he'd been that whole time? *Jail.* Told me he got locked up for a DUI and was too ashamed to call me because he didn't want to hear my mouth. Come to find out, that shit was all a lie. Nigga was cooped up in some bitch house, passed out and high as hell in Pasadena. He found out about my father when he called the house phone looking for me because I wouldn't answer my cell, and my mother told him what had happened.

Looking back on it now, that should have been the deal breaker in our relationship, and I should've left then.

But we stayed together for a few years after that, and probably would've still been with each other today if he hadn't slept with LaLa and gotten her pregnant. Will not being there for me when my father passed was hurtful to my heart, but him having a baby with my sister was damaging to my soul. Toby coming into my life and showing me love like his helped with my healing, but there was still a small part of me affected by what Will and I had.

Shaking my hand from his grip, I walked around the large black sectional that was in the middle of the room and sat down. Aspen, who was on the other side of the couch, stirred in her sleep a little bit but didn't wake up. The small curl on her lips and the slight tick of her jaw caused me to smile. Her cute little butterscotch face was so smooth and innocent. The big curls from her ponytails were wild and spread over the decorative pillow. Her little thumb tucked inside of her mouth and nestled against her tongue. She looked peaceful as she dreamed, no doubt about unicorns, rainbows, and candy, the three things that this little girl was obsessed with.

"Maybe we should go into the kitchen," Will whispered. "I don't want to wake her up."

Nodding my head in agreement, I bypassed Will's outstretched hand and waited off to the side for him to lead the way. A small smirk played on his lips as he shook his head and started for the kitchen. While we walked through the dining room and down a short hall, I took in more of Will's spacious home. Frames of all shapes and sizes decorated the white walls with beautiful black wood crown molding. Professional photos taken of him and Aspen in a park somewhere was on one side, while candid photos of him and his family members were on the other. Newspaper clippings from his high school football days were also framed and hung, as well as a few pieces of colorful artwork that contrasted with the black-and-white theme of the house. Whoever he hired as his designer must've gone to Pinterest for some inspiration, because Will's home was absolutely breathtaking on the inside and out. I was even impressed with the charcoal-stained maple wood that covered every inch of the floor we were walking on. It was crazy how some parts of his home screamed bachelor pad, while the rest was on the modern family side.

Once we entered the kitchen, I took a seat on one of the bar stools around the center island and grabbed a banana from the fruit bowl to snack on. An awkward silence wafted through the air as our eyes connected.

"So are you going to talk or what?" I looked down at my watch. "You already wasted three minutes not saying anything. Don't let these remaining seven minutes pass the same way."

Will chuckled. "You still have that smart-ass mouth, I see."

"And you still wasting my time with bullshit, I see." I stood up from my seat, laying the empty banana peel on top of the counter. "Look, if you don't have anything else to say, we can do this staring match some other time. I gotta go home and get ready for the club's opening tonight. My dress is probably wrinkled by now laying in the back seat of my car, and I still gotta do my hair. Plus, traffic is about to be a bitch trying to get to Sunset Boulevard."

"Do you have everything you need for tonight in the car with you?"

"Why?" I asked, grabbing my purse and keys.

"Because you can use my bathroom to get ready and leave from here. The 101 freeway is right down the street. And you'll get to the club a lot faster from here than going back to the other side of town."

I thought about Will's offer for a minute. It would make more sense to get ready here then to go back to Toby's loft in downtown L.A. Traffic was going to be a bitch coming and going. It would probably take me two hours to get to the club from down there and only an hour or less from Will's house. All I needed to do was take a quick shower, put on a few layers of makeup and curl the ends of my hair over, and I'd be ready to go. I looked at the time on my watch again and bit my bottom lip. Something inside of me was telling me to leave now and get ready at home, but the idea of sitting in all of that traffic and wrinkling my dress up before I walked down the red carpet in Toby's arms had me doing the complete opposite.

"Do you have a guest bedroom or something I can use to get ready in?"

Will rose up from leaning against the counter, the muscles in his arms flexing as his hands gripped the marble edge. My eyes roamed down his body, and I unconsciously licked my lips. Images of the way Will used to lift me in the air as if I weighed nothing while we had sex began to play in my mind. I shook my head and felt my cheeks heating up.

Will squinted his eyes and then raised one of his eyebrows. "I do have one that you can use, but you might do better in my bedroom instead." I opened my mouth to protest, still embarrassed from my thoughts a few seconds ago, but Will raised his hands, cutting me off. "Before you even try to curse me out, I only offered my room because it has the master bathroom with that full vanity mirror shit you women like. You can get dressed in there, do your hair and do your makeup all at the same time. If you use one of the guest rooms, you will have to go back and forth across the hall." I nodded my head in understanding. "Oh, and in the closet next to the shower, there's a steam machine on the floor, so if your dress has wrinkles in it, you can handle that in there too."

Again, I nodded my head without saying a word to Will. Grabbing my keys, I headed toward the front of his home and out to my car to retrieve my things. Once I came back in, Will led me to his bedroom, where he already had a few towels and some toiletries lying on his bed for me. I looked around his room at the dark cherry wood furniture and black, red, and white color scheme, Los Angeles Sabor memorabilia hanging everywhere. There was even a jersey with his last name framed on the wall.

"I take it you're a Sabors fan?" I asked, grabbing my curlers, body wash, and lotion from my overnight bag.

"Something like that," Will answered, picking up a few of Aspen's toys out of the walkway.

"It's a little more than *something like that,* isn't it? Your damn room is practically covered in Sabor stuff. Then you have the black-and-red color theme going on."

Will stopped whatever he was doing and looked around the room, a small smile tugging at the corner of his handsome face. "You remember back in the day which team I said I wanted to play for whenever I made it to the NFL?"

I sat on the edge of his king-size bed and removed my shoes from my feet. "You said you wanted to play for the Sabors, even though your dad was a die-hard Raiders fan."

He laughed. "Yeah. Pops said he would disown me until the day I died if I ever played for anyone other than his beloved Raiders. I think he stuck to that promise too."

"What do you mean?" I asked, walking into Will's master bathroom, the heated tile on the floor instantly warming up my feet. The double vanity and makeup counter was the first thing that caught my eye, followed by the jetted tub, separate shower with frameless glass door, and two walk-in closets. Everything was white, except for the small tufted chair that was under the makeup counter. It was a little red vintage number with dark wood legs and rhinestones around it.

"That's what I wanted to talk to you about that time I invited you out for dinner. I wanted to let you know about everything that's been going on in my life since the last time you and I talked."

Plugging my curlers into the outlet, I placed my make-up and everything else on the counter, then hung my dress in the doorway of the first closet. Grabbing the steamer from where Will said it was going to be, I hooked that into an outlet and then wrapped my hair with a scarf before placing a shower cap over it. The grand opening started in about an hour and a half, so I was going to give myself forty-five minutes to get ready. I walked back out into the bedroom and faced Will.

"Look, I'm pretty sure you've been doing well for yourself. I can tell from the way you take care of Aspen and from your house that you're making money. I always told you that if you didn't make it in the NFL, you were smart enough to figure out some other way to make those millions. Now, if you don't mind, I need to get ready for tonight and get out of here if I want to make it to the club on time."

I turned to walk back into the bathroom but stopped when Will tugged my arm. For some reason, a warm feeling shot through my body, and I didn't like it one bit. Snatching my arm from his grip, I stepped back a few feet, giving us some much-needed space. "What the fuck, Will?"

"Niecey, I know you're in a hurry, but just give me five minutes of your time . . . Please. I promise once I'm finished saying what I got to say, I'll leave you alone."

"You got five minutes, Will," I said, turning back around. "By the time I finish steaming my dress, you need to be done with whatever it is you have to say."

"Cool." He tried to walk into the bathroom, but I stopped him before he took another step.

"Uh-uh, nigga, from out there." I pointed to his bedroom. "I can hear everything you're saying loud and clear."

"You a cold piece of work, Niecey. But that's the one thing I've always loved about you." There was an awkward silence between us before he cleared his throat and continued. "Anyways, what I wanted to tell you was that I got picked up by the Sabors."

I stopped steaming my dress and looked at Will, excitement all over my face. "You what?"

"I got picked up by the Sabors. Been on the team for about two years now."

I stood up from my hunched position and walked toward Will. "When . . . How did this happen?"

He had a big smile on his face. "After getting clean from doing drugs and drinking and doing years of some intense physical therapy, I tried out for the team and got picked."

I don't know what came over me, but the next thing I knew, my arms were around Will's neck, and we were embraced in a hug, both of us jumping up and down. Well, mainly me. He lifted my weight from off of the ground and swung me around, causing me to squeal in laughter . . . something he used to do all the time when we were together. Once we broke apart, I slapped him in his chest and bit my bottom lip as I looked at him.

"Damn, Will. Congratulations. I had no idea you were playing for the Sabors. Nobody told me."

He had a sheepish look on his face. "Would you have cared? I mean, I'm pretty sure your moms mentioned it at some point. She knows I play for them."

"Nah, she hasn't. After that whole thing with you and LaLa, I made it quite clear to my mother and everyone else that I didn't want to hear about anything having to do with you. Wow . . . the Sabors . . . Totally explains the decor in your room now. *That's* what's up, though. You always said that you'd make it to the NFL, and you finally did, even after being told that you wouldn't." He nodded his head. "So, is that why my mother has Aspen the majority of the time? Because you have practice and stuff?"

Will licked his lips and sighed. "Well, that's one of the reasons. The other reason is your sis . . . I mean, LaLa, disappearing and not showing up until weeks later." He wiped his hands over his face and blew out another breath, a more serious look on his face now as he looked at me, coffee-colored eyes a little darker. "Niecey, I don't know how to tell you this, but I think LaLa's on drugs . . . again."

My heart dropped at the same time as the towels I was holding slipped from my hands and hit the floor. I searched Will's face to see if he was lying but knew that he wasn't when I saw the remorseful look in his eyes. "Drugs? Will, what are you talking about? LaLa doesn't do drugs."

"When's the last time you talked to your sister? Didn't you cut her out of your life at the same time that you cut me?"

"What the fuck does that have to do with her being on drugs?"

Will walked into the bathroom and sat on the edge of the tub, his head low and nestled between his palms. "After that whole thing went down with us, LaLa was really upset with you not talking to her and pretty much acting like she didn't exist. Whenever I would go to pick Aspen up, it was always Ray who I dealt with because LaLa started staying out late and not coming home. Ray voiced his concerns to me about LaLa and the drug use. But like you, I didn't believe it. It wasn't until I went to this party with a few of my teammates and saw her there, hugged up with this cat that I knew was a dopehead. I confronted her. Asked her was that the reason why I had to deal with the next nigga when it came to my daughter.

"She looked bad. Her nose was red as hell. Her eyes were glossy and rolling over. Whenever she would open her mouth to speak, she would swipe at her nose and sniff." He shook his head. "I knew she was high then. Same way I used to be whenever I snorted a line or two back in the day. I threatened to take full custody of Aspen. Even went to your mom and did a little intervention. Paid for her to go to rehab and everything. Shit was going good for about a year. She was being a mother, taking care of home and trying to get her life back together. But something happened a few months before Aspen's third birthday that triggered her to start back up using again. And then, if that wasn't enough, when Ray decided to move to Texas without her, it just took her over the edge. I'd come home some nights from a game or practice, and Aspen would be lying on my porch with a blanket and her teddy bear under her arm. Sometimes I'd go to pick my baby up, and she'd be in the living room by herself while her mom was blacked out, lying in a pool of her own vomit on the bathroom floor. And then the one time when she almost died—"

"Almost died?" I yelled, not even recognizing my voice. "What the fuck do you mean almost died?" All of this was news to me. My mother didn't tell me anything. She never told me about LaLa being on drugs and being on them so badly to the point that she wasn't taking care of my niece. Whenever I would ask my mother why *she* had Aspen and not my twin, she would always say, "*You know your sister. LaLa is just being LaLa.*"

My head began to spin, and I could feel my breath becoming shorter. Moisture was in my eyes, but the tears hadn't fallen yet. I didn't know how badly I was shaking until Will gently grabbed my hand, and his arm started to shake.

"You need to have a seat, Niecey. Maybe it wasn't such a good time to talk about this. Your whole body is shaking." Will smoothed his hands up my arms and then over my shoulders. I felt the vibration of my body start to slow down. "I know you have to get ready for the grand opening, and I don't want you to be any later than what you are now. We can talk about this later."

I shook my head. "No . . . no . . . I'm good. I still have a little more time." I looked around for my cell phone but remembered I left it on the charger in my car. "I-I wanna hear the rest. But what time is it?"

Will stepped out of the bathroom and then back in. "It's a quarter to eight. I know the club starts in about an hour, so we can talk later."

"No." I grabbed his wrist. Will's eyes went down to my hand, then back up to my face. "Please, just finish telling me the rest, and then I'll get ready."

After searching my face for a quick second, Will led us over to the tub and sat back down on the edge, pulling me down beside him, my hand still cradled in his.

"Well, there isn't much more to tell you. A few weeks ago, she overdosed, and your mother found her. Called 911, and they got to her in time. We tried to get her into another rehab, but she disappeared again."

"Where was Aspen when all of that happened?" My stomach turned just waiting on his response. All sorts of questions started running through my mind. Was I the reason why my niece's mother was choosing drugs? Did my cutting off all communication with my twin cause her to start doing drugs? And most importantly, why didn't my mother say anything to me?

"Aspen was actually with me. I was on my way to drop her off when your mother called and told me what happened."

I blew out a sigh of relief. "So, no one has seen her since she overdosed?"

Will shook his head. "We haven't seen or heard from LaLa in almost a month. Thought she would show her face when she noticed I hadn't dropped that child support payment in her account, but nothing."

"Well, we need to call the police, the sheriff, or somebody. What if my sister is out there lying in some ditch dead?" I shot up from my seat. "What if she needs help, and we don't know where to find her?"

I started picking up my things and throwing them back into my overnight bag. "I need to call Toby. He'll know what to do. I hate to ruin the night of his opening, but my sister's whereabouts are more important than some club."

"Hold on. Wait a second, Niecey." Will grabbed me by my waist and turned me around. I didn't like the way my body started to react to his touch, so I stepped back. "We may not have heard from her, but we know that she's alive."

I screwed my face. "How do you know that if no one has talked to her?"

"Because she's been using the credit card that Ray gave to her. He checks it every week, and LaLa has been making cash withdrawals."

"But that doesn't—"

"And . . ." He cut me off. "She's been seen around with that dopehead dude I told you about at a few other industry parties. So, like I said, she's okay. She just doesn't want to be a mother right now or deal with life."

With that admission and knowing that I was probably the reason why LaLa was acting this way, the tears that I had been holding in finally started to fall down my face. My knees hit the heated tile floor in the bathroom hard, and I started to sob uncontrollably. If anything ever happened to my sister behind my actions, I didn't think that

I would be able to forgive myself. Yeah, LaLa was in the wrong for fucking Will and having a baby by him, but was that betrayal worth her life? No . . . It wasn't. I should've picked up the phone or called her back after all of those times she tried to reach out to me. I probably should've taken my mother's advice and sat down and talked to LaLa to clear the air. Regardless of what she had done to me, LaNiece was still my twin sister. Someone I shared my mother's womb with for nine months. Someone who would've probably forgiven me sooner if the tables were turned. The same someone who always had my back whether right or wrong. I felt the scream that ripped from my throat as I continued to cry on Will's floor. It was my fault that my niece was suffering. It was my fault that my twin was out there trying to kill herself. It was my fault that my mother now had to take on the burden of raising a child again when the ones she had were already grown.

I tried to pull myself up from the floor to get ready for the party but fell back down. The tears I was trying to control were still sliding down my face.

Will kneeled on the floor beside me hesitantly, not knowing if I was going to let him comfort me or not. When he reached his hand out and I didn't shrug away, he lifted my upper body into his strong arms and pulled me into his chest. He rubbed his hand up and down my spine.

I buried my face in the crook of his neck and continued to cry. I don't know how long my sobbing went on for, but once I stopped, my head was throbbing with pain. The last thing I remembered before I closed my eyes and fell asleep was Will wrapping me tighter in his arms, and the evening gown I bought to match Toby's suit was fading into darkness.

Tobias

The night had finally arrived for the grand opening of my new club venture, and I couldn't have been more excited. Everything was in place and looking exactly how I expected it to thanks to Koi and all of her hard work, the party planning crew that she hired, and the three men who took a chance and invested their money in this exclusive gentlemen's club with me. Cairo, Finesse, Beano, and I were going to be some very wealthy men within the next couple of years, and the membership fees that we'd collected already had shown that. Add in the profits we would be making from the 24K Gold champagne, private VIP parties, and 10 percent house fee the dancers had to pay, and I could already see the dollar signs in my future. The two-night event was sure to bring in a shitload of money, and I was already thinking about the next city to expand in.

Walking through the kitchen, I spoke with the chef to make sure that night's menu was on point. Each VIP room had a different theme, and I wanted the food and decor to match. Although our normal menu would consist of American and Jamaican food, I wanted our guests to experience what all Decadence had to offer should they select a different type of menu other than the norm. Chef Rollin was a beast in these L.A. streets, and I was happy to have him on the team. It cost me a pretty penny to get him to leave his successful food truck company, but it would all be worth it in the end. After going over a few things with him and sampling some of his creations from the recipes Mama Faye sent over, I headed to the back of the club and into my office to see if Niecey had returned any of my calls. It had been two hours since the last time I spoke with her, and I was starting to become a little bit annoyed.

In no way was I insecure about the love that Niecey had for me, but when it came to her ex, Will, there was something about him that she just couldn't let go of. Yeah, she cried on my shoulder all of those nights and claimed to be over whatever feelings she had for him, but I knew from personal experience that it was hard to let go of your first love completely. That person would always hold a special place in your heart, regardless of how bad the breakup was or who you moved on with. I accepted that with Niecey because I loved her and would do anything I could to heal the broken heart that she came to me with.

I blew out a frustrated breath and plopped down into my office chair. After loosening the tie from around my neck, I laid my head back and closed my eyes. Tonight was supposed to be one of the best nights of my life, but all I could do was wonder where in the hell Niecey was, and why she wasn't there to celebrate with me. A light tapping on the door caught my attention.

"Yeah?" I called out, still with my eyes closed and my head back.

"Toby, it's Koi. Can I come in?"

"Come in."

After fidgeting with the knob a little, Koi finally pushed through the door and into my office. Dressed in a black, knee-length strapless number, Koi looked beautiful. Her hair was swept to the side in a cascade of curls that fell over her shoulder. Her makeup was light, not taking away from her natural beauty. The colorful tattoos on her arms and back were on full display, showing off the koi fish and other Japanese artwork. Pulling the clipboard from behind her back, Koi wrote something down and then said something into the headpiece that was wrapped around her head.

"I'm in his office now. . . . Well, tell them to hold off for another ten minutes. . . . What do you mean they don't want to wait?" She smacked her lips. "Okay, give me five minutes, and I'll hit you right back. . . . Okay, okay. No, if he brought some extra guests, they need to pay. I don't care who Beano Cooper is. Extra heads mean extra money, so tell him to pay up. I'm sure he has it." Koi pushed the microphone piece above her head and then turned her attention toward me.

"Has she called you back?"

I slowly shook my head and then sat up in my chair. "Has she responded to you?"

"I've tried over ten times. Still no answer. Do you think she's okay?" A worried look crossed her face.

"I hope she is. I mean, I feel in my heart that she's okay." I shook my head. "Niecey should've been here two hours ago. She said all she had to do was drop Aspen off, and then she would be on her way."

Koi closed the door to my office and came and sat in the chair on the other side of my desk. Her eyes searched my face for a few seconds before she spoke. "Look, Toby, I know some crazy shit is probably starting to cross your mind about Niecey being at Will's house, but don't even feed into that bullshit. Niecey loves you and would never do *anything* to break you two apart."

I could feel my eyebrows crease and dip. "She might not do anything, but Will . . . That's a different story."

Before Koi could respond to what I said, her phone went off, and she looked down at the screen. As if she were reading my mind, she shook her head and mouthed that it wasn't Niecey as she answered the call.

"Yeah. . . . Okay. Here we come right now." She released the call and then stood up from her chair. "Come on, Toby, my assistant said that the press is getting restless out there waiting on you. All of our VIPs have walked the red carpet, including your brother and his wife. Now everyone is just waiting on the man of the hour."

"But I don't want—"

Koi cut me off. "I know you wanted Niecey on the red carpet with you, Toby, but she's gonna have to miss out on this one." She came around the desk and straightened my tie. "It's opening night. We need to let the press and everyone else get these shots of you for the papers tomorrow. I'm sure by the time you finish doing some interviews and posing for a few pics, Niecey will be here. At that time, you can pull her on the carpet with you to get some shots in, or we can have the photographer I hired snap a few and post them to all of the social media sites I set up. Whichever one, you and my cousin will be photographed together looking good in y'all's matching outfits."

I laughed and pulled Koi in for a one-armed hug, then let her go. In the weeks before the club opening, she and I had become a lot closer than we were when I first met and hired her. I actually considered Koi as my cousin too, even though Niecey and I weren't married yet. She and I had great working chemistry and a great platonic friendship. She understood some of the concerns I had about Niecey and Will having to see each other in regards to Aspen and didn't judge me at all. I felt like a lame when I told her about how I felt at first, but Koi reassured me that it was natural. Even with me being secure in Niecey's and my relationship, she knew just like I knew that Will was still a soft spot for her, even though Niecey claimed that he wasn't.

Walking over to the full-length mirror on my closet door, I straightened out the pant legs of my suit and buttoned the one button of my jacket. Turning to the side, I made sure that there wasn't a wrinkle in place or a piece of lint hanging somewhere before I tightened my tie and turned back toward Koi.

"So, how do I look?" I asked, brushing the fine hairs of my beard and making sure my man bun was in place.

Koi gave me the thumbs-up. "Never imagined a white boy looking as fly as you do in a wine-colored three-piece suit. It fits you nicely and screams *I got money*."

I chuckled. "Well, maybe I need to change. I don't want people all in my finances like that."

"Boy, please." She waved me off. "We all know you ain't broke. Which reminds me, what's up with me getting a raise? Not only am I the club manager, but it seems that I've taken on the responsibility of being your PR, your assistant, your club promoter, and interior designer. Last time I checked, I only got hired on for one position at Decadence."

"I thought you already talked to Beano about that."

Koi's brown face turned red. I didn't know the extent of her and Beano's situationship, but I did know that they were spending a lot of time together. I'd dropped by the club on many occasions and found him here. If he wasn't back there chopping it up with Storm and Halo, he was following Koi around like a love-struck puppy. When I asked him what was up, he said that they were just friends getting to know each other, but when I asked her, her face always heated up the same way it was doing now.

"Beano isn't the man who hired me. You are."

"That is true, but he owns part of the club, so you can talk to him about raises and shit too." I picked up my phone and sent a text to Niecey, asking where she was again. "Let's go out here and get this stuff over with so I can figure out if I'm going to stay for the rest of the night or leave."

A worried look crossed her face. "Leave? You can't leave, Toby. It's opening night. People will be expecting to talk to you and see you face-to-face."

"I hear all that, Koi, but if I don't hear from Niecey by the time I walk this red carpet, I'm going to Will's house to find her ass."

"Toby, this way."

"No, Toby, over here."

"Mr. Wright . . . Mr. Wright, can we get one word with you?"

"Looking good, Toby. Can we get a side pic now?"

It was a media frenzy outside on the red carpet. My eyes were burning from all of the flashes that were going off second after second. As soon as the first photographer saw me, the flashes started up and hadn't stopped yet. I stood in front of the backdrop that had Decadence's new logo all over it and posed for the camera. At one point, I had to pause when my phone started ringing in my pocket. Thinking it was Niecey, I turned my back to the press and answered my phone, only to be disappointed when I heard my father's voice. After he congratulated me a few more times, I put my phone back in my pocket and turned around to take more pictures.

Koi, who was standing at the end of the red carpet, was talking into her mouthpiece and giving out orders to a few workers who had come out to ask her questions. All I needed to do was get five feet closer to her, and this shit would be over.

"Toby . . . Toby . . . How does it feel opening up another successful club?" a reporter asked. I remembered her from the opening of my other spot, the Lotus Bomb, a few years ago. She was a cute redhead who tried to hit on me a couple of times, but she wasn't my type.

I smiled for the cameraman filming me behind her and walked up to the outstretched microphone. "Uh, it's actually a blessing. This is our first night being open, and I can already tell you that we've exceeded the revenue we thought we'd make."

"Is it true that Club Decadence is a members-only club?"

I nodded my head. "It is. You have to be invited to become a member."

"So, it's not open to the public?"

"Unfortunately, it's not. We only deal with an exclusive clientele at this location; however, my other club, Lotus Bomb, isn't as exclusive as Decadence. There are no exotic dancers there, but you don't have to have a membership either."

The redheaded reporter nodded her head and smiled. Stepping closer to the metal gate that separated her from me, she poked her chest out as far as she could and leaned over the rail a bit. The white blouse she wore under the blue blazer was unbuttoned and showing off a little of her cleavage. When she drew her bottom lip into her mouth, I knew she was about to dig into my personal life.

"So, Toby,"—she looked to her left and then her right—"I see you're walking down the red carpet at another one of your grand openings alone . . . again. Have you not found your future Mrs. Wright yet?"

Unbuttoning my jacket, I placed my hand in my pocket and chuckled. "Are you flirting with me . . . again, Ms. Reporter Lady?"

She smiled and licked her lips. "It's Sharon . . . and I'm just asking the questions any single lady would like to know."

I nodded and looked over to Koi, who was on her phone arguing with somebody. When her eyes caught mine, she pointed to her phone and mouthed, "Niecey." Pulling my phone from my pocket, I checked my phone for any missed calls and became a little upset when I didn't see any. Why would she call Koi before she called me?

"So, Toby, are you going to answer the question for all of the single women who are watching right now? Is there a future Mrs. Wright?"

My eyes turned back toward Koi. "Ummm, I—"

"He's in a very committed relationship," a sultry voice said from behind me, her arms sliding around my waist. "So all of you desperate and thirsty broads out there wishing and hoping that you can get a chance with him , keep it moving because he's already taken."

The reporter's face dropped, and her eyes squinted before they rolled at the person behind me. "And who the fu—I mean, who are you?" she asked, a fake smile plastered on her face.

"If you must know, my name is Raven, but my stage name is Storm."

"Stage name? So, what? Are you one of the exotic dancers here?"

Storm came in front of me and pushed me back with a bump of her ass. The green sequined dress she had on hugged every curve of her body from the top to the bottom. The sweetheart neckline left very little to the imagination, while the split on the left side of the dress was exposing her full leg as well as the fact that she didn't have any underwear on. Her platinum-gray hair was in spiral curls surrounding her face, and her skin was sparkling from whatever lotion she put on.

"I am a Decadence dancer. In fact, I'm one of the best."

"And . . . are you . . . the future Mrs. Wright we were just talking about?"

Storm looked at me over her shoulder and then back at the reporter. "I'm not the future Mrs. Wright, no, but I could be if Toby here—"

"Okay, that's enough," I interrupted, snatching Storm's arm and walking off of the carpet, the flashes from the photographers' cameras going crazy.

"Toby, are you dating a stripper?"

"Toby, does she pay you in lap dances?"

"Storm, where are you from?"

"How long have you and Toby been seeing each other?"

The reporters were screaming to our retreating backs. Koi, who was still on the phone, rushed into the front entrance of the club behind us and closed the doors.

"Just hurry up and get your ass here," she screamed into the phone before she marched over to where Storm and I were standing. "Bitch, you really must want your ass beat, huh? My cousin ain't here to stomp a hole in your ho ass, but I will gladly do so in her absence."

"What the fuck are you talking about?"

"Bitch, you know *exactly* what I'm talking about. That shit you just pulled on the red carpet. Grabbing all on Toby and addressing the press like they were here to see you."

Storm shrugged her shoulders. "I was just trying to help. Toby here looked pretty lonely out there all by himself. And since I was dressed for the part, I decided to help him out. Your cousin can thank me later."

Koi lunged at Storm, but I caught her before she was able to pounce on her, her hair now all over her head. The doors that led into the main room of the club opened and Cairo, Ness, Beano, and Cairo's wife, Audri, walked out.

"What's going on out here? Why are you all standing at the entrance with the doors closed?" Audri asked, her eyes going from Koi to Storm. "Toby, who are these ladies. And where is Niecey?"

"Audri," Cai called, pulling his wife by the waist, but she walked out of his hold.

"No, Cai, I need to know what's going on right now. Toby is out here with one woman in his arms who looks like she's ready to beat the brakes off of her." She pointed to Storm. "Now, this is all fine and dandy, except for the fact that neither one of these women is my homegirl Niecey. And since she's not here to speak for herself and her man, I'm damn sure about to do it for her."

I let go of Koi after she assured me that she was cool and turned to address my sister-in-law. "Audri, it's not what it looks like. This"—I pointed behind me—"is Koi, Niecey's cousin, that I'm sure she told you about. And this"—I pointed at Storm—"is one of the girls who dances here."

"You need to fire that bitch. What she just did was totally out of line," Koi fumed.

"What did she just do?" Audri asked. Her attitude turned toward Storm.

I raised my hands. "Look, everybody, we can deal with what just happened later. Right now, we got a club full of members in there enjoying themselves, and I don't want to ruin the night. The media is still out there trying to get some picture or story for some bad publicity, and I don't want to give them anything to run with right now. Storm, you go to the back and get ready for your set. Everyone else go back into the party, and Koi and I will join you in a minute."

Cai raised his head to me, silently asking if I was really okay. After nodding my head to assure him that I was, he grabbed a reluctant Audri's hand and headed back into the club, followed by a still-confused Ness. Beano, who was staring at Koi, finally took his eyes off of her and looked toward Storm.

"Didn't you hear what he said? Take your ass to the back and get ready before you do not perform tonight at all."

Storm smacked her lips. "Really, Beano? You wanna act like a boss in front of him and her. Your ass wasn't talking to me like that the other night when I was sucking your—"

Beano snatched Storm up before she could finish her statement and pushed her through the employees-only door. When I turned back to Koi to gauge her feelings on what we just heard, she just shook her head and started to write something down on her clipboard.

"Look, Koi, whatever she was about to say about her and Beano—"

"Doesn't even matter, Toby. He and I aren't even . . . We're nothing. So, he can do whatever the hell he wants to do with whomever he wants to do it with. I already knew with him being in the NFL that being a one-woman man wasn't anywhere in the cards. I was . . . I was just hoping that he was a little different, but I guess not."

"Koi, don't count him—"

"Do you wanna know what Niecey said or not?" she asked, changing the subject. I could tell that she was a little hurt by what had just happened but didn't want me to know it.

"Did she say where she was at or if she was okay?"

"She should be on her way here. She found out some shit about LaLa that caused her to break down, but she's good now and should be here any minute. When I talked to her, she said she was like twenty minutes away."

I wanted Koi to elaborate on this LaLa situation, but I didn't push. I was sure whatever was going on, Niecey would tell me as soon as she got there. I knew there had to be some reason behind her missing the first part of my grand opening. I was just happy it had nothing to do with Will. I already beat his ass once, and I would have no problem with doing it again. He needed to understand that Niecey was mine, and I was not about to lose her to him.

I paced the floor for a few seconds, lost in my thoughts when the employees-only door opened again.

"Aye, bro, let me talk to Koi for a second," Beano said as he walked over to me. His suit was almost identical to mine but blue, and where I wore a striped silk tie, Beano had a blue bow tie to match his outfit.

"You don't have shit to talk to me about. Just make sure your bitch stays out of my way before she gets that ass beating she almost got tonight." Koi didn't even wait for Beano to respond. She turned toward the main room of the club and disappeared through the door. Whatever perfume she had on lingered in the air.

Beano looked at me and shook his head. I could tell that he was a little embarrassed by what happened earlier. As I said, I didn't know too much about what he and Koi had going on, but I could tell that they liked each other. And him letting Storm suck his dick just fucked shit up for whatever they were trying to start.

Clapping my hand on his shoulder, I smiled at him. "You wanna go grab a drink, man? You look like you could use one."

Beano wiped his hands down his face. "Toby, bro—"

"I already know, man." I laughed. "We both having women problems tonight."

"At least you get to have sex on the regular when you're going through things with your girl. Koi and I only had sex one time, and I swear to God, I wish sometimes it didn't happen."

That was news to me. I wasn't mad that my club manager and partner were fucking. I just hoped that this pleasure did not cause any bad business on either end.

We walked into the club and immediately became surrounded by the huge crowd of people in attendance. Not only were the members who paid for full membership there tonight, but there were also their plus threes, a

small perk we added after receiving their 20K membership fee. Everyone was dressed in their after-five attire,
talking, drinking, and dining on the delicious food that
was prepared, while enjoying the dancers that were on
the stage in the middle of the room. Money fell from the
sky like it was raining. Beano and I moved through
the crowd as best as we could, grabbing a few of the beef
sliders and some truffle fries that the waitresses were
serving. When we made it to the bar, the bartender took
our drink orders and handed us our shots several minutes later.

"To a successful night," I toasted.

"To a successful night," Beano returned and downed
his shot. "We should head over to where Cai and them
are and make a toast with them. I mean, the night is
successful for them as well, right?"

I nodded my head and laughed. "You go ahead, and I'll
meet you there as soon as Niecey comes in."

Beano agreed and then turned toward the VIP area. I
scanned the crowd and watched as the faces of our guests
beamed with delight. A few people came and shook my
hand, while others started conversations about buying
into the club that I quickly declined. I looked at the time
on my phone, noticing that twenty minutes had come and
gone. Niecey should have been here by now, according to
Koi. Sending out a text to her for the hundredth time, I
continued to wait by the bar until Niecey walked in or at
least texted me back.

"Toby, Toby," Koi frantically called behind me, making
her way through the crowd. It was crazy how I heard her
voice over the loud music, but something in her tone put
me on alert. "Oh my God, Toby, we gotta go."

"Why? What's wrong?" I yelled as I let her lead me to
the exit.

"Niecey just called me—"

I stopped in my tracks and turned Koi around, both hands on her shoulders, trying to calm her down. I could feel my heart starting to beat superfast. If anything happened to Niecey, I didn't know what I'd do.

"Niecey just called you? Where's she at? And why hasn't she called me?"

Koi blew out a nervous breath. "She didn't call you because she was embarrassed to say where she was."

"Koi, what's going on? Where's Niecey?"

I could see the lump in her throat as she swallowed. "I don't know what or how it happened, but Niecey's in jail. She just called me collect on my cell phone."

In jail? What the fuck was Niecey in jail for? And better yet, what could have possibly happened in an hour to cause her to be put there? Not waiting for a response from Koi, I took my phone out and texted my driver to bring my car to the front. As soon as we stepped outside, the camera flashes from the press started going off again. When my car came to a stop in front of the club, Koi hurriedly slid into the passenger seat, phone pressed to her ear, trying to find out some information on what station Niecey had called her from.

After my driver threw me my keys, I hopped in the driver's seat and took off like a bat out of hell. *In jail?* My mind was still trying to figure out how Niecey ended up there. Did Will do something to her that caused her to react? To my knowledge, Niecey didn't have any record or warrant out for her arrest. Whatever she did, I had the money to bail her out tonight, and if need be, an expensive-ass lawyer on retainer to fight whatever charges she could be facing.

ShaNiece

The pungent stench of urine and the ungodly body odor of the woman who sat next to me were the only things I could smell as I sat in the holding tank of the NoHo Police Station. Women dressed in nothing but bras and skirts or dingy clothes walked around scratching their arms, no doubt going through withdrawal. A blond chick who looked more manly than I'd ever seen was biting the nubs on her fingers and spitting out whatever piece of skin or nail she could get her teeth on. I put my wrist up to my nose to try to get a whiff of the perfume I had sprayed on earlier but had no such luck when the lady sitting next to me uncrossed her legs and then crossed them again. The bile at the back of my throat threatened to come up, but I tried my best to hold it in. The small toilet in the corner of the tank looked like it hadn't been cleaned in weeks. Tissue, pubic hair, and some weird black residue decorated the top of the seat, while streaks of yellow and red ran down the sides. There was no way in hell that I would stick my head over it or touch that thing with my hands.

"Smith," the female police officer who took my finger-prints yelled. "You're up."

"Up for what?" the brunette, who obviously was high on something, stuttered as she backed into the corner where the toilet was. Paranoia filled her face as her eyes traveled around to everyone who was standing near her. She pulled at the short denim shorts she had on and then tugged on the arm of the thin sweater that obviously couldn't be used for warmth anymore. "Am I going home?"

The police officer shook her head. "You were caught shoplifting again from the same store the judge told you to stay away from."

"But I didn't take anything. They stopped me before I could make it out of the store."

She shrugged her shoulders. "Doesn't matter. You disobeyed a court order. So now, you have to sit in jail for a few weeks." The officer waved her hand. "Now, come on, so we can process you and get you into one of the cells."

The brunette shook her head for a few seconds and then slowly started to inch her way toward the open door. When she finally stood in front of the police officer, she tried to make a run for it but was caught by the burly male officer I hadn't noticed standing to the side. Before the female officer closed the door again, I stood up and walked over to her as fast as I could, the organza ruffled train of my velvet V-neck mermaid gown dragging across the filthy floor. I wanted to bend over and pick it up but didn't want to miss the opportunity to ask the question I had. We'd been sitting in this holding tank for the last two hours without so much as a peep from these officers, and I couldn't wait for another two.

"Excuse me, Officer."

A low huff escaped her lips. I can only imagine the eye roll that followed it before she turned to me. "Yes, inmate."

"Inmate? I don't have any charges pressed against me, do I?"

"You have three warrants for your arrest, ma'am. I'm pretty sure by this time tomorrow the name 'inmate' will refer to you."

"I told you that I didn't get those tickets."

"Just like everyone else in here, right?" She ducked her head and looked at the women behind me. "Look, I have a job to do, so if there's nothing else—"

"Have I been bailed out yet?" I asked, eagerness all in my tone. I'd called Koi an hour ago, yet I was still there. I had tried to call Toby's phone first, but it went to voicemail both times I tried.

"Obviously not. You're still here."

"Well, can I get another phone call? Maybe my cousin got lost or something."

"You only get one phone call. And seeing that you already had yours, you need just to sit back and wait."

We stood at the door, staring at each other, my frame easily towering over hers with the five-inch heels I had on. The officer quirked her eyebrows and shifted to the right a little, her free hand resting on the butt of her Taser gun. I bit my bottom lip, contemplating if I should try to make a run for it like the brunette just did, but visions of me falling to the ground and shaking uncontrollably from being tased nixed that idea. Plus, with the way that my dress hugged my body, I didn't have any leg room to run as fast as I needed to.

"Is there a different bathroom I can use? I don't want to get my dress dirty."

The officer laughed. "Sweetheart, this isn't the Ritz Carlton. If you have to use the bathroom, you're more than welcome to use the toilet that has been provided to you in the corner. If that isn't to your liking, you can hold it until you get to your cell, where I'm sure you will find the latrine in no better condition." With that, she laughed again and closed the door in my face.

"What a bitch," the Gothic-looking chick mumbled as I passed by her.

Thankfully, when I walked back over to the bench I'd been sitting on earlier, the woman who smelled of spoiled milk and rotten fish had moved to the other side of the room. Her smell still lingered a little, but it wasn't as strong as it was when she was sitting next to me. Smoothing the back of my gown, I sat in my vacant spot and sighed. Had I listened to my first mind and went home to change like I wanted to instead of getting dressed at Will's, maybe this shit would have never happened. Then again, who was I kidding? I would've probably run that same red light trying to hurry and get to the club like I had before I got arrested. What I thought would have been an easy ticket that I would pay as soon as the letter came in the mail ended up being some different shit that I wasn't expecting.

"License, insurance, and registration please," the officer asked as I rolled down my window.

"Here's my license and insurance." I handed the cards to him. "Let me get my registration out of my glove compartment." I bent over the armrest, knocking over my purse, and retrieved the paperwork. After handing it over to him, I spoke again. "I'm sorry, sir, but I'm interested in knowing why you are pulling me over right now."

His "bitch, please" face was pretty evident when he looked at me and responded. "You don't remember running not one, but two red lights back there?"

I shook my head, feigning ignorance. I did remember running the light after I got off of the freeway, but not another one after that.

"Uh . . . No, sir, I don't remember running any light."

"Well, you did. I was right behind you the second time too. Saw the second you noticed me in your rearview mirror also, before I turned the lights on."

Shit. He was right. I did see him behind me, but I could've sworn the light I went across that time was on yellow. I wasn't expecting him to turn on the red-and-blues, either. When he did, though, I was scared as shit.

"I'll be right back. I need to walk to my car and make sure everything here is legit."

I nodded my head, content that once he ran my name and came back to my car to give me my things, he would just hand me a ticket and I would be on my way. But, boy, was I surprised when he walked back to the driver's side and asked me to step out of the car. Confused and not ready to die from some "accidental" shooting, I unhooked my seat belt and stepped out of my car onto the side of the busy street. I bent over to pick up the bottom of my dress but dropped it when the officer tugged at my free arm and pulled it behind my back.

"Wait! What the fuck? Wait! What are you doing?" I yelled, fear pumping all through my body.

"Ms. Taylor, you are under arrest."

"Under arrest? For what?"

The officer grabbed my other arm and pulled it behind my back, causing my dress to fall to the dirty ground. I twisted a little from the uncomfortable angle that I was in and tried to reposition my arm but got rewarded with a hard tug and a knee to my ass as he pressed me up against the side of my car.

"What am I under arrest for, Officer? I have the right to know that." Tears began to pool from my eyes, and I could hear the shakiness in my voice. "You can't arrest me without telling me why. And why are you so rough?"

"Miss, you have three outstanding warrants for your arrest right now. One for a failure to appear, another for possession with intent to sell, and a third for disorderly conduct."

"But I've never gotten a ticket in my life. Even when I was younger."

"That's not my problem to figure out." The officer pulled me up and started walking me toward his car. By this time, another squad had pulled up, and two more officers got out of the car.

"Wait a minute. What about my car, my purse? Look at the way I'm dressed! I was on my way to my fiancé's grand opening. Please, this is all some kind of misunderstanding. Run my name again. Shit! Call my mama. She'll tell you that I haven't done anything."

The back door to his squad car was opened, and I was "lovingly" pushed into the backseat. My hair, which was in a goddess braid updo with curls on the side, was all over the place as my head hit the hot leather seat. When the officer closed his door, he snagged the bottom of my dress in it. I tried to pull it out carefully but stopped when I thought I heard the sound of fabric ripping.

I had stayed in the back of the police car for what seemed like an hour before he drove me to the police station I was in now, then I was thrown in the holding tank. After being read my rights, getting my picture taken, and being fingerprinted, I was ushered to this smelly-ass room and waiting on Koi to bail me out.

Toby was going to be pissed the hell off. Not only did I ruin one of the most important nights for him, but I knew he was probably wondering where I'd been for the last five hours. All I was supposed to do was drop Aspen off at Will's and then get ready for the club. I shook my head. I should've called him back.

When I had finally made it out of Will's house after getting ready, I checked my phone and saw that I had over ten missed calls from Toby and a dozen text messages asking if I was okay. I knew I should have responded, but I only wanted to make it there and tell him face-to-face about everything that happened: about my break-down, about everything I found out about LaLa, and about how Will did seem like he'd changed for the better. Instead of arguing over the phone like I knew we would've had I called, I wanted to concentrate on driving while I swerved in and out of traffic, trying to avoid any head-on collision.

Toby had always been understanding, especially when I was going through something. Then again, this something included Will, so the conversation might not blow over the way I wanted it to. Damn. We'd just gotten back on track with our relationship, and now, because of me and my need to hear what Will had to say, I was sure we were headed for another bump in the road.

Sitting back in my seat, I lay my head against the brick wall and closed my eyes. Millions of thoughts ran through my head. The most important ones surrounded what I was doing in jail. *A warrant for my arrest? How in the hell did that happen? How could that have happened? What did that officer say that the warrants were for? Failure to appear, disorderly conduct, and . . .* I thought about it for a second. *What was the last one? Oh, yeah, possession with intent to sell. What the fuck?* I had never possessed or had any intent to sell any drug. The closest I'd ever come to drugs was the 800s I popped now and then whenever I got one of those crazy migraines. And those were prescribed by my doctor. *Disorderly conduct? Isn't that another way of saying disturbing the peace? What peace have I disturbed besides the ones of Toby's neighbors when he's fucking the shit out of me?*

I was exhausted from trying to figure this jail shit out; then my mind went to LaLa and everything Will told me about her. Drugs? There was no way my twin was out there like that on drugs. She loved Aspen, and she had never done any drugs to my knowledge. Even though she and I didn't talk after she gave birth to my niece, I still got updates about her and her well-being from my mother. Not once had she ever said anything about drugs being in the mix.

What's crazy was things that I didn't necessarily care for about LaLa, my mother would tell me. Like when she reenrolled in school. That's what I thought she had going on for herself since she dropped out when we were in our second year of college. I was happy that she was serious about her education again, but she wasn't going to know that. As a matter of fact, that was one of the reasons why I thought my mother was watching Aspen so much. With Ray getting a job working on the refineries, and me assuming Will was missing in action, how else could I explain my mother having my niece so much?

Come to find out, my twin was out there wildin' with dopeheads and everything else that came along with do-ing drugs. Will said he would see her at clubs high as a kite. I wondered how many times she was out in public disturbing the peace. Or how many times she may have possibly gotten caught up holding some shit if she was hanging around the dealers and such. Seeing how irre-sponsible she was with Aspen, I was pretty sure if she ever got busted for some shit, she wouldn't even show up to court. I shook my head. I didn't like my sister, but I loved her and hoped like hell for her daughter's sake that she got her shit together.

The door to the tank opened again, and the same Sherri Shepherd police officer walked in with a clipboard in her hand. "Okay, Jones, Marks, Bullis, and Taylor, come with me."

As soon as I heard my last name, I hopped up and rushed to the door, pretty sure that Koi had posted bail for me and I was about to be released. Passing through the heavy door, I looked at my passing reflection in the small window and saw how the curls in my hair had fallen and my once flawless makeup was smeared and in need of a touchup. I pulled at a few strands of my hair and tried to save some of the curls but stopped after I noticed that my makeshift curlers were not doing me any justice.

The female officer grunted as she passed me by and shook her head. Falling in step with the other women whose names were called, we walked down a long, dark hallway until we rounded the corner and ended up in a small room where another female officer stood in front of a high desk, and a male officer was pacing behind a gated room.

"All right, ladies. All of you have posted bail. You have a few forms to fill out and a few more forms that will explain your court date and things like that. Once you are done with that, Officer Luca has another piece of paper you have to sign to get your things. After everyone has filled out their paperwork and gotten their things, we will let you out one by one. Please know that there are a few more inmates before you who have already finished this process, so it will take a minute before you can smell that fresh L.A. air that will be awaiting you outside. Now, first up, Margaret Jones. The rest of you, please wait in a line behind the yellow tape on the floor."

While we waited in line to be released, the ladies who were in front of me and I made small talk. Well, it was mostly them telling me how beautiful my dress was and how good I looked in it. When the next chick was called, we kind of all went back to minding our own business. I didn't know why, but LaLa and this drug thing was plaguing my mind again. I was still trying to figure out how she ended up falling so bad.

"Hey, Taylor. Haven't seen you in a while," the officer who was behind the desk said to me as I walked up to fill out the necessary paperwork. "I thought you were going to get your act together after that last arrest and you didn't have anyone to go pick up your daughter."

I looked at this lady like she had two heads. "Seen me in a while? I've never seen you in my life."

She laughed and shook her head. "I see you still out there sniffing that shit up your nose."

"Excuse me?"

She held her palms up. "Look, ShaNiece, I was just hoping you was going to keep your word on getting your shit together seeing as you had a baby to take care of, but I guess not." She shoved a form in my face. "Sign everything that's highlighted. Right here is your court date. You have to be present, or they will issue a bench warrant for your arrest this time. Oh, and if you don't want the person who bailed you out to have to pay any extra fees or lose whatever they put up to bail you out, you better be there."

I signed the papers she put in front of me, then took the little card with my card date on it. "I'm sorry, but this has been all a misunderstanding. I will most definitely be in court on this date to clear my name, and that's it. I have no idea why I'm here in the first place."

The officer didn't say anything else to me before she turned around and walked to the copy machine on the other side of the desk. Officer Luca, who had opened the gate, walked over to me with what I could see as my purse, wallet, and phone in a clear bag.

"Sign right here, Ms. Taylor." I did as I was told and grabbed my things. "Oh, and before I forget, you left some things here from the last time. Give me one moment."

He quickly turned around and walked through the gate and then back out, a small plastic bag in his hand this time. "If you can sign right here, you can go ahead and take this too."

I looked at the small bag that looked to have some jewelry in it. "That isn't mine."

His eyes squinted as he read whatever was written on the front. "ShaNiece Taylor. Arrest date October 15, 2016. Female . . . Height five foot eight . . . Weight 178 . . . DOB . . ."

"Yeah, that's me, but I don't—"

The female officer behind the desk cut me off. "Girl, as much as you were crying for that damn locket in there the last time, I would think you'd be happy to get it back, seeing as you never came to retrieve it after you left it out there on the bench."

Last time? What was this lady talking about? Instead of arguing with her any further, I signed for the small bag and took it out to the area where we were waiting to be released in. Once I found a vacant spot on the wall, I opened the bag and shook its contents out into my hand. A small gold ring fell out first with a solitaire two-carat diamond. Although it was simple, you could tell that it was an engagement ring. Next came a link bracelet that looked familiar, but I couldn't remember where I'd seen it before. The last thing that fell out was the heart-shaped locket that the officer must've been talking about. It was hanging from a thin, gold chain necklace which could use a dip in some of that jewelry cleaning solution.

Curious to know if it opened or not, I turned the locket to the side and stuck my nail through the small opening. When it opened after I applied a little pressure, I damn near fell to the floor when I saw the two pictures nestled in it. On one side, my niece's beautiful face was smiling brightly as if she were the happiest child in the world. Front teeth spaced out and full of life. And on the other side was a picture of LaLa, Ray, and Aspen looking like one big happy family. They were at some amusement

park. I could tell by the balloons and ride in the background—smiles on each of their faces. A pink princess
hat with a long veil and round silver ears on the side sat
on top of my niece's head. LaLa's face was thinner than
what I remember, and her hair wasn't as thick and coarse
as it used to be, but she still looked the same. Ray, who
was always smiling, had a content look on his face, but it
wasn't the same smile I was used to seeing from him.

This shit was crazy. Besides me getting arrested, what
in the world would LaLa's jewelry be doing here and
under my . . . I stood up straight from the wall, the blood
in my body getting hotter by the second.

"Hell nah!" I shook my head. "She wouldn't . . . She
wouldn't do that to me," I said to myself. "Getting arrested and using *my* name instead of her own?" I shook my
head again, then stopped the pacing I was doing along
the wall when the realization hit me smack in the face.
"If she had a baby with my ex, why wouldn't she use my
name when it came to the police?" Tears brimmed at
my eyes. "I'm going to fucking kill her," flew from my
mouth. My teeth clenched, and I damn near grinded the
enamel off.

"Taylor, you're free to go," an officer called from behind
me.

Picking my things up and shoving the locket and other
jewelry into my purse, I marched out of the holding room
and into the lobby of the precinct. My eyes scanned
around for Koi and landed on her as soon as I looked
toward the exit doors. Pulling the front of my dress up
in my hand, I briskly walked toward my cousin, trying to
control the anger that was building up in my body.

"Koi, you will not believe what the hell I just . . . What
the fuck is wrong with you?" I stopped my sentence to ask

when her eyes kept going behind me and then back to my face. "Why are you looking like that?"

"Ummm" was the only thing she was able to get out of her mouth before I felt a warm presence on my back side.

The minute I smelled his cologne, I already knew it was Toby. My heart started to flutter when his arm wrapped around my waist, and he pulled me farther into him. All of the anger, heartache, and frustration that I was going through instantly melted away from just being in his arms. I laid my head back on his shoulder and closed my eyes. My hand came up from the side and intertwined with his. It wasn't until I didn't feel the squeeze I'd just given him reciprocated that I opened my eyes and turned around. The smile I was expecting to see on his face was nowhere to be found. Instead, there was a blank stare and a look in his eyes that I wasn't familiar with.

"Toby, are you okay? Babe, what's wrong? I'm sorry about pulling you from the grand opening. I knew this was a big night for you . . . For us . . . and I just messed it up. But, baby, you will never believe what happened," I said all in one breath. I was still searching his face, trying to make sure that he was okay.

"Where were you tonight, Niecey? And don't lie to me."

I looked over my shoulder to Koi and then back at Toby. In a rushed way, I told Koi how I fell asleep in Will's arms after hearing all of that shit about LaLa and breaking down, but I didn't think my cousin would dime me out like that. Trying to figure out the right things to say, I jumped when Toby asked me the same question again, but with a little more bass in his voice.

"I . . . was at Will's house dropping Aspen off, and then . . . instead of going all the way home to get ready, Will kind of made sense when he offered a room for me to get ready there instead of driving back home and being in heavier traffic." I licked my lips and stepped toward him, but Toby stepped back. "I-I was on my way to the grand opening . . . and you . . . when I got pulled over by the police for running a couple of red lights. The officer ran my name and said some warrants popped up, and he brought me here."

Toby's intense gaze tore through my body and my soul. I couldn't tell what he was thinking or what he thought about what I'd just told him. We stood in awkward silence, those beautiful greenish-blue eyes still staring at me. When he reached out to me and pulled me closer to him, I finally released the breath I'd been holding and wrapped my arms around his waist. After I finished hugging him, Toby lifted my head to his lips and pressed them gently against my forehead. We stayed like that for a few seconds before he released me and stepped out of my embrace. Toby gazed into my eyes one more time before he nodded his head and backed away.

"Toby!" I cried out when I noticed him turn around and head for the exit on the other side of the room. I started to walk after him but stopped when Koi pulled my arm back.

"Niecey, I think you should give him a little space right now. Some shit went down before you were released that almost had Toby arrested right now."

"What are you talking about?" I asked, turning back to the exit to catch another glimpse of Toby's retreating back, but he was gone.

Koi cleared her throat and then sat me down on the bench facing the large glass windows. Police cars were lined up in the parking lot, ready for the next set of officers to start their shift. A K-9 officer and his dog were walking up the sidewalk and heading into the precinct. I turned to the lobby and watched as small lines were being formed for the people who were waiting on an inmate to be released or trying to find out some information on their loved ones. My attention turned back to Koi, and my eyebrows raised, trying to see when she was going to explain what had just happened.

"Niecey, when you called and told me that you were in jail, Toby was the first person I ran to. Even though you told me not to bother him and let him enjoy his night, I didn't think that was the right thing to do." She shook her head and chuckled. "I wish I would've listened to you."

"Why you say that, Koi?"

"When I finally got the information we needed to bail you out, we found a bondsman not too far from here."

"Okay . . ."

"When we get to the bondsman, he informed us that someone had already bailed you out."

"Wait. What?" What Koi said had me confused. My mother was gone, and LaLa's trifling ass wasn't trying to bail me out, so I didn't know who else she could have been talking about. "Koi, I'm lost."

Biting her bottom lip, Koi stood up and pressed her back against the glass window, arms crossed over her chest. The little black number she had on looked cute on her, no doubt a dress she picked out to woo Beano. My cousin thought she was slick hiding their little relationship, but after I walked in on them making out in the bathroom of my old apartment, I knew something was up with them.

"Niecey, Will was at the bail bond's office. *He's* the one that bailed you out."

I jumped from my seat. "Will?"

"Yeah. From what he says, your phone butt dialed him, and he heard the whole arrest when it happened. Instead of reaching out to me like he should've, he took it upon himself to find out where you were being held and came down and paid for you to get out."

My head began to spin. "And you and Toby were there too?"

"Yep. We were, and after Will told us how he had to comfort you after your breakdown, I knew some shit was about to go down. The nigga started smiling and telling us how you fell asleep in his arms and woke up the same way 'like old times.' Even said you two kissed at some point, but stopped when Aspen came in the room."

I didn't remember kissing Will at all. I do remember my niece coming into the room and snuggling up to me in bed—but a kiss? Nah.

"And what happened next?" I asked, already knowing the answer to that question.

"He and Toby got into some shouting match that almost came to blows. Me and the bail bondsman broke them up by the time the police got there. When I explained that Toby was there to pick up his fiancée, the police asked Will to leave. At first, he was saying that he wasn't going anywhere, but once the officer threatened to take him in for disorderly conduct, his ass hightailed it out of there. Said something about the L.A. Sabors and some clause in the contract."

"You gotta be kidding me." I picked up the front of my dress and began walking toward the exit, leaving Koi where she was.

"Where are you going, Niecey?"

"To find Toby and explain to him that what Will said didn't happen like that."

Koi caught up to me and grabbed my shoulder, stopping me in my tracks. "Look, cousin, I know you want to make things right, right now, but I think you should hold off on going after Toby at the moment. With the stress of the grand opening, and then everything that went down here, I don't think his mind is in the right place, and he might say something to you that you both will regret later."

Before I knew what was happening, the tears that I was trying so hard to keep at bay began to fall, and I fell into my cousin's arms. I would take her advice and give Toby a few days to cool off, but after that, I was going to find my man and get us back on track.

Koiya

I stumbled into my apartment and threw my purse and keys on the floor. Kicking the door closed with my foot, I walked into the living room and flopped down on the couch, my eyes barely open and mind focused solely on sleep. It had been a long weekend and an even longer sleepless one for me. The two-night grand opening for Decadence went by smoothly as planned, and I was finally able to sit back and not have to worry about any club business until Tuesday morning when I clocked in for another crazy week. Pulling my shoes off, I crossed my left leg over my lap and started to massage my aching feet. Damn near forty-eight hours in some six-inch Brian Atwood stilettos did some major damage on my poor soles, and I needed some relief.

I rested my head against the couch and let out a slow breath. The headache I could feel coming on was thumping at the side of my head. My phone went off in my purse, but I didn't move an inch to get it. At six o'clock in the morning, it couldn't be anyone worth talking to on a Monday morning. They'd leave a message if it were that important. I felt around the couch for the TV remote but couldn't find it anywhere. Although the morning sun was starting to peek through my blinds, it was still kind of dark in the apartment, and I needed some extra light to help me navigate through the mess I'd left on the floor.

"Fuck," I swore to myself after stepping on whatever sharp object in front of the coffee table burrowed into the bottom of my foot. "I need to clean this shit up."

Shaking my head, I continued my limp step toward the kitchen, stepping over clothes and shopping bags along the way. Reaching for the switch located on the hallway wall, I turned on the overhead light and squinted when the brightness of the fluorescent bulb almost blinded me. The smell of two-day-old egg sandwich swirling in the air turned my stomach but didn't propel the vomit that I was sure was ready to come up at any second. I leaned against the counter for a second, trying to get my insides to settle down. I didn't have time for this shit. I shook my head and picked up the sandwich and the rest of the mess that was spread across my counter that didn't need to be there. Sweeping the crumbs into the palm of my hand, I turned on the faucet to wash away the dirt and germs but had a hard time doing that due to the pile of dirty dishes in the sink.

"I love you, cousin, but you need to go back home," I mumbled to myself as I went through my refrigerator to find me something to snack on before I went to my room. "Got my house smelling and looking like death."

After placing a piece of turkey meat and cheese on a slice of bread and squirting a dab of mustard in the middle, I folded my breakfast in half and finished it in two bites. Grabbing a fruit punch Snapple from the freezer, I turned the light off in the kitchen and headed toward my bedroom with thoughts of everything that happened over this weekend running through my mind.

Out of everything that kept swirling around, Niecey being in jail was the one that kept popping up the most. I didn't know the extent of the situation she and LaLa were going through, but I had heard the story from both sides. My take on the whole thing was they needed to sit down and talk everything out. In no way was I excusing La's behavior or what she did, but after finding out about the drug abuse and everything else, I wonder how long that had been going on and if being high was a factor in what led her and Will to sleep together. In some ways, La did hint around that fact to me, but never really fully said that drugs were indeed the reason. I didn't know; maybe their relationship could be saved. Then again, maybe not. What I *did* know was that life was too short, and either ShaNiece or LaNiece would hate themselves if something happened to the other and this family drama wasn't resolved.

And speaking of ShaNiece, I stopped in front of my guest bedroom and placed my ear against the closed door, trying to see if she was still awake or if she had finally cried herself to sleep. When I left there Saturday night, she was a complete mess, crying and eating nothing but donuts and vanilla bean ice cream while the movie *Selena* played on repeat. I tried to get her to perk up a bit and even offered to skip out on work to take her out to eat last night, but she declined. All she wanted to do was lie in bed, cry, and rewind the end of the movie when Selena's song "Dreaming of You" came on. My cousin could be so dramatic at times. But I did understand how she was feeling right now. Toby wasn't answering any of her calls or texts. When she tried to go by his loft to pick up some clothes, he had the bellhop bring down a box with some of her things in them.

I kind of thought Toby was doing her a little dirty with completely ignoring her and not having any communication with her, but I understood where he was coming from in this situation too. Niecey knew to be at Will's house without calling Toby was going to cause some problem. I mean, would she be okay with Toby falling asleep at one of his ex's houses and not having any contact with her? Again, I felt sorry for my cousin, but I understood Toby's hurt too.

I pressed my ear a little closer to the door. When I didn't hear a sniffle or the sound of the TV coming from the other side, I twisted the knob and let myself in. The room was dark and quiet. Only the small light seeping through the blinds allowed me a clear path to see. You could tell that there hadn't been any happy moments in here. It felt sad. Not only was the cheerful vibe of my cousin off, but so was the smell. Three nights and four days without a bath or brushing her teeth had Niecey's room reeking of bad hygiene. Although it smelled a little better in here than it did the kitchen, my stomach still flipped a little the farther I walked inside. I had to cover my nose when I reached the side of the bed she was lying on, and the other half of that egg sandwich was in there. There was only a small piece, but the lack of clean air circulating in here caused a sour stench.

Walking over to the window, I cracked open the blinds and then raised the window. The cool breeze that entered the room gave a small amount of relief to my stomach and pushed some of the stale air out.

"Can you close the blinds back, please?" Niecey's hoarse voice asked. "I just went to sleep an hour ago."

"Niecey, you need to get up and take a shower or some-thing. Change the sheets on the bed. Empty the trash and spray some damn air freshener in here. It stinks." I moved some of her blankets to the side and sat on the edge of the bed.

"I was gonna straighten up today, so don't start that shit."

"What shit am I starting? Am I wrong for wanting you to wash your ass and brush your teeth?"

She smacked her lips and turned over, pulling the cover over her head.

"I'm serious, Niecey. You need to get up and do some-thing with yourself. What if Toby came by right now wanting to talk? Do you think he'd want to sit up in this funky-ass room and try to work things out?" She mumbled something, but I couldn't hear what she said. "What you say?"

"I said he's not coming over here anytime soon."

"How do you know?"

"Did he tell you that he was?" she asked, turning her body back to me, eyes wide with hope.

Honestly, I hadn't had any time to talk to Toby to see where his head was at. The one time that I did try to bring up him, Niecey, and what happened, he told me that my job description didn't include *relationship expert,* so I needed to mind my own business. He didn't say it to that effect, but I got the message loud and clear. After that, the only time I ever said anything to Toby was if it was about the club, or I had some information on a potential member. Toby and I had developed a cool relationship, but I guess it wasn't that cool to talk about him and Niecey.

I shook my head while looking around the room, answering her question. When my eyes went back to Niecey, I could see the tears already starting to build up again. I rolled my eyes.

"Man, don't start this crying shit again, Niecey."

"But-but-but you don't un-understand, Koi. I really think it's over between us. Three days . . ." her voice cried above a whisper. "Toby hasn't responded or said anything to me in three days. We've never gone that long without some form of communication. Even when I'm mad at him, he always makes it a point to text me and tell me how much he loves me. He-he hasn't said he loves me in three days."

"Niecey." I placed my hand on her thigh and rubbed it back and forth. "you need to give him a little more time. From the look on Toby's face when Will told him what happened, he was hurt. It was almost like something broke inside of him."

"But we didn't do *anything*, Koi."

I sat for a moment in my own thoughts. Niecey was real adamant on saying that nothing happened between her and Will, but I wasn't too sure if I believed her. The way he was describing her breakdown and how she fell asleep in his arms . . . I could see him kissing her, trying to calm her down, and she accepted it. Although it was at a time of weakness for her, it was still wrong. She shouldn't have been in Will's house in the first place, knowing he would do anything to get that old thing back. And if that meant fucking up what she and Toby had to do that, he wasn't about to let the opportunity slide.

"Niecey, how sure are you that that kiss didn't happen? Or anything else, for that matter?"

Her eyes rolled around for a second as if she were trying to picture that night in her head. "I'm 100 percent sure. Our lips never touched. Neither did our bodies in any sexual way. After I woke up in his bed—"

"You woke up in his *bed?* Were your clothes on?"

She slowly shook her head. "No . . . I was only in my bra and panties, but Aspen was in bed with me. When I woke up, her small body was nuzzled against mine." Her eyes squinted. "I already know what you're thinking by the look on your face, Koi. Will wouldn't do no crazy shit with his daughter in the bed next to me."

"How do you know that? I mean, the nigga was pretty convincing that the kiss happened. He never said that y'all fucked, but he alluded to it."

"What do you mean he alluded to it?"

I took a deep breath and sighed. "Niecey, Will made it seem like you two were so caught up in the kiss that y'all may have done something before you fell asleep in his arms."

"What?" she scoffed with a laugh. "You're lying. Will would never do anything like that. He knows how much

I love Toby and that he and I will never be anything but friends."

"Are you *sure* about that? I remember the stories you used to tell me about—"

She cut me off. "That was back in the day when we were young. Will has grown a lot." She shook her head. "He-he's different from how he used to be. He's not on drugs anymore. He's a father. A great one at that, regardless of how Aspen was conceived. And he's finally playing for the NFL, something he's always dreamed of doing. Will seems happy for once in his life, and I don't think me being with him would change any of that. I mean, it hasn't in all these years."

Sitting and listening to Niecey praise Will the way that she was struck me as odd. It wasn't too long ago that she was screaming "Fuck Will and his whole being!" Hell, she pushed her sister out of her life because of him. If she couldn't forgive LaLa for what she did, why was it so easy to forgive him? Her niece's DNA shared his too. I felt myself becoming a little upset with my cousin. What the hell happened that night to have her seeing this nigga in a whole new light? *He isn't on drugs anymore* . . . Good for him. *He's a great father* . . . Shit, he should be. Aspen belonged to him. *He's playing in the NFL* . . . Shit, that was barely. According to Beano, he was only on the practice team. Yeah, they got paid, but his ass could get dropped at any time. Regardless of any of that, I still couldn't understand this praise Niecey was giving him. It seemed as if she were #TeamWill now and that he wasn't the same nigga who was a big part of the drama she'd been through these last couple of years and when they were teenagers. The same man who blamed her for his NFL career ending in the first place. I needed to talk some sense into her ass before she fucked around and let those blinders cost her the man she was supposed to be with.

"Niecey, I don't know why, and I don't care how changed you may think Will is, but I don't trust him, and you shouldn't either." She opened her mouth to say something, but I continued speaking. "I don't know what he said or what he did to cause you to see this big change in him, but you need to congratulate the nigga and move on. Don't let him come between you and Toby like that. Yeah, you may see the change and think that's great, but Toby won't see it like that. All he will see is your first love trying to get back into your life."

Niecey sat up in her bed and turned on the TV. After setting Pandora to the Anita Baker channel, she got out of bed and started to pick up the trash that was on the ground. I watched as she hummed along to "Caught Up in the Rapture," giving me no response to what I just said. The pink shorts she borrowed from me a couple of days ago stretched across her ass, and the white wife beater was more stained than it was a day ago. Her hair was in a low ponytail and tangled like crazy. She was going to have a field day trying to comb that shit out.

When I tried to say something to her again, she turned the TV up a little louder, basically drowning me out. Once she finished picking up the clothes and empty bottles of soda from the floor, she muted the TV and started to pull the sheets off of the bed. I stayed seated in my spot until she began to jerk the fabric from beneath me.

"You could say excuse me," I snapped as I stood up and faced her.

"I thought that was what I was doing by pulling the sheet."

I laughed. I didn't know why she had an attitude with me for telling her some real shit. Hell, I was only trying to help.

"I didn't know that's what that meant," I said over my shoulder as I began walking toward the door. I needed to get some sleep, and trying to talk some sense into her was delaying that. "Look, Niecey, I wasn't—"

She held her hand up, cutting me off. "Koi, I know you were trying to help, and I thank you for that. Shit, you didn't have to let me stay here, but you did. I appreciate everything you've done and said to me these last couple of days. I heard you, but please know that I got this. I told you before that my position with Toby is solidified. We are going through a small bump right now, but we *will* get it together. Especially after I explain to him what really happened. Toby knows he doesn't have to worry about Will, or any other man, for that matter. My heart belongs to him just like his belongs to me. I know I made a mistake by going into Will's house and breaking down in his arms, but please believe me when I say nothing else happened or ever will happen."

I looked at her for a second and then nodded my head. Yawning, I lifted my arms over my head and stretched. "I heard you, cuz. I just wanna make sure you don't fuck up a good thing behind some bullshit like I did. Just remember you have to be smart with your head—"

"I know," she interrupted.

"I'm pretty sure you do, but also know that you have to be smart with your heart too. Don't let the good you see in Will fuck up the good thing you have with Toby. I'd hate to see another sista come up on all that rich, smooth . . . delicious . . . white chocolate."

Niecey laughed and threw a pillow at my head that I blocked and swatted down to the floor.

"Don't be describing my man using the word 'delicious' if you don't want your ass whipped."

I shrugged my shoulders. "Hey, you can't blame a girl for noticing how fine he is."

"He *is* fine, isn't he?" she replied with a dreamy look in her eyes.

"That he is. I'll see you in a few hours, okay? I need to get some rest."

I didn't hear Niecey's response because I had already closed the door and headed to my room. After taking a quick shower and throwing on one of my old T-shirts, I hopped in my bed and lay down without bothering to wrap my hair. The second my head touched the pillow, I was out like a light and dead to the world.

I woke up a few hours later to a quiet apartment, the smell of Pine-Sol and Lemon Lysol in the air. I walked past Niecey's room and noticed the door was open. Peeking in there, I saw she had completely cleaned the room. Her things were still packed in the corner, but the room smelled and looked good. She even vacuumed and wiped down the entertainment center. When I walked into the living room, the same results greeted me. My things that were on the floor were folded and sitting on the back of the couch, and my shoes were neatly lined up against the wall. She Windexed the hell out of my coffee and end tables because they looked brand-new. The trash had been taken out, the kitchen was spotless, and the guest bathroom had been cleaned and sanitized. I must've been knocked out for real because I didn't hear Niecey doing any of this while I was asleep.

Opening the fridge, I noticed a note on the door.

Hey, Koi,
I went to run a few errands and pick up some things for dinner. I'll be back in a couple of hours. If Toby stops by while I'm gone, please tell him to wait for me.
Thanks for the talk,
Niecey

I crumpled the note up and threw it in the trash, then grabbed me another Snapple out of the fridge. Plopping down on my couch, I turned on the TV and tried to find something worth watching. After settling on some HBO movie, I grabbed my purse from the coatrack and fished out my phone. I knew I'd have a million emails and missed calls because although I was off today, business never stopped; especially, when you were running a cash machine like Decadence. I returned a few calls and responded to a few emails before I tossed my phone on the other side of the couch and promised to answer the rest of my messages tomorrow.

The movie I was watching ended about two hours later, and Niecey was still gone. My hunger pangs had grown tremendously, so I decided to order a small pizza from the Italian spot up the street. I had just found another movie to watch when there was a knock on the door. Expecting it to be the delivery guy, I grabbed my wallet and went to answer the door, thankful that the forty-five-minute wait time was only twenty.

"You guys must be slow today," I said before opening the door fully and dragging out the last word. However, I wasn't staring into the eyes of the short Italian boy who normally delivered to me, but a pair of dark, sexy ones that were slanted and had a hint of lust in them.

"From the way that your nipples are getting hard, I can tell that you're happy to see me."

I rolled my eyes and tried to hide the way his smooth yet deep tone in his voice traveled down my spine and caused my body to shiver. "Beano, what the fuck do you want? Or should I address you as Mr. Cooper, seeing as our relationship is strictly professional now?"

"Are you going to invite me in, or are you going to cuss me out, out here?"

"I don't think I want you in my house. As a matter of fact, how do you even know where I live?"

"Uh, this is where we had sex a few weeks ago, or did you forget?"

I shook my head. "No, I didn't forget, but obviously, you did. We never made it out of the restaurant you took me to that your friends Langston and Shaylor own. We fucked right there in the private room and then parted ways after I ate some dessert."

Beano smiled that breathtaking smile of his and bit his bottom lip. His eyes trained on me again, with a different look in them this time. I tried to make out what it was, but couldn't when he lowered his head and then looked the other way.

"You're right. We did have sex there. One of the best nights of my life, if I'm being honest."

"Oh, so your little snow bopper sucking you up wasn't as memorable?"

He blew out a breath and wiped his hand over his chocolate face. The red L.A. hat was sitting low on his head. His facial hair was neatly trimmed. His red-and-white button-up was fresh out of the cleaners I could tell because the creases in the sleeve were superstraight. Dark denim jeans covered his long bow legs, and some red-on-red suede Puma classics covered his feet.

One of the things that I admired about Beano was his need not to be flashy and to keep some things low key. With all of the money he made playing professional football, his whole outfit wouldn't cost more than several hundred dollars at the most. The most expensive thing he wore was the black diamond Cuban link bracelet and matching necklace he bought when he got his first player's check . . . something he promised himself to buy whenever he made it.

He licked his lips and looked to the side before setting his dark eyes back on me. "So you still ain't gon' let me in?"

Before I could answer his question, the delivery guy walked up, holding my pizza and the extra crushed peppers I asked for.

"Holy shit. You're Beano Cooper. What are you doing here?" he asked, trying to keep some of his *fan*demonium down. "Oh my God, is this pizza for you? Can I get a quick pic to post on IG? My friends will never believe I delivered a pizza to you."

Beano looked at me and smiled before taking the pizza from fan boy's hands and posing for a few snapshots. After signing a few napkins and paying for my food, he leaned against the door frame and handed me the pepperoni and cheesy goodness.

"I pay for your food and you *still* not going to invite me in?"

Stepping to the side, I allowed Beano to enter my home and closed the door behind him. I watched as his eyes traveled around the living room and then into the kitchen.

"You got some Vitamin Water or orange juice?"

"Only Snapples, some smoothie shit Niecey drinks, or regular bottled water."

"Well, can I have some regular water?"

I passed by him and sat back on my couch. Opening my pizza box up, I grabbed a slice, folded it in half, and took a huge bite.

"You can get it yourself," I managed to get out, strings of cheese falling all over my chin and shirt.

Beano walked into my kitchen and grabbed a bottle of water for him and one for me. After drinking more than half of his and opening mine, he sat down next to me and grabbed a slice of my pizza.

"Um, this is a small, which means it's only for one person—not two."

He ignored me and grabbed the remote off of the coffee table, changing the channel to ESPN.

"Uh, excuse me. I was watching that."

"He kills that ugly wizard dude at the end and marries the redhead girl. Oh, and they have a few kids too."

I rolled my eyes and ate some more of my food. We watched highlights from his game last night for about half an hour and then turned on the rerun of *Game of Thrones*.

"So, how is Niecey?" Beano asked after *we* finished my pizza.

I shrugged my shoulders. "She said she's good, but I don't think she is."

"Why do you say that?"

I folded my legs underneath me and turned my body toward him. "What's your take on Will Davis? I know you said he's cool and all, but does he seem like he's on the up-and-up to you?"

He thought about my question for a second before he answered. "The dude is all right with me. Brags a lot about stupid shit, but he's cool." Beano paused for a minute. "A lot of the team fucks with him, but that might change now."

"Why you say that?"

"Because he got bumped up to the playing squad now. Andre Steward is out indefinitely, so the higher-ups called a meeting this morning and gave the spot to him. No more practice team. He's stomping with the big dawgs now."

"I wonder if Niecey knows," I said to myself but loud enough for Beano to hear.

"More than likely she does. My boy Armell said that he's been calling everyone he can think of. He was at his house a few hours ago and had to leave because Will said he was going out to celebrate with his daughter and some more family."

I nodded my head and sat back in my seat. I hoped Niecey's ass wasn't a part of that "family" he was talking about. I mean, I was happy for him and all. It's good to see people accomplishing something or living out their dreams, but Will needed to realize that Niecey was no longer a part of his.

After *Game of Thrones* went off, I picked up my trash and took it to the kitchen. I could feel Beano's eyes on my ass, so I gave him a little show. Yeah, I was mad at him for letting that slut bucket Storm suck him off, but we weren't together or hadn't agreed to become exclusive after that one time we fucked. I realized now that I was expecting for Beano to read my mind and be on the same wavelength as me when it came to whatever it is we were doing, but I was wrong. The man was just as much single as I was and could do whatever he wanted with no objections from me.

"You keep shaking that ass like that, I won't be responsible for what happens next."

I smacked my lips. "Beano, leave me the hell alone and go text one of your other little female friends with that bullshit. What you and I did was a one-time thing. We sampled each other, and that was it. No strings or anything attached."

I was laughing in my head with what I just said and not paying attention to my surroundings. When I turned around to leave the kitchen, Beano was in the doorway blocking my path, and I ran right into his hard chest. My eyes ran down his fit body with no shame, every memory of the dark tattoos lining his arms, chest, and neck reeling in my mind. The way he laid me on top of that small table at the restaurant and ate *his* dessert had my clit thumping against my panties like crazy. I tried to swallow the lump in my throat but ended up coughing instead.

"You need some water?" he asked, voice low and almost in a hum. His cool breath blew across my forehead.

I know this may sound crazy, but when he brushed his lips past mine, I could taste a small hint of the mint gum he was chewing in my mouth. I tried to move back, but whatever cologne he had on caused me to have temporary paralysis. Beano took my disability as a cue to wrap his arms around my waist and pull me closer to him.

"Wh-wha-what are you doing?" breathlessly came from my mouth.

"About to show you why you should answer the door fully clothed the next time I pop up."

Before I knew what happened, Beano had my ass stretched out on my countertop, feasting on what he claimed as his "new home" from now on. I came three or four times before he got up from off of his knees and grabbed another bottle of water out of the fridge. When I thought he was finished and tried to get down, Beano turned me over and dove his thick tongue in my love from behind. As if that wasn't enough, when I felt the weight of his heavy dick press against my opening, I completely lost it. In one smooth stroke, Beano had filled me up and began to fuck the shit out of me.

"Just in case you were wondering," he said in between strokes, "this pussy is mine. Act like you don't know and watch what happens to you."

I bit my lip to keep the moan I could feel in my throat from coming out and nodded my head. At this point, Beano could tell me to pledge my soul to the devil and I would, just as long as he didn't stop hitting my shit the way that he was.

We fucked all over my kitchen, dining room, and living room for the next two hours. After we were done, I went straight to sleep. Didn't know if Niecey came back or not. At this point, I really didn't care. My mind was still on a fuck high, and all I could see was Beano Cooper's fine ass being my supplier.

Tobias

I massaged my temples with my fingers and shook my head, just thinking about the bad press I could get if this small mishap that I now had to deal with ever got out. As if the stress of what Niecey and I were going through right now wasn't enough, I had to deal with the repercussions of a thieving asshole I trusted to run my other business.

"I appreciate everything you just said, Chase, man, but is there anything I can do to get my money back?"

"If it's still available, I'm pretty sure that there is something you can do, but I can't give you the full details. You have to talk to a lawyer who deals in criminal law."

"Then why did Cai refer me to you?" I asked, wondering why my twin even offered up Chasin's attorney services if he couldn't help me.

I didn't mean to snap on him, but shit was going crazy in my life right now, and it seemed like everything started to happen at the same time. Niecey doing God knows what at her ex's house when she should've been at the grand opening with me. Raphael, the damn general manager over Lotus Bomb, had been taking money from me for God knows how long. And then there was that whole *"exotic dancer bags rich club owner"* thing with Storm that the press won't let go of. Even after telling a few reporters who had followed me to the grocery store that I was happily engaged to Niecey, they still found a way to twist the story and have me connected to Storm for some reason.

"Toby, man, everything will be okay," Chasin reassured me, pulling me from my thoughts. "I have a few colleagues who are some great criminal attorneys and have represented clients on both sides, so they understand the situation from every angle. Before I leave for the day, I'll go through my contacts and then forward you their names and numbers. You can Google them and see which one you wanna roll with. But off the top, I'd tell you to hit my boy Jeffery Townsend up. Not only is he my frat brother, but he has an exceptional win rate."

I pulled at the thick hair on my chin and then wiped my hand over my face. Pressing charges, finding a good lawyer, and then having to go to court was going to be more shit added on to the stressful events of my life.

"Thanks, Chase. Just one quick question. I know you said you don't know everything about what's about to go down, but worst-case scenario, what *could* happen?"

The other end of the line was silent for a second. "Worst-case scenario? Ole boy doesn't have any of the money he stole from you to give back. In that case, the judge may require him to pay restitution in addition to the fines he might get slapped with or while he's doing some prison time."

"*Some* prison time? What's the most he can get?"

"He's going to get some years. No judge in the world will give him only a couple of years when he's stolen a little over $150K from you. My guess, he'll spend somewhere between seven and twelve years, more or less. But like I said, my boy Jeffery or one of the other attorneys you pick will be able to tell you a more definite answer."

I drank the last of my watered-down scotch and poured me another shot. "All right, man. Thanks for the info, and I'll see you around."

"You already know. Oh, are you coming to the couples dinner Cai and Audri are having in a few weeks?"

"Honestly, I don't know. Me and my fiancée are going through a little something right now."

"Is that right?"

"Yeah, man."

"If you don't mind me asking, what's going on? Maybe I could give you some sound advice seeing as I don't know the two of you that well. I'm not at liberty to pick sides."

I thought about it for a second. "Nah, man, it's okay. I'm not about to bore you with that shit. I just need to figure some things out on my own."

"That's cool, and I respect that. But before I go, let me hit you with this . . . Whatever is truth to you will be truth to you, even if that truth is a lie." From my lack of response, Chasin laughed. "I can tell you don't get what I'm saying with that, so let me break it down in layman's terms. Your girl obviously did something you felt betrayed your trust. How you found out, I don't know. But don't let what you *assume* is the truth blind you to what *really* happened. Give your girl a chance to explain and then go from there."

"Wait. How do you know she's the one that needs to do the explaining?"

Chasin chuckled. "The only time a dude sounds as sad as you do over the phone is when his girl done broke his heart. We just had a thirty-minute conversation about your general manager who stole a shitload of money from you, and the tone in your voice didn't raise once. You haven't threatened to beat his ass, and you haven't asked a ton of questions about your money. The only thing that can have your mind that occupied is your girl."

Damn. Going over our conversation in my head, I realized Chasin was right. Although a part of my mind was on Raphael's bitch ass, thoughts of Niecey controlled the others.

"I got a client walking in right now, Toby, so let me—"

"*Boy, who the hell are you talking to?*" the feminine voice seductively said in the background.

"Bree, I'm on a business call right now. I'll get with you in a minute."

"Can't be too much business the way your dick just sprung to life when I walked in here."

"Why wouldn't it? You don't have any damn clo—Aye, Toby, man, I'll holla at you later. Be looking for that list later on today, okay?"

Before I could even respond to him, Chasin hung up the phone. The last thing I heard was him swearing in a low growl before the call was fully disconnected. Whoever that was in the background was most definitely *not* a client. It must've been his scientist girlfriend Cai told me about. I remembered him saying her name was Bree or something like that.

I laughed just thinking about the pop-up visits Niecey used to do while I was at work. It didn't matter when, either. Lunch breaks, before work, in the middle of the day, after she clocked out. When I wanted it, Niecey had no problem showing up to give it to me. My dick pressed against my thigh as it began to grow harder, and I groaned. Maybe I should give Niecey a call so that I could relieve myself from some of this stress. I picked up the phone and dialed half of her number, but hung up after giving it a second thought. Niecey was still on time-out, and I would just have to handle this built-up frustration the same way I had for the last couple of days . . . in the shower. Pressing the "do not disturb" button on my office phone, I gathered up a few of the unpaid notices that were spread over my desk and bit my bottom lip, highly irritated.

For a whole year, Raphael had been overseeing everything at Lotus Bomb, and in return, he was robbing me blind. The only way I found out what was going on was because the liquor distributor refused to bring me my monthly shipment of alcohol last week. When I got on the phone to ask him what was going on, he told me that we were behind six months on paying him for deliveries. That little piece of information prompted me to get in contact with my accountant to see why no payments were being issued. I mean, I had more than enough money, so there was no reason for this to be going on.

When I tell you that I was mad as fuck after finding out that Raphael had been promising to pay all of my vendors and pocketing the money in return, I lost it. The asshole had even given himself monthly bonuses for some shit he didn't even do. I confronted him about the whole thing, and he confessed but then tried to change his story up when I called the police. Needless to say, he was arrested, and now we have to go to court to figure this shit out.

Like I said earlier, shit in my life was going crazy, and all I wanted to do was be up under Niecey to feel some type of familiarity with being okay. But I couldn't do it. In my heart, I felt like she betrayed me, and I couldn't trust her to not do it again, especially, with Will's snake ass slithering around. For some reason, Niecey wanted to believe that he had changed after all these years, but I didn't believe it. That little fight he and I had before Decadence opened should have told her that, but I guess she saw something in him that I never would.

Now, don't get me wrong. I still loved Niecey with every breath in my body, and I still intended on marrying her. I just needed for her to once and for all get this bitch-ass muthafucka Will out of her system so that we could move on with our lives and continue to build on us.

"Speak of the devil," I said to myself as I picked up my ringing cell phone and declined the call.

As much as it hurt me to ignore my baby, I needed her to get her shit together. She couldn't do that if she was sitting on the phone trying to explain herself to me all day. Did I think she slept with Will that night? I mean, it was a possibility, but I seriously doubted it. The look on Will's face at the bail bondsmen wasn't one of a man who had just had sex with ShaNiece Taylor. Niecey's pussy was golden and could have the hardest man whimpering for just a taste. Will's whole demeanor screamed tension that day, something he shouldn't have had if he was able to bust a nut.

With thoughts still lingering on Niecey, I managed to get a little work done. Paying out these old invoices and apologizing for the inconvenience of it all, I was on the right path to having everything back to normal. The only thing I needed to do now was find another GM who would do his or her job right and not steal any more money from me.

After hours of returning more phone calls, Googling the list of lawyers Chasin sent me, and responding to emails for a good portion of the day, I was finally ready to head home and get me something to eat. I had already informed the personal chef that I would use from time to time that I had a taste for some comfort food and nothing too fancy. Hopefully, he had a full understanding of what comfort food meant and wasn't about to serve me any braised lamb or something like that. All I wanted to do was go home, eat, take a shower, and then hop in bed— my schedule of sorts since Niecey was no longer there.

Gathering my things, I made sure to grab my laptop and cell before I turned off my office light and locked the door. Tonight at Lotus Bomb was Karaoke Night, and I wanted to be out of the vicinity before people started to get drunk and sing off-key. I had just walked out of the hallway that led to my office and stepped into the back of the main room when a voice halted my stride.

"You gon' cry, you gon' pay me in tears.

You gon' cry, you owe me for all these years. . ."

My eyes scanned the stage for the source of the power-ful voice that was belting out the K. Michelle song. I was shocked when my gaze landed on a familiar sight. I almost didn't recognize her at first because her hair was pulled back in a half-up, half-down style that showed off the beautiful features of her face, and she was fully clothed. Some jeans and a V-cut blouse with one of those colorful scarves that loosely hung around the neck. No makeup and only some regular heels. Her brown skin glistened under the spotlight. With her hand pressing lightly into her diaphragm, she sang the bridge of this "Cry" song and then went back to the chorus. Tears were now slowly falling down her face. This song must have meant something to her or whoever she was singing it for.

I watched as she captivated the small audience with her version and hurt. When she was done, the crowd, including some of my employees, gave her a standing ovation. I clapped my hands together a few times for the great performance and then turned to walk away. Before I could make it out of the exit, a soft voice called my name, which I heard over the next track that the karaoke machine began to play.

I turned around and acknowledged her presence with a head nod.

"What are you doing here?" she gushed with squinted eyes.

I held up my laptop. "Had to do some work."

"Work? Like what?" She looked around the dimly lit lounge. "Odd place to get some work done, huh?"

"Not when you own the place. The walls in my office are soundproof."

"Your office?" She had a confused look on her face. "You own this club too?"

I smiled, never answering her question. "Did you need something, Halo? You called my name for a reason, I'm assuming."

"It's Kategory."

"I'm sorry."

She licked her lips and nervously pulled at her fingers. "My, my real name is Kategory. I know." Her eyes playfully rolled to the back of her head. "I don't know what my mother was thinking, but here I am. Kategory LaChay Thomas." When I didn't respond, she turned her eyes over and continued. "No one calls me Halo outside of work except for Storm. So please, call me Kategory, or Kat for short."

I nodded my head. "Okay, Kategory. Did you need something?" I pointed to the door. "I was actually on my way out."

"Uh . . . I just wanted to say hello. I was a little surprised to see you standing back here while I was singing. And then to find out that this is your spot . . ." Her head nodded up and down as she looked around. "Now that I'm paying attention, this looks like a club you would own. Sorta has that *I'm rich but still like things low-key* look about it." I furrowed my brows, and she lifted her hands. "I hope I didn't offend you with what I just said."

"Nah, you good. And as far as the look goes, I don't like a lot of flash. The main focus is to have people enjoying the atmosphere and spending money here, not wondering how much money was being spent to decorate." We shared a laugh. "Hey, it's getting late, and I need to go. It was nice running into you. And before I forget . . . Your voice is amazing." I turned to walk away, but she grabbed my arm.

"Do you really think so? I'm only asking because my singing is what brought me out here in the first place. I figured since I wasn't getting anywhere in Atlanta with my singing, I could come to Los Angeles and do something with it. You know, run into someone famous and hand them my demo."

"Old school, huh?"

She nodded her head and smiled.

My eyes diverted from hers and went up to the stage. The new person who was up there had the mic entirely too close to their mouth as they slurred the words of Rihanna's "Kiss It Better." When my eyes returned to Halo, we both busted out laughing.

"Please tell me I sounded better than that," she said. Her smile and high cheekbones gave Tyra Banks a run for her money.

"You sounded ten times better than that. Have you put a demo together yet or uploaded some videos of you singing on YouTube?"

"I have, but no one is checking for me—especially when they find out that I dance for a living. You don't know how many of these dudes have invited me to a session only to try to get some puss—" Her eyes grew big. "Oooh. I'm sorry, Toby. I didn't mean to . . . I mean, I wasn't trying to . . . Fuck. Um . . . I'll see you at work tomorrow." She covered her mouth with her hand. "Oh my freaking God. I talk too damn much. Bye, Toby."

Halo turned to walk away, but I called her name, and she turned around. "Aye, if you're really serious about this singing thing, I have a studio you can record your demo in. As a matter of fact, I have a few songs that I wrote and produced that you would sound great singing."

"Are you serious? Like, for real?"

I nodded my head. "Yeah. But only if you're serious."

"Oh my God. I'm *super* serious." Her eyes became misty. "Thank you, Toby. You just don't know how much I hate dancing. Yeah, it helps me with maintaining my lifestyle, but I'm so ready to hang those thongs and stilettos up."

She jumped up and down, excitement all over her face. "Oh my God. Wait until I tell Stor—"

I cut her off before she could finish. "About that. If I help you do this, Storm can't be anywhere around. I'm already trying to get the media to stop associating me with her. So, if we do this, no Storm."

Hopefully, she understood the weight of my words. Although Storm was one of the top performers at Decadence, I wouldn't hesitate to fire her ass in a heartbeat. That little stunt she pulled on the red carpet almost got her ass thrown out, but Beano told me that he talked to her, and she promised that she would never do it again. As a matter of fact, Storm had been staying clear of me since that night. The couple of times that I was at Decadence and she was there, she didn't utter a word to me or look my way. Either the talk she had with Beano changed her mind or the ass whipping Koi promised scared her ass straight and away from me.

"My lips are sealed," Halo said, causing me to turn my attention back to her.

I pulled the strap of my bag over my shoulder and turned toward the exit.

"Do you want my number or something so that we can schedule this session?"

I continued to walk but answered her over my shoulder. "I don't think my girl would appreciate me taking your number even if it's for business reasons. I know where you work, so I'll get at you in a few days."

"Smart girl," I heard her say as I walked out of the club and to my car.

"So you still not answering Niecey's calls or texts?"

I shook my head and bounced the basketball around Cairo, trying for a layup, but missed. My reaction was quicker than his, so I grabbed the ball again and dribbled over to the half court line.

"I don't think she's ready to talk to me."

"Oh, so now you know what she's ready to do?"

"Man, I know Niecey like I know the back of my hand. I think I know her more than she knows herself."

Cai reached in and tried to steal the ball from me, but I crossed him over and took the three-point shot. *Swish.* Nothing but net.

"So, do you think she did anything with him?"

I shrugged my shoulders. "I don't think she had sex with him, but I do think they kissed at some point. Probably wasn't initiated by her, but it happened."

"So, if you know that, why aren't you speaking to her yet?"

I dribbled the ball a bit and then threw it to Cai. "Because even though she didn't initiate it, there was still some part of her that gave him the impression that it was okay to do. Yeah, I know she was having a nervous breakdown after being hit with that news about LaLa, but still."

Cai tried to make the same three-point shot as me but missed. He retrieved the ball after running it down the other half of the court and threw it back to me.

"Did your source ever get back to you with the information on that situation?"

I shook my head. After finding out about Niecey's sister being MIA and strung out on drugs somewhere, I put in a call to one of my friends who could locate just about anyone who was missing, but I hadn't received a call back from him yet.

"I'm still waiting on him to get back to me." I threw the ball from the free throw line and missed the shot.

"Well, I think while you're waiting on him to hit you back, you should talk to your girl."

"Bro—"

He cut me off. "Man, before you even say she still needs some time to get her shit together, let me tell you this. You don't want to leave your girl out there too long wondering if y'all relationship is still a relationship. Because, believe me, while you're giving her the silent treatment and ignoring her calls, there's another man that's not. And while she's pouring her heart out to him, crying over you, she might mistake his fake concern for something that it isn't."

I swiped the ball out of Cai's hand and dribbled back down the court. What he was saying made sense. Maybe I did need to talk to Niecey. At least, give her an explanation about why I hadn't been answering her calls or texts. The shit was crazy, though. The one problem that almost caused me to lose her at the beginning of our relationship was the same thing causing problems in it now.

My mind was reeling, and this basketball game wasn't helping to alleviate these thoughts. I threw the ball back over to Cai and walked over to the bleachers, grabbing my towel and wiping the sweat off of my face. Pulling my phone out of my gym bag, I scrolled to Niecey's name to call her but stopped when a curvy shadow hovered over me.

"Well, well, well. Fancy running into you here." The purr in her tone was suggestive, but then again, it could've just been how she talked.

My eyes rolled up her toned stomach, over her breasts, and then to her face. "What's up, Storm?"

"Nothing much. Just had to come to make sure that all of this stays in tip-top shape." Her hands lightly ran over the silhouette of her frame. In a pink, two-toned yoga outfit, Storm's body was a sight to see: a small waist that expanded out to some wide hips, triple-D breasts that didn't need the support of a bra, and an ass that was round like two melons. Her thighs weren't as thick as they should have been for the build she was going for, but that didn't take away from the reaction she obviously wanted to get from men when they saw her.

"*That's* what's up." Cai walked up and grabbed his towel. "Storm, this is my twin, Cairo. Cai, this is Storm. She dances at the club."

Cai extended his hand, and she took it. "I remember her. You almost had my wife coming out of her shoes."

Storm waved him off. "I get that a lot. Jealous housewives who feel threatened by me for some reason. Anyways . . . Twins?" Her eyes went between Cai and me. "Damn. I bet the two of you broke plenty of hearts back in the day."

Cai looked at me and shook his head. He already knew what time it was with Storm and this flirty question asking, but he wasn't fazed by it, and neither was I. We had two of the finest women in Los Angeles and would never mess it up for anyone, including Storm. Lying back against the bleacher, Cai opened his bottle of Gatorade and took a sip, ignoring Storm's statement completely. The look in her eyes held nothing but pure lust as she eyed his sweat-drenched body up and down. When Cai licked his lips after finishing his drink, her breath hitched.

"Was there something else you needed besides saying hello, Storm? My brother and I were busy," I asked as I pulled my T-shirt over my head, the sweat on my back and chest instantly dampening the cotton fabric.

She bit her bottom lip and twisted the ends of her silver hair with her fingers. "I hope you're not as mean as your twin here, Cairo."

"Nah, I'm not—but my wife is." He grabbed his gym bag and stood up, his black Nike basketball shorts identical to mine. We would've almost been dressed the same, but Cai chose to rock a pair of some custom red-and-black Retro 3s that matched the Bulls jersey he had on. "I'm about to go hit the showers and head on home. Audri can smell when another female is within five feet of me, and I don't feel like having to post bail for her tonight."

"You guys and these insecure females. I'm not doing anything but having a friendly conversation with my handsome boss and his equally handsome twin brother. No laws are being broken here. So why would she be mad?"

"The fact that you even asked that tells me that there's a lot you don't know about our wives."

"You mean your wife. Toby here isn't married yet. Well, according to all of these newspaper articles he and I have been pictured in, he isn't."

Cai turned his attention to me. "Aye, man, you can sit here and entertain this shit, but I know better." His phone started to ring. "See, what I tell you. Audri's ass is all the way on the other side of town and is already calling me."

I laughed. "That doesn't mean she knows a female is around."

"She does when her nosy ass wants to FaceTime. Look, I'm outta here. Remember what I told you about your girl. Handle that before it's too late." Cai grabbed his things and walked off before he answered Audri's call. "Hey, baby."

"Don't 'hey, baby' me, Thad-deus. Who is that bitch you just walked away from?"

"Baby, what are you talking about?"

"I can see some silver-haired ho in the—Is that that same bitch who Niecey's cousin was about to fight at the grand opening? Wait. Is that To-bi-as back there too? Thaddeus, turn that damn phone back around so I can see."

"Stop being nosy, babe. And stop calling me Thaddeus. You know I hate that shit."

"Turn the phone around now, Cai."

"You need to stop screaming before you stress my baby out!" was the last thing I heard before he disappeared behind the locker room wall.

"Wow . . . But she isn't insecure."

I grabbed my things from the bleacher and stood up. "That's your problem, Storm. Always speaking on shit you don't know about. How is she being insecure because she wants to know what women are around her husband? Shit, Niecey does me the same way."

She smacked her lips. "Niecey. What's up with you and her anyway? Why wasn't she at the grand opening?"

"That's not any of your business. And if you want to keep your job, you'd be wise to stay out of my personal life. You have already been warned once. Don't let it happen again."

She lifted her hands in surrender. "Oh, shit, my bad. I just assumed that you guys had broken up with all of these rumors I've been hearing going around about her and Will Davis."

I scoffed and shook my head. When Storm didn't get the response she wanted out of me, she continued.

"Oh, so it's true? Her and Will are hooking back up again? I mean, Beano and his boys were talking about it the other day, and I was floored. The way she was all in my face and telling me to stay away from you when all I was doing was introducing myself. Kind of makes you wonder why she was so riled up, doesn't it? In my experience, I've learned that females only tend to get superterritorial when they've been doing dirt themselves. You might wanna think about that before you go running back to the woman who still holds a torch for her ex." Storm smiled and then turned to walk away, but not before winking her eye and waving over her tanned shoulder.

Cai and Niecey were right. I was going to have to fire this chick, but not until Koi could find a replacement. A few of our exclusive members had already booked events in the next few months and Storm was being requested left and right. The girl was good for business, but this poking into my personal life and pushing up on me had to stop. I'm not gonna lie, though; some of the things she said did get me to question some shit. Was Niecey still communicating with Will behind my back while acting like she wasn't? We never had the type of relationship where we felt the need to go through each other's phones, but was that a mistake?

I shook those thoughts out of my head. That shit wasn't true. I knew Niecey. I knew her heart. Then again, what if I was wrong? Was my love really not enough these last two years to make her completely be over Will? I groaned as I walked farther into the locker room. This second-guessing myself was starting to give me a headache, and I was ready to go home and go to bed. Skipping over taking a shower at the gym, I sent a quick text to Cai and told him that I was out.

Walking to my car, I assumed the person who was calling my phone was my brother and went to answer it but stopped when I saw Niecey's name flash across my screen. As much as I wanted to talk to her, I declined the call. Niecey still needed a little more time before we had this conversation on what we were going to do about this Will situation. Hopefully, this time apart wouldn't come back to bite me in the ass like Cai said. But even if it did, I wasn't about to go out without a fight.

ShaNiece

A week and a half had gone by, and I still hadn't heard from or seen Toby. The only way that I knew that he was still breathing was because of a few newspaper articles Koi and the celebrity blogs wouldn't stop talking about regarding Mr. Wright, his new club venture, and the hot platinum-silver-haired dancer who was at his side on the red carpet. When I first saw the pictures of Toby and Storm on the front cover of *Hollywood Weekly* with the new couple alert headline, I was ready to hunt both her and him down to fuck up both of them. But after Koi told me the full story of what happened and how she was about to snatch that ho's head off, my anger calmed down a bit. However, that didn't stop me from sending him a nice little text message telling him he needed to fire the bitch before I used my fist and fired on her ass. I waited a whole day for him to send me some response in regards to that message, but just like all of my other texts before, that one also went unanswered.

I was all for giving Toby some time, but a week and a half without any communication was stretching it a bit. In my heart, I could feel that we weren't over, but in my mind, I wasn't so sure. Yesterday, Koi brought some of my clothes from his loft home, with a note saying that anything else that he found of mine along the way would be sent either through the mail or through my cousin if I needed it. When I asked her if he had said anything before he gave her my things, she shook her head and changed the subject.

Not satisfied with that response, I showed up at Decadence the following day to try to get some type of conversation out of Toby, but when I got there, one of the security guards informed me that he wasn't scheduled to come in that night. When I asked Koi where he'd been, she told me that Toby had only come to that club twice since the grand opening, once to help the new bartender do inventory and another time to drop my things off. According to her, Toby was spending the majority of his time in the a.m. at lunch meetings with potential investors for another spot he wanted to open in Vegas and spending his nights at his other club, Lotus Bomb, trying to get everything there back on track after having to fire his general manager for stealing.

Of course, I sent him a text message in regards to that whole situation, telling him that if he needed me to come and help him close out on some nights and do receipts that I would, but from his lack of response, I guessed he didn't want or need my help.

I sighed as I sat on the bench at the park around the corner from Koi's apartment and watched Aspen play on the swings. I had my niece for the whole week, watching her while Will was away doing media for his new starting position on the team and practicing for the Sabors away game on Sunday.

My mother, who decided to stay on vacation for another week, called to check in on her granddaughter and me but didn't stay on the phone long enough for me to ask her anything about LaLa and this drug business. The day I left Koi's apartment after cleaning up my room and everything else, one of the errands I had to run consisted of me dropping by LaLa's house and seeing if she was there. I took the key she gave my mother for emergencies and entered her house unannounced. The condition of her home mortified me. La was never the cleanest person in the world, but she wasn't the dirtiest either. Her house looked like it hadn't been cleaned in months. There were toys, clothes, trash, and take-out containers everywhere. Mail addressed to Li'l Ray was spread over the dining room table with *"this muthafucka doesn't live here anymore"* written across the front in crayon. Sippy cups with old juice and spoiled milk were stacked on any flat surface. My niece's little toddler bed sitting next to the couch had dingy-ass sheets with holes in it. There was a small pallet on the floor next to it, where I assumed LaLa would pass out whenever she was there.

I walked into the kitchen and opened the fridge but had to close it back when an awful smell smacked me in the face. I guess with there being no electricity, everything in the icebox and freezer spoiled. Wasn't no telling how long that had been, either. I tried to wash my hands after touching the dirty metal, but when I turned the faucet on, nothing came out, which meant the water was off too. I shook my head just thinking about my niece living in this condition but was glad that she had me, my mother, and Will as choices to fall back on.

I sat in my car in front of LaLa's place for a couple of hours, waiting on her to resurface so that I could give her a piece of my mind, but she never showed up. Her phone was disconnected, and all of her social media pages were shut down. I reached out to her friend JaNair to see if she had heard from her recently, but Jay said that she and La had not spoken in almost six months—around the same time that Will said he suspected her of being back on drugs. This shit was crazy. My sister was wildin' out in these streets, smoking or sniffing that white girl up her nose, and my fiancé didn't want to speak to or see me. The only positive I had in my life right now was Aspen. Seeing that smile on her face had gotten me over a few of these sad days in this last week.

"A few more times down the slide, baby, and then we have to go," I told her as I looked at the time on my phone.

Her cute round face looked over at me with a smile that could brighten up the sun. "We go eat, TeTe?"

I shook my head. "No. We gotta go see your daddy before he leaves."

Today was Thursday, and the team had an evening flight out to New York. Will called and asked me if I could bring Aspen by his house to spend some time with him before he left, but I didn't think that would've been a good idea. So I opted to bring her to the airport instead. That way, she could see him off and also see the airplanes that she was now starting to obsess over. I figured after we got us something to eat from McDonald's, we could head over to LAX, and then she could spend about an hour with Will before he had to leave.

I'd just gotten through reading over a few of the workers' comp emails I needed to respond to on my phone when the Wale and Usher ringtone I had set for my baby started to play.

"If there's a question of my heart, you got it.
It don't belong to anyone but you."

The butterflies in my stomach began to flutter like crazy, and my heart seemed to skip more than a few beats. Toby was finally calling me back, and I was more than excited to hear his voice.

"Hello," I anxiously answered on the third ring, my breathing a little short.

"Hey." A comfortable silence followed after his response. "How are you, Niecey?"

"I'm fine, babe. How-how are you? I miss you."

He hesitated before he answered. "I'm doing good . . . And I miss you too."

I didn't want to say anything to piss him off or bring up the whole Will situation, so I decided to bring up the shit going on at Lotus Bomb. "So, I heard you had to fire Raphael."

Toby yawned, and I could tell by the way that it sounded that he was tired. His voice was a little strained and at the same time raspy. I could imagine the facial hair on his face being a little longer than it was the last time I saw him and his curly blond locks wild and all over the place, his greenish-blue eyes red from another sleepless night. I could see his fingers pinching the bridge of his nose as he sat back in his work chair, shirtless, muscled arms, chest, and colorful tattoos on full display for the world to see. I could picture his lounge pants falling just below his waist, showing off that delectable V-shape and the light trail of dark, curly hair leading from the middle of his abbed stomach down to the shaft of his curved dick.

My throat hitched.

"Niecey, are you okay?"

I nodded my head as if he could see me. "Just got a lot of things on my mind."

"Seems like we both do."

"You-you wanna talk about it?" I asked, my nerves starting to play on me.

While I waited on his response, my eyes wandered over to Aspen, who was now on the swings. Some little boy whose father was sitting on another bench pushed her as she rolled her head back and laughed.

"I do wanna talk about it, Niecey, but not over the phone. Are you able to meet for dinner in a couple of hours?"

I looked at the time. It was almost four o'clock, and I had an hour before I was supposed to meet Will at the airport.

"Uh, yeah. But you know I still have Aspen with me."

"Oh, yeah?" I could hear the smile in his tone. "And how is my beautiful princess?"

"She's fine, considering some of the shit I found out." I waved it off. "But we can talk about that later."

I could hear some paper shuffling in Toby's background, and then the sound of a few keys being stroked on a piano.

"You're in the studio?"

He chuckled. "You heard that, huh?"

"I did. When did you start playing again?"

Toby paused for a second and then replied, "About two weeks ago."

Two weeks ago was when our problems started. Whenever Toby was overwhelmed with a project or just work in general, I could always find him late night in his studio playing the piano as he sang whatever song was on his mind. A lot of people didn't know that Toby played instruments and could sing. It wasn't a talent he talked about a lot but something he would share with me whenever he was going through something or if he wanted to find another way to get my panties off. The first time Toby ever sang for me was the first night we had dinner together at his loft. It was our first date, and I sure wasn't expecting him to serenade me, but when he did, I fell in love and had been falling ever since.

"I thought we can meet somewhere close to the airport, if possible. I'm on standby for a flight to Vegas, and I need to be close just in case they call me."

"Vegas?" I felt my eyebrows furrow.

"Yeah. Thinking about opening a club out there."

"So Decadence must've been a big hit?"

"It was, and I have you, Cai, Ness, Beano, and Koi to thank for that."

I blushed. "Well, you know I would do anything to make sure you accomplish any of the goals you have in life." When Toby didn't respond, I asked, "Is Koi going with you?" I did remember my cousin telling me about the potential Vegas move, but I didn't remember if she said whether she was traveling too.

"Nah, Koi got her hands full right now helping me with both clubs. I don't want to put too much more on her. She's already going above and beyond her job description as it is."

"So who's going with you to Vegas?" I pushed again.

"Just me and a business associate, Niecey."

I don't know why my first thought went to Storm's ho ass, but Toby had another think coming if he even thought he was going to leave L.A. with that bitch.

I sarcastically replied, "I hope this 'business associate' isn't your new girlfriend the media can't get enough of."

"If you're talking about Storm, Niecey, you already know what time it is with that. Let's not play that game. We may be going through our shit right now, but I've never looked at another woman since I laid eyes on you." He chuckled. "You just don't get it, do you? Niecey, you are it for me. When I told you I loved you the first time we made love, I meant that shit. When I told you that I would do anything in this world to make you happy, I strive for that shit. When I told you that you would be the woman I would marry and carry my seeds, I intend to make that shit happen. There isn't a woman alive that could take your place in my heart, my mind, my soul, or on my dick. You just need to be sure that you're ready to be on the receiving end of all of that. Are you ready, Niecey? Are you ready to be just mine and only mine? Are you ready to give your complete heart all to me?"

I sat on the park bench, stunned by everything Toby had just said. I could feel my eyes start to tear up and tried to hide my face when Aspen ran over to me.

"Go see Daddy now?" she asked as she plopped down in my lap and wrapped her arms around my neck. The pink sweater that matched the pink sandals on her feet felt fuzzy against my cheek. I pulled her little shorts down and pulled her closer to me.

"Give me one second, baby. TeTe talking to Uncle Toby right now." She nodded her head and wiggled her little self out of my lap. Running over to the slide, she climbed up the small stack of stairs and slid down.

"Toby . . ."

He didn't answer me at first, but I knew he was still there because I could hear him moving around and closing doors.

"So, you're about to go see Will?" he asked. His tone was even, but I could still hear a little anger in it.

"I-he . . . wants to see Aspen before he leaves. My mom is still on vacation, so I still have her." Toby didn't say anything. "Babe, I still want to meet with you, though. And we can talk about everything you just said. Will's flight leaves in about an hour and a half. I'll be at the airport already anyway, so maybe we can meet at one of the spots there so that we could talk. Toby?"

"We can meet up when I get back. I see you have something else you need to handle that's more important than talking about our relationship."

"Toby," I cried.

"I'll hit you when I get back, Niecey." And with that, the call was released, and I sat in my seat, stunned by how fast shit had changed in a matter of two minutes.

When I tried to call Toby back, of course, my calls went straight to voicemail, and my text messages went unanswered. After he refused to answer my fifth call, I gathered up Aspen's and my things and then left the park. Hopefully, by the time Will finished saying his goodbyes to his daughter, Toby would answer my call, and I could find him before he left.

I walked through the airport in search of the terminal Will and the rest of the Sabors were scheduled to leave from. With my niece's hand tightly clasped in mine, we navigated our way through the droves of people who were waiting to either depart from the City of Angels or come in.

Aspen and I walked for what seemed like thirty minutes before we finally found the small secluded area where the players, coaches, physical trainers, and everyone else who traveled with the team were standing. Carry-on bags, duffle bags, and small suitcases were everywhere. A few press people were interviewing some of the players, while others sat in the small airport seats, scrolling through their phones and listening to God knows what kind of music on their Beats by Dre.

It took a few seconds, but I spotted Will the minute the camera lights began to flash. Mr. Hot Shot was smiling wide and posing for the cameras as he spoke into the small recorders that were shoved in his face and hammed it up for the reporters who were trying to get an exclusive. Before I could stop her, Aspen let go of my hand and ran straight to her dad, jumping into his open arms. The small crowd that stood around him oohed and aahed as the two hugged and kissed all over each other.

"Hey, baby girl. You came to see your daddy off?"

Aspen bashfully hid her cute little face behind her stuffed unicorn and nodded her head. The crowd was loving every minute of it and taking pictures of the two while asking more questions. A redheaded reporter whose skirt was a little too short and blouse was a little too tight walked up to Will, placed her hand on his forearm, and gave it a gentle squeeze. The way she stared up into his eyes all lovingly told me that they were intimate somewhere along the line. From the look on her face, the girl had it bad. I just hoped she was ready to handle everything that came along with Will Davis.

"So, Will, who is this adorable little lady who has you smiling like this?" she asked, her breasts pushing up on his free arm.

"This is my daughter, Aspen. She came to give me my good luck kiss before I leave."

"Why isn't she coming to your first game? I'm sure you can afford to bring some of your family out to watch you help the Sabors with this win," another reporter asked.

"That contract you just signed is big," someone else shouted from the back of the room.

Will's eyes traveled to me and then back to the crowd in front of him. The redheaded reporter followed his line of vision, and when she saw me, I didn't miss the small roll of her eyes and the stank look that crossed her face.

"I mean, it can be arranged"—his eyes found me again—"if *she* wants to come." To anyone who was listening, they may have assumed that the *she* Will was talking about was Aspen, but from the way his gaze stayed stapled my way, I knew that he was directing that comment toward me.

The whole room seemed to go quiet as everyone waited in anticipation for Aspen to answer her daddy's question. Will smiled and looked down at my niece.

"So what you say, baby girl? You wanna come watch Daddy play football and be his good luck charm?"

Aspen held up her stuffed unicorn. "Can Bucky come too?"

"Of course, Bucky can come. And he can have his own seat too."

The press went wild, and the camera flashes started again when Aspen screamed in joy and pulled her daddy's face to her lips.

"Charming muthafucka," I mumbled to myself as I pulled my phone from my back pocket and called Toby's phone again.

"You've reached Toby. Leave a message after the beep, and I'll hit you back as soon as I can. Beep!"

"Hey, babe. I'm here at the airport. Let me know where you're at so Aspen and I can come meet you. It's crowded in here, but I'm pretty sure we'll be able to find each other. Okay . . . Call me back. I love you. Bye."

Releasing the call, I stood in the middle of the next terminal for a few more minutes before I returned to where Aspen and Will were. The crowd had thinned out a little bit. Reporters were still around, but they were talking among themselves and looking at pictures on their cameras. I spotted Will sitting in the corner with a sleeping Aspen lying in his arms. He kissed her forehead and whispered something in her ear, causing her to smile. When he felt my presence, he looked up and nodded for me to sit in the seat next to him.

"Thank you for bringing her, Niecey," he whispered.

I shrugged my shoulders. "I'd do anything to see her smile."

He nodded his head and looked down at my niece. The Sabors beanie on his head was pulled down low, but you could still make out the handsome features of his face. A strong jawline, luscious full lips, smooth brown skin, and the prettiest copper eyes you've ever seen. Even dressed down in a Sabors T-shirt, some gray sweatpants, and a pair of Nike slides, I couldn't deny that Will was still sexy as hell. A little tingle shot through my spine, and I didn't know why.

"So, have you decided yet?" he asked, breaking me from my crazy thoughts.

"Decided on what?"

"If you were going to come to New York?"

"Will, I don't think that that would be a good idea. Especially since you are the reason why Toby and I are having problems right now."

"*I'm* the problem?" he asked and I nodded my head. "How is that, Niecey?"

"Telling Toby you and I kissed and that I fell asleep in your arms."

"But you did."

"Yeah, after I had an emotional breakdown. That was the only reason why I fell asleep in your arms. I wasn't in my right state of mind at that time. And as far as the kiss, I don't know why that happened."

"So you're admitting that you and I kissed. And that you wanted it as much as I did?"

I opened my mouth to object, but then shut it back. Did I *want* to kiss Will? Had it happened before my breakdown, the answer would've been no. But when I woke up to Will sitting on the edge of the bed, shirtless and pushing the loose strands of hair behind my ear, we had a moment. Something about what he was doing felt familiar and on instinct had me sitting up and moving my face closer into his. When our lips touched, I closed my eyes and moaned. Our kiss deepened, but when Will's fingers started caressing my neck and then went down to my shoulders, something felt off. My body wasn't responding the way it should have. I didn't feel any goose bumps, my clit didn't thump, and my head didn't spin—all the things it did whenever Toby touched me.

I pulled back from the kiss, trying to make sense of what just happened but couldn't. My mind was a little foggy. Embarrassed by what had just happened, I carefully moved Aspen to the other side of the bed and left Will sitting there with a confused look on his face. He called my name, but I never stopped my hurried stride into the bathroom. After getting dressed and doing my hair as best as I could, I left Will's house without so much as a thank you or goodbye to him or Aspen. I hightailed it out of there, wishing the whole time I drove to the opening that I could take those last few seconds of my life back—and then to get pulled over and arrested. I was so in my own world thinking about what had just happened that I probably did absentmindedly run those red lights.

"Hey." Will nudged me, drawing my attention. His hooded eyes looked down at my lips, then back up to my line of vision. "We're about to board the plane. I had my assistant purchase a couple of tickets for you and Aspen to meet me out there tomorrow evening. The game is on Sunday, so I figured after practice, we could go to the zoo or something."

I shook my head. "Will, I can't. I have to work. And, frankly, I don't think we're in a place where we should be taking family trips together. Where is your mother? Can't she come?"

His eyes rolled to the back of his head. "My mom is still in Florida handling her business." He slowly stood up from his chair and cradled Aspen in his arms. "Do you think I'd be asking you to do this if I had anyone else? Your mom is still gone, and LaLa . . . Well, you know I can't depend on her. Niecey, just do this one thing for me, please. It's my first game, and I want my baby to be there."

The sad look in his eyes tugged at my heartstrings, but I still wasn't moved. "Will—"

"All right, fellas, it's time to go. You got two minutes to get your asses on this plane, or you won't be playing in Sunday's game," the coach yelled over the loud talking voices of the other players and everyone else in the terminal.

Will slipped Aspen into my arms and kissed her cheek. Our faces were so close when he looked up that I could smell the tropical scent of whatever gum he was chewing. Our eyes locked on each other's, and I swallowed the lump that formed in my throat. I opened my mouth to say something but stopped when the flash of someone's camera went off.

"Now, isn't that a picture worth a thousand words," that bitch Storm sassed in her purrlike tone. "You two look so cozy. Like one big happy family . . . except for one thing. He"—she pointed at Will—"doesn't look like the man you told me to stay away from."

"That threat is very much still valid, ho. Try me if you want to," I warned between clenched teeth.

She shook her head and tsked. "And to think, he had all this good shit to say about his fiancée at the gym the other day. Him and his fine twin brother with the dreads." Storm didn't try to hide the lustful look in her eyes. "Never seen a white boy who looked like that. Talk about doubling the fun."

I was ten seconds from lunging at that bitch with my niece still asleep in my arms and everything, but Will stood in front of me, blocking my view of her tacky ass.

Who comes to the airport in six-inch thigh-high boots and a dress short enough to see the gap between her legs? The silver mess on top of her head was in short spiral curls. Her makeup was over the top like a drag queen's, and the jewelry she had on looked like the fake shit you get from the beauty supply.

"Aye, yo, Carl," Will called to the security guy standing by the gate. "Come get this girl and escort her out of here."

I peeked my head from behind Will and watched as Carl walked toward our direction. His eyes focused on the target in sight, but before he could get close enough, one of Will's teammates grabbed Storm by her arm and pulled her away, whispering something in her ear. She rolled her eyes at whatever ole boy was saying and walked out of the area without a problem.

"Look, I'm sorry about all that. I don't know why she even did that, but I gotta go." He kissed Aspen on the cheek again. "Please think about coming out to New York this weekend. It would mean the world to me."

"We'll see, Will," was all I said as he said bye to his sleeping beauty one last time and waved goodbye to me.

Once he and half of the team were out of the terminal, I pulled out my phone to call Toby again. When he didn't answer, I checked my notifications for the text message I'd missed thirty minutes ago.

My Love: Rain check on meeting up today. Your phone was going straight to voicemail, so I guess you must be busy. Just hopped on a flight to Vegas with my associate. When I get back Monday, maybe we could meet up for lunch or dinner . . . if you have time.

Toby was trying to be funny. But there wasn't a need for him to be. If I had time? Why wouldn't I have time for him? He was going to see me on Monday, for sure. We needed to talk and get this shit together. Our wedding was in three months, and I'd be damned if I wasn't walking down the aisle to him.

"Where's my daddy, TeTe?" Aspen asked as she sat up in my arms, yawning and looking around.

"Daddy left already. He had to go on a big plane so he could play football on Sunday."

"But Daddy said me and Bucky can come."

"I know, baby, but—"

"I want to go see Daddy play his football game, TeTe. Please . . ."

I bit my bottom lip. Saying no to Aspen was one of the hardest things for me to do. The sad look on her face and those little lips quivering got to me every time. I rolled my eyes and shook my head. Pulling my phone out, I sent Will a text.

Have your assistant send me the info for the flight.

After pressing *send,* I placed Aspen on the floor and grabbed her hand. Walking back through the less crowded airport, I couldn't help but wonder who this associate Toby mentioned he was going to Vegas with was. Koi, I assumed, was still at work, and I had already X'd Storm's ho ass out of the picture. Hopefully, while I was in New York, I'd be able to find out that little bit of information so that I could at least make the weekend enjoyable for my niece.

William

It seemed as if everything I ever wanted in life was coming full circle for me, and I was so thankful to God that he didn't count a nigga out yet. Even with all of the bad shit that I'vd done in the past, he was still making sure that I was straight. I guess the few changes that I did make since becoming sober were starting to pay off in a good way. I mean, I had my baby girl full time now. Although I wasn't involved in her life as much as I should've been when she was first born, she was truly the light of my life now. And then there was this whole thing with Niecey. That kiss we shared when she woke up in my bed told me that she still had feelings for me the same way that I still had feelings for her. The only thing that was stopping us from being together was Toby's bitch ass. But I had a plan for that. And after all was said and done, Niecey was going to be mine again.

I threw my duffel bag on the floor next to the bathroom and walked into my room. We were staying at some hotel close to the stadium, and it wasn't too bad. I was expecting to see Beano since the coach decided to room me with him, but he was nowhere in sight, and neither were his things. Picking the bed closest to the window, I threw my body across the plush queen mattress and tried to close my eyes for a few minutes, enjoying the peace and quiet.

Sunday was going to be a big day for me, and I needed all of the rest that I could get. Especially with Niecey and Aspen flying in tomorrow evening. After practice on Saturday, I had a whole day planned for the three of us, and it was going to be fun. Niecey made it clear that she would only come to the game on Sunday, but I was pretty sure my baby girl could get her to change her mind. I rolled over on my back and smiled. My mini me had Niecey wrapped around her little finger, and I was going to use that to my advantage in every way possible.

The sound of someone unlocking the door had me sitting up on the edge of the bed. When Beano came into my sight, I lifted my head, and he did the same.

"What's up, man? You ready for Sunday?" he asked as he threw his sweater, headphones, and overnight bag onto his bed.

"Yeah, I'm actually hyped. I finally get a chance to show the world that I still got it."

"The world?" He looked at me and chuckled. Taking his hat off, he placed it on the nightstand that sat between our beds and then walked over to the mirror where he laid a towel down and removed his jewelry. "You saying that like the world has seen you play before."

"They have. I mean, in high school, I was pretty popular."

"The golden boy, huh?" He smirked.

I nodded my head. "Something like that." Changing the subject, I asked. "So what you getting into tonight?"

"Nothing really. Curfew is at eleven, and it's already 9:30. I'll probably just have room service bring me a protein shake, work out a little, and then get some sleep. I got a few endorsement meetings in the morning before practice, so I want to get a couple of hours of sleep. What about you? You have any plans?"

"I'ma go down to the bar for a few seconds and then come back up."

He looked at me over his shoulder. "About to go fishing, huh?"

"Man, is it always like that?" I asked, referencing all of the women who were standing outside of the hotel waiting for us to come in. There were even some waiting in the lobby, but security got a hold of them before they could touch any of us.

"It gets crazy sometimes. But if you're a single man, it's the way to go. Just make sure you strap up and have her out of the room before the morning wake-up call. Coach will definitely bench you if he finds a groupie in your bed."

I laughed. "Man, you said that like you're talking from experience."

He removed his shirt and toed off his shoes. "I am. Why do you think I sat out of the first playoff game last year? Coach walked in on me beating the frame out of this sexy-ass chocolate goddess."

"Yo . . . Fo' real?"

He nodded his head.

"What you do when you noticed Coach was in the room?"

"Shit, got my nut and told ole girl to get the fuck on. I wasn't about to have blue balls on national television."

I couldn't help but laugh. The look on Coach's face had to be priceless. To walk in on your star player having sex and not stopping after he notices you standing there . . . Wow. Beano was all right with me. I mean, he'd always been all right with me. We'd hung out a few times before, but never really kicked it like that. I had a whole new respect for this cat.

He walked over to the bed and opened his suitcase, then grabbed his shower bag.

"Aye, man, if I'm still in the shower before you leave, make sure you lock the door. These groupies are clever as hell. I don't wanna walk out to one butt-ass naked in my bed."

I got up from my seat and walked over to my bag. Grabbing my L.A. Sabors sweater, I pulled it over my head and then straightened my beanie up.

"Would that be a bad thing if there was a fine-ass naked woman on your bed when you got out?" From what I remembered, Beano had mentioned that he was single the last time we hung out.

"Probably wouldn't have been some weeks ago, but now, I don't think my girl would go for that."

I smiled. "Your girl? Someone done tied your ass down, huh?"

He blushed and pulled his bottom lip into his mouth. "I'm not about to say that I'm tied down, but she does have my attention in a real way."

I grabbed my wallet, phone, and room key. "That's what's up. I'm happy for you, man. If all goes right with me, I'll have my girl back soon. Be blushing and shit like you whenever someone brings her up." I put my fist out to him, and he pounded it. "I'll be back in about forty-five minutes, bro. Don't latch the top lock trying to keep these groupies out, and keep me out in the process."

He nodded his head and turned toward the bathroom, giving me the peace sign as he disappeared. I wanted to ask him about the look on his face when I mentioned that shit about me getting my girl back, but I was probably overthinking things.

Once I made it to the hotel lobby, I walked past the large reception area and straight to the bar. Ordering a cranberry juice from the bartender, I waited on a stool for the person I was coming down to meet. Ten minutes later, the text I was waiting to receive came through, and I walked to the back of the bar. Although it was dimly lit, my eyes found who they were looking for the second I stepped down into the dark room.

Her hair was straight now, and the outfit she had on was a little less revealing. The makeup on her face was still heavy, but it didn't take away from her beauty. I slid into the booth and took a sip of my juice, waiting for her to finish talking on her phone.

"So, what's up, Raven? Did you send the picture or what?"

She took a pull of her cigarette and blew the smoke out of her nose. "We should just send it to the newspaper. Let them throw around their speculations and assumptions. I think it would hit harder that way and cause more damage."

I scooted closer to her. The light scent of her fruity perfume assaulted my nose. "I told you I don't want the paparazzi to get involved. If we do it that way, they will be dying to get pictures of Niecey and my baby, wondering who they are, and I can't put my daughter in that type of danger."

She laughed. "Danger? Since when is there a danger in getting your picture taken?"

"Man, you know how these paparazzi are. They will do anything to get the perfect angle, and I don't want my daughter to be the object they're going after."

"Sending the picture to his phone isn't going to do shit. Especially when he figures out it came from my phone."

"We'll send it from someone else's, Raven." She was starting to get on my nerves.

When I came up with this plan to break Toby and Niecey up by any means necessary, I wasn't expecting it to be this hard. I thought that red-carpet shit was going to start some drama, but it didn't. That's why I told Toby about the kiss me and Niecey shared that night at the precinct. If bailing her out wasn't enough, that info about the kiss should've been the nail in the coffin. What man can stay with a girl who slept in another man's bed and kissed him at that?

"Whose phone can I send it from? You know I don't have any friends like that out here."

"Use your homegirl's phone . . . Halo."

Raven waved me off. "That won't work."

"How do you know?"

"Because Toby is supposed to be helping her with this singing shit she wants to do."

"Wait. She sings?"

Raven nodded her head. "Only reason why she moved out here with me. She didn't want to strip anymore either, but when she saw how much her half of the rent was going to be, she changed her mind."

"Rent? Y'all staying in my old town house rent free."

"*I* stay in your old town house rent free. *She* has to pay."

I shook my head. Ever since I knew Raven, she hasd always been a coldhearted bitch. I'd met her a few years ago when I moved to Atlanta to stay with my brother Ruben for a few months. We went to one of the strip clubs down there, and there she was, looking good enough to eat. I was still on drugs and out there basically fucking everything that looked good to me, and Raven wasn't the exception. I tipped her off real good one night, and she returned the favor by fucking my soul out of me the next morning after we left the Waffle House. We tried to have a relationship for a couple of weeks, but Raven was too money hungry for me. When I stopped breaking her off the way she wanted, she quickly moved on to the next. We remained friends after all that and kicked it on a few occasions whenever I went out to Atlanta to visit.

When I came up with this idea to get between Niecey and Toby, she was the perfect person to use as a pawn when I learned about this new strip club he was opening. All I had to do was get Beano to recommend her and Halo, and I knew the rest would be history. They got hired on the spot, and my plan was slowly setting into motion.

The only thing was, I needed Raven to turn it up a notch if I wanted Niecey to call everything—including this wedding—off.

"Look, whatever. Just use her phone to send the picture. And when you send it, say something like 'I'm only looking out for you since you looked out for me with this singing shit.'Ssomething to make him think she sent it."

Raven put out her cigarette and then looked at her phone screen. "What time does Niecey and your daughter get out here?"

I sat back in my seat and drank the last of my juice. "Sometime tomorrow evening. Why?"

Her bare foot slowly made its way up to my dick, and she rubbed him to life. "Because I wanna have a little fun before they get here."

I pushed her foot off of me. "Didn't you come here with my boy Armell?" I only knew that because he kept bragging about her on the plane ride over there.

She shrugged her shoulders. "And? Me messing with another man has never stopped you from fucking me before."

I thought about what Raven said for a second, and she was right. I never really cared if she was messing with another nigga, just as long as she never said no to me. But things were different now. I was trying to change for Niecey, and I couldn't keep having sex with her if I was.

"Naw, I'm good. Just hit me when you send that text so I can put my next phase into action," I said, scooting back over to the other end of the booth and getting up.

"Are you for real, Will? You really gonna leave me hanging?"

"I already told you, Raven, I need to get my shit together if I have any chance of this working out for me and Niecey. She has to see that I am a changed man."

Raven pulled a few bills from her purse and placed them on the table. She stood up and pulled the skintight catsuit she had on from between her legs.

My eyes roamed her body up and down. Not an ounce of fat or belly pudge sticking out anywhere. Her breasts were spilling over the lace up top, and her waist looked tiny as hell.

She pulled the silver strands of her hair out of her face and looked me straight in the eyes.

"It's funny how you wanna be this changed man for a bitch who clearly doesn't want your ass, but you will see. Don't come crawling back to me when the shit doesn't go your way."

I threw a bill on the table. "I won't. Niecey and I will be back together. It's only a matter of time."

Raven smirked and walked up closer to me, standing on her tippy toes to reach my ear. "Even if you do cause her and Toby to break up, once she finds out that you're the reason her sister is strung out on dope, she'll never forgive you. You better pray she doesn't resurface before all is said and done, because if she does, Niecey probably won't speak to your ass ever again."

I pushed Raven back from out of my space, and she laughed. This was why I shouldn't have involved her in my plans. She knew too much. I wasn't worried about her spilling anything to Niecey, but in the back of my mind, I knew I would have to get rid of her before she grew a conscience or some shit like that.

Niecey could never find out that I was the reason why LaLa was on drugs, or that I'd known where she was at this entire time. LaLa knew that as long as she stayed away, I would keep supplying her with money for her habit. Once Niecey, Aspen, and I were settled into our new lives, LaLa would be free to come back around. Hopefully, by then, she would be too gone even to try to start up a new relationship with our daughter . . . or dead in someone's morgue from an overdose.

ShaNiece

"So, how are you liking the Big Apple? See anyone famous yet?"

"Koi, I've only been here for literally a few hours. Who could I have possibly seen in that small amount of time?"

"Hell if I know. I figured with that expensive-ass hotel Will got y'all in, you would've seen someone in passing already."

I coughed and cleared my throat. "Naw, I haven't seen anyone yet. When and if I do, I'll be sure to let you know."

Koi was quiet for a few seconds. "You still not feeling good, huh?"

I nodded my head as if she could see me and continued to look out of the floor-to-ceiling windows in my hotel room, enjoying the beautiful views of Times Square and the Chrysler Building. This was my first time in New York, and as much as I hated to admit it, I was a little excited. Although we were only going to be there for basically one day, I couldn't stop the smile that formed on my face as my eyes scanned the busy streets of the Big Apple. There were so many people already out and about enjoying their day, and it sucked, because I, unfortunately, wasn't going to be one of them.

I pulled my robe tighter around my body and double knotted the belt. The cool air from the air-conditioning was giving me the chills. I would have turned the damn thing off as soon as I got in last night, but I couldn't find the controls for shit. And when Will came by earlier to pick Aspen up, I didn't want to have him in the room any longer than he had to be. Since we arrived late last night, he had been trying to find some excuse to come to our room, and I declined his every advance. With the jet lag, a whining toddler, and my head pounding like crazy, all I wanted to do was find a bed and go to sleep. After Toby and I texted each other for a minute and I took a quick shower, Aspen and I were both knocked out as soon as our heads hit the pillow.

"Do you think you need to go to an Urgent Care or something? I can look one up on the computer right now while I'm in front of it."

I coughed again. "Nah, I don't think it's that serious. At the most I might be coming down with a slight head cold. With the difference in weather from the West Coast to the East, it's possible."

Koi tsked. "Difference in weather? Niecey, knock that shit off. We both know what the hell is wrong with you," she laughed. "Difference in weather . . . So *that's* what they're calling it now?"

I walked back into the living room and sat on the plush couch. My body immediately sank into the fluffy cushioning as I pulled my legs underneath my ass. Picking up the remote, I switched on the television and left it on the news channel.

"What are you talking about now, Koi?" I asked, rolling my eyes to the back of my head. She'd been talking crazy ever since the night I told her I was coming to New York, asking all kinds of questions and shit, with the first being "Have you told Toby or not?" I lied to her and said that I had, but I didn't think she believed me at all. Toby knew I was going out of town; he just didn't know the reason why and how.

"You know damn well what I'm talking about, *ShaNiece*. You can call it a head cold all you want, but we both know the real reason behind this sickness out of the blue."

I sucked my teeth. "For the last time, bitch, I'm not pregnant."

"Oh, I know. You pop those birth control pills like candy. I'm referring to something else."

I flipped through a few channels until I landed on a rerun of the TV series *Person of Interest*. Picking up the crystal mug room service brought for me to drink my tea out of, I took a sip and situated the phone between my ear and shoulder.

"Well, please enlighten me with whatever it is you're referring to, dear cousin. I really want to know what could possibly be the *real* reason behind me coughing, having a headache, and a stuffy nose if it isn't a head cold, *Koiya?*"

I could hear Koi typing something on her keyboard and laughing at something before she responded to me. "Your ass is lovesick, Niecey. Plain and simple."

I shook my head and scoffed. Only Koi would say some shit like that. "Lovesick? Girl, how do you figure—"

"Before you even start, there is such a thing as being lovesick, and you, my dear, are it. Not only do you have that headache and shit, but your ass has been throwing up and crying at the drop of a hat for no logical reason other than missing Toby. I've hardly seen you eat anything, and your stress level is beyond high. Shit, you just told me the other day that you fucked up some important papers at work, and you've *always* been one of those chicks who stays on her job. Your moods have been swinging all over the place, *and* don't think I haven't noticed your ass up all night watching movies and not getting any sleep."

Everything she had just said about me was true. For the last month or so, I had been battling insomnia, making small mistakes at my job, and hardly eating like I normally did, but I chalked it all up to being overcome with *everything* going on in my life, not just what Toby and I were going through. I mean, I was basically playing mama to my niece, and the new position at my job had my workload heavier than it previously was. Then, if that wasn't enough, who wouldn't be a little stressed out and not tending to their basic needs after finding out about their sister and her drug problem, being thrown into jail behind some stupid shit, and then this whole thing with Will?

I took another sip of tea and lay back on the couch, closing my eyes, the phone still being balanced on my shoulder and thoughts of everything I just said running through my mind. I could feel the thumping in my head start to progress. I rubbed my temples, already trying to soothe the headache that I knew was on the way. Finally, I took a deep breath and sighed.

"All right, Koi, I think I'm about to take a nap. I can already feel this headache coming, plus Will texted me a little while ago and said that he and Aspen would be out for a few more hours. I want to get as much rest as I can before the game tomorrow."

"Yeah, yeah, yeah. You be careful with Will and his slick ass too. I know you said you see a change in him, but I don't trust his ass for shit. A lot of the stress you have in your life now didn't start happening until he came back into the picture. You remember that shit." She paused before she continued. "Oh, and before I forget, I asked Auntie if she could get you from the airport tomorrow instead of me. I have to handle some business at both clubs and won't be done before your plane lands."

"Wait, I thought Toby was coming back tomorrow night?" At least, that's what he told me when I talked to him yesterday before I boarded my flight out of Los Angeles. We didn't get to talk long, but we spoke long enough for him to tell me that he was coming home on Sunday night instead of Monday like he said. We even made plans to have dinner at his place. So now I was confused about what was really going on. "Why do you have to be at both clubs? Toby told me himself that he would be back sometime Sunday evening."

"He was, but something came up."

Something came up? Something like what? Koi was very vague.

"Look, Niecey, I'm about to get off the phone and finish up the rest of this work that I'm behind on. Stop thinking too far into shit. Toby is handling business. That's it; that's all."

"I didn't say anything."

"You didn't have to. I know you, and I know you still feel guilty about that kiss with Will, so you're going to over analyze everything Toby does to justify the sneaky shit you've done."

"Whoa, Koi, now you're really out of—"

She cut me off. "I'm not out of line with shit. I'm just keeping it real with you. Your ass is fucking up with trying to help Will out and shit with Aspen. You keep allowing him to put you in these situations where he's going to try to come between you and Toby. And for the life of me, I don't know why you don't see that shit yet.

"Yeah, he's a good dad now. But do you remember when LaLa first had Aspen, his ass was nowhere to be found? He gets kudos for stepping up and taking care of his responsibility, but as a man, that's what his ass is supposed to do. I also understand that he's clean now and on some real shit. I commend him for that, but his sobriety doesn't mean that his inner soul has changed. He looks all good and fine on the outside, but that ugly inside still looks the same to me. Niecey, you need to open your eyes. You told me that day at the club that your position with Toby was solidified, right? Well, don't let Will—*your damaged past*—break up your solid future."

I thought about everything Koi just said. "I hear you, cousin, and I won't let things get that far."

"Yeah, you better not. Oh, and while you're out there, keep an eye out on my boo for me. I'm pretty sure those hoes are already swarming around, and Beano's ass shouldn't be anywhere near them. I don't care if you sick or anything. You owe me. I almost ruined one of my favorite dresses having your back with that bitch Storm, so I need you to do the same for me. Try to land a few punches in between throwing up is all I'm asking."

I laughed. "I got you, cousin. I'll call you before we board the plane tomorrow night."

"All right, girlie, talk to you later."

I hung up the phone and started to think about everything Koi had just said again. Was I allowing Will to put me in situations where he could potentially come between Toby and me? I mean, we did kiss that one time at his house, but that was it. Like I said, when I didn't get that feeling all over my body like I did whenever Toby touched me, I knew that Will and I were no longer right for each other. When my heart did not react in the way that it did whenever Toby was just around me, that told me that whatever Will and I could ever have was over. My whole purpose for interacting with him now was solely because of Aspen. Anything else would be shot down at the front door.

Laying down on the couch, I pulled one of the decorative pillows under my head and yawned. A few hours of sleep would probably help me to feel a little better. With thoughts of Toby and our relationship getting back on track swimming around in my mind, I easily dozed off. Our wedding was a few months away, and although Toby not calling it off was a good sign that he still wanted to marry me, I needed to get my shit together before that all changed.

What was supposed to be a two-hour nap ended up turning into three. Those sleepless nights must've caught up with me because I was dead to the world. The only reason why I woke up was because whoever the chick was that was talking on TV had a high-pitched voice that annoyed the hell out of me. Rolling over, I checked my phone for the time and saw that it was twenty minutes after five. Two hours after the time Will said that he was going to bring Aspen back, but I wasn't tripping. She was with her father, so she was in good hands.

Getting up from my comfortable spot, I went to the bathroom and splashed a little water on my face before drinking a handful of it to wet my dry throat. It was evening time in New York, and the lights were already illuminating the semidark skies. Walking back over to the large windows in my room, I looked out over the scenic view, still mad that I couldn't enjoy it in person.

My phone chirping told me that a new text message had come in. Hoping it was Toby replying to the I Miss You message I'd sent before I dozed off, I walked back over to the couch in a hurry, tripping over the leg of the coffee table in the process. I laughed at the screen when I opened up a selfie of Toby in his hotel room, lying in his bed with a picture of me on top of the pillow next to him with the caption: Wishing you were here.

My heart started to flutter, and I could feel my stomach start to turn. Maybe I was lovesick like Koi said because before I knew it, I hauled ass to the bathroom and stuck my head all the way in the toilet, throwing up the contents of an empty stomach.

"Fuck," I whispered as I sat down on the tiled floor, my back against the wall, and my head tilted toward the ceiling. I counted to ten, praying that the dry heaving spell was over. I didn't think my chest or stomach muscles could take it anymore. "What the hell is going on?"

I tried to get up from the floor when I heard my phone ringing, but my arms were so weak that I couldn't lift my body weight. Sweat beads were starting to form on my forehead, and I could feel my body temperature increasing. I took deep, labored breaths to try to control the anxiety that was starting to rise, but my throat was so dry that I began to cough uncontrollably.

My phone rang again and again until the caller must've realized that I was not about to answer it. With my thighs pulled up to my chest, I folded my arms around my legs and lay my head on my knees. All I wanted to do was get over this small attack and go back to sleep. And since I couldn't return to my comfy spot on the couch, the cool tiled floor was going to have to do for now.

I don't think my eyes were closed for five minutes when there was a loud banging noise on my door. The first thought that came to my mind was that Will and Aspen must've been back. I cursed myself for not giving him the room key like he asked, because now I had to find a way to get up to let them in. After two unsuccessful tries to lift myself on my own, I was finally able to hoist myself up on the toilet somehow and then use the granite countertop to help me fully stand up.

As soon as my eyes landed on my reflection in the mirror, I had to do a double take. I looked a mess and almost didn't recognize myself. My hair was all over the place, one side still in a loose ponytail at the top of my head, while the other side was in a disarray of tangles. My skin was ashy and almost pale, while my lips were cracked and dry as hell. I stuck my tongue out and tried to moisten my lips, but I felt a light sting of pain every time I swiped. With the way that I was feeling and looked right now, I don't think Aspen and I would make it to the game tomorrow. Will would for sure have to find a plan B, or she and I would just have to watch him play on the television right here.

"Who is it?" I sluggishly asked as I walked closer to the door. My head was spinning lightly, and my eyes squinted low. Instead of answering my question, the person on the other side of the door decided to knock again. Assuming it was Will who was playing around, I pulled the silver handle down and pulled the door open without looking through the peephole. I turned to walk away but stopped when a pair of hands grabbed me by my waist and pulled me back into a hard body.

The rise and fall of my chest began to speed up as my body started to tingle from head to toe. The nausea I had been experiencing was now replaced with a lustful yearning in my belly. I could feel my nipples hardening and trying to push through the thick fabric of my bathrobe. The friction of the two caused my pussy to thump. I lay my head back on a strong shoulder and closed my eyes. A familiar scent cleared the stuffiness in my nose. I licked my lips and could taste his essence all around me. He didn't have to speak or make a single sound. His presence . . . my instant cure to whatever was ailing me a few seconds ago. I tried to take a deep breath, but instead, let out a small moan when he snaked both of his hands around my waist and pulled me tighter into his frame. Goose bumps decorated my body as his lips brushed against the nape of my neck.

"How," I swallowed the lump in my throat, "how did you—"

"Shhhhhhhh," he whispered into my ear as we began to walk into the room, his arms still wrapped around me tightly, and my steps guided by his.

For a brief moment, our bodies disconnected as he backed away to shut and lock the door. The carry-on bag he had on his shoulder dropped to the floor and made a small sound. My breath hitched the second I felt his body heat radiating into my back again. I stood still as his hands caressed my hips and then made their way to the front of my robe. After untying my belt, he removed the terry cloth material from off of each shoulder and let the fluffy, white garment fall to the floor. Raising my arms high in the air, the thin T-shirt that I had on was slowly lifted from over my head and was the next to go. With nothing left to cover the top part of my body, I stood in the middle of my hotel room, half naked in only my boy shorts and some colorful-striped kneesocks. With my arms back down to my side, I patiently waited for him to remove the remaining two items.

"I missed you," came out of his mouth a little above a whisper. The deep rumble in his cords sent the thumping of my clit into overdrive. "Do you know how hard it was for me to stay away from you, Niecey?" I quickly nodded my head yes, and he lightly smacked me on my ass. "You needed to be taught a lesson. Probably wasn't the best way to teach it, but I hope it was effective." He kissed me behind my ear. "Was it effective, Niecey?"

I licked my lips and tried to say yes as loud as I could, but my throat was so dry that it came out choppy and strained. A low groan escaped his lips when he trailed his fingers up my arms and down to my breasts. My nipples became harder the second his knuckles brushed against them.

"Damn . . . I can't wait to feel your soft velvet walls wrapped around my dick and tongue."

I laid my hand over his, guiding it down to the top of my boy shorts. "I . . . I can't wait either. It's right here for you."

"Oh, yeah?" he questioned with a chuckle, and I nodded my head. "So she still belongs to me?"

"Always has and always will," I answered with conviction all in my tone.

"And how do I know that?"

"Because she only cums for you, Toby."

"Just like I will always *come* for you," he declared as he swung me around and pressed his lips to mine.

Maybe Koi's ass was right about that lovesick shit. Because here I was, feeling 100 percent better just from being in his presence alone. The headache, the stress, the anxiety, and the sickness—all gone. All I needed was a dose of Toby, his vitamin D, and a heaping spoonful of some bed medicine to get me right.

Tobias

I got up from the bed in Niecey's hotel room and stretched my arms above my head, the sound of my back cracking flowing through the air. The sweet smell of whatever body wash Niecey was showering with caused my dick to stir a bit. I swayed my head from side to side, trying to loosen the tension I could feel around my neck. Maybe I did go a little overboard with the way I was eating Niecey's pussy a couple of hours ago, but I had some lost time to make up for.

Pulling the white cotton sheet around the lower half of my naked body, I walked over to the large floor-to-ceiling window and looked down at the busy street traffic. The sun had gone down a few hours ago, and the bright lights of the city were now illuminating the sky. Buildings as tall as mountains hovered above me and practically stacked on top of each other. New York wasn't my favorite place to visit, but I'd had some good times while on business trips out there.

I stretched my arms high above my head again and yawned, still enjoying the view before me. My eyes were low and red. My limbs slowly started to shut down. In the last twenty-four hours, I had been running on nothing but fumes, and I was tired. The minute I stepped off of the plane in Vegas, I was in nonstop meetings. Vendors needed to be interviewed, spots needed to be seen, and permits had to be discussed. And with Las Vegas being a city where no one ever slept, some of these meetings took place at crazy hours. The only good thing to come out of that trip was securing a prime location inside the Aria Hotel.

The bad thing, though, was getting a picture message sent to my phone from an unknown number of Niecey and Will looking pretty cozy at the airport. The shit didn't bother me at first, because you could see that Niecey wasn't affected by Will's closeness. The look in her eyes told me that up front. However, the gaze in his told me something completely different. He looked at Niecey as if she were the best thing in his world, which was kind of funny seeing as her heart, mind, body, and soul belonged to me. There was also something in his smirk that caused me to become very irritated. It was pretty evident that this muthafucka still thought it was okay to try to weasel his ass back into my girl's life. But not on my watch.

When Niecey mentioned that she was going out of town, I didn't think anything of it. After being promoted to her new supervisor title, she would sometimes fly out to the job's sister company to handle things in their HR department personally. I assumed that she was on her way to one of those trips, so I never asked where she was going. It wasn't until I received a call from Koi that I knew Niecey was taking Aspen to see her father in New York instead. I finished up the meeting I was in, checked out of my hotel room, and hopped on my cousin's private jet to the Big Apple.

Now, here I was, finally back with my fiancée and enjoying the fruits of our makeup sex sessions. When Niecey opened the door earlier, I couldn't help the way my body gravitated to hers. All I wanted to do at that moment was bury my dick so far into her pussy that she forgot about these past few weeks of us being apart.

***

My hands possessively gripped Niecey's hips as she rocked back and forth to the rhythm we had going. Her melon-sized breasts bounced up and down with every movement. I sucked one of her nipples into my mouth and swirled my tongue around it slowly. The small mound of joy grew harder with every lick. A low growl escaped from my throat when her pussy muscles began to contract around my dick, pulling me deeper into her love. The tight, wet, slick feel of her insides was warming up by the second. I wrapped my arms around her waist and pulled Niecey's body farther into mine, thrusting my hips up at the same time as she swayed hers down.

"I'm so sorry, baby," she moaned. "I promise it will never happen again."

Before we made it to the bed, Niecey and I sor of talked about the reason for our separation these last few weeks. And although we did a lot more kissing and taking each other's clothes off than talking, we were still able to get a few things off of our chest, finally putting an end to all the bullshit. We were due to be married in a few months and needed to get everything hindering us from going through with this wedding on the table. I didn't believe for a second that Niecey wanted to get back with Will, but I had to be honest and admit that I was kind of shook for a minute. Your mind can start to make you believe some crazy shit if the communication in your relationship isn't on the up-and-up.

Not really knowing the full story behind the kiss was something that always bothered me, and as much as I didn't want to know, for my sanity's sake, I had to ask her about it. To say that I was surprised at her honesty would be an understatement. I was shocked when she told me about the kiss between her and Will, but even more shocked when she admitted to kissing him back.

Her admission was like a douse of water that put the fire burning inside of me out, but my dick was still hard and in need of her loving.

"Fuck, Toby, I swear to God I'm sorry, baby."

"I know," I assured her, making sure she felt my acceptances of her apology every time my dick burrowed deeper into her pussy. I was on a mission to fuck all of our pain away and then move on with our lives, leaving all of this shit in the past.

"I-I'm . . . ooooh . . . I'm about to cum," came from her mouth breathlessly as she closed her eyes and let her head fall back, the movements of her hips speeding up a bit. I lay my body back and raised my arms behind my head, giving Niecey total control over both of our orgasms. "Fuck, Toby," she screamed, her rocking becoming harder and harder before releasing a tsunami of her juices over my dick and lap. The combination of her heated core and her vibrating walls clenching my shit for dear life was enough to bring me over the edge, spilling every last drop of my seed into her.

Niecey collapsed on my chest, and for a few moments, we lay there in silence, basking in the feel of our bodies being connected.

Niecey's phone vibrated on the nightstand, bringing my thoughts back to the current moment. There were still a few things that we needed to go over, but nothing that would cause that big of a problem between us.

"Yo, Niece. Your phone's going off again," I yelled over my shoulder as I sat back on the bed. The scent of our sex still lingered in the air. I picked up her phone and looked at the incoming call, instantly irritated by the name that was flashing across the screen.

Since I got there a few hours ago, Will's bitch ass had been calling her phone nonstop, trying to get her to join him and Aspen for dinner. The last time he called and Niecey answered, I had her pussy in my face at the time, and when I sucked her clit into my mouth and bit down on it, she declined Will's offer and released the call. I would've thought he'd gotten the picture with the way she moaned from me lapping up her sweet juices, but his ass was still calling. Already fed up with bullshit, I decided to answer the phone two seconds later when he started calling again.

"What's good?" I asked—no signs of pleasantry in my tone.

"What's good? Who is this? And why you answering my girl's phone?"

"*Your* girl? Bro, last time I checked, every part of Niecey inside and out belonged to me."

"Belongs to you, huh? Well, she wasn't saying that shit last night."

I laughed at his pathetic attempt to make me mad. "Look, man, Niecey's in the shower right now. Is Aspen okay?"

"Muthafucka, don't speak on my daughter. She ain't your concern, white boy."

"Anything that concerns my fiancée concerns me. You might want to take note of that for future references. Now, if this phone call doesn't have anything to do with Aspen and what time you're going to be dropping her off, I suggest you stop calling this phone."

"And if I don't, what the fuck are you going to do, Ryan Seacrest? You know, you should be nice to me. I mean, it's my dime you're on while Niecey's giving you some goodbye pussy. I paid for that room, all of the room service she's been ordering, and her plane ticket out here. You actually should be thanking me for swooping in and taking her so easily off of your hands. Pining over a woman that's still in love with her ex is not a good look for you. Now, be a good little boy, get your shit, and get the fuck outta my room before I call security and have them throw you out."

While he continued to ramble on about calling hotel security, my mind drifted back to the conversation Niecey and I had almost thirty minutes ago.

We lay in the bed, tangled in each other's arms, basking in that sex afterglow. I ran my fingers through Niecey's hair as she lay lazily on my chest, her fingers slowly tracing the tattoo on my rib cage . . . something she always did after we finished loving on each other.

"So you kissed him back, huh?"

I felt the second her body froze and then released into its relaxed state again. A few moments of silence passed between us before she responded.

"I did."

"Did you feel something in the kiss?"

She shook her head. "No."

"Are you mad that you didn't feel anything?"

Again she shook her head no.

Kissing her forehead, we lay in silence for a few more minutes, my fingers still digging in her scalp. I took a few seconds mentally to prepare myself for this next question. Her answer would determine our future from this point on, and my nerves were already on edge.

"Do you still love him?" I asked barely above a whisper, confidence there, but not all that high. She stopped fingering the side of my body and lifted her head, turning her gaze to mine.

"In my heart, even after all he's done, I will always have a love for Will because he was my first in a lot of things. But do I still love him enough to leave you alone? No. Will I ever love him enough to leave you alone? Never.

Do I love you? With all my heart. Am I in love with you? Undoubtedly so. Will I ever do anything to jeopardize our relationship again? Hell no. These weeks apart from you have been hell, Toby, and I don't like the feeling of being without you. I promise from this day forward, you don't have anything to worry about when it comes to my love and devotion for you. You are my life, and I cannot wait to become Mrs. Tobias Wright . . . if you will still have me."

Her eyes looked deep into mine and connected to my soul. I knew at that moment that everything Niecey had just said was coming straight from the heart, and she meant it.

"You know I was never going to let you go. I told you, you were mine for life after our first date, and I meant that." I kissed her ring finger and then the engagement ring I presented her with six months after we got together. Will did me a huge favor by fucking this relationship up. Not only had he lost the love of his life in the end, but he had also blessed me with my future wife.

The door to the bathroom opened, and Niecey walked ou,t wrapped only in a towel, water droplets still on her shoulders and neck. Her hair, which was all over the place when I arrived, was now washed and in a high bun on top of her head. I watched as she walked around the bed and grabbed her pear-scented lotion out of her overnight bag. Unhooking the towel and dropping it to the floor, she looked at me and smiled, knowing what she was doing. My dick was getting harder by the second. Rubbing some lotion between her hands, she smoothed it all over her body, making sure to cover every dry spot. She lifted her head toward her phone and asked me who I was talking to.

Instead of giving her an answer, I smirked and put the call on speaker.

"Aye, man. Now, see, I'm kind of confused. I need you to explain to me again how security is going to throw me out of a room that *I* paid for?"

"Muthafucka, that room is under *my* name, *not* yours. Your ass ain't making the kind of bread to afford to put Niecey up in a place like that with your whack-ass clubs. You would have to own twenty of them bitches to ever get on my level. I know you heard about the contract I just signed. I promised Niecey that I would take her with me when I made it, and I'm not about to fall back on that shit."

Niecey tried to grab her phone from me, but I moved my arm that was holding it out of the way and flipped her onto the bed with my free arm, quickly moving my body over hers. I grabbed both of her hands and locked them with mine over her head. The breath that caught in her throat when she felt my dick poking against the inside of her thigh told me that she was ready for another round, but before that could happen, I had to get some shit straight with this fuck boy.

"Believe me when I tell you that you *don't* want to compare bank accounts with me. I don't have to brag on my shit because big money always moves in silence. But just to educate you on some things real quick . . . That money I pull in from my clubs every week is what I put in an account for Niecey to play with. But seeing as my girl has her own money, that shit I put up for her is just sitting there collecting interest—interest that has her already sitting on several mill, and we ain't even married yet. That small account I set up for her will shit on that bullshit-ass contract you signed any day. And as for me, all I'm going to say is that I'm good over here, man. Been good since I turned eighteen. I could retire from working today, and my great-great-great-grandkids could live off of their inheritance."

I laughed at the shocked look on Niecey's face. "Oh, and by the way, you should see a credit on your credit card statement in three to five business days. My girl wasn't about to stay in a room that some other man paid for. Not while I still have breath moving through my body. And please be expecting a cashier's check in the mail for her and Aspen's plane tickets. Round-trip, right? I'll even add in a few more dollars for the inconvenience. We appreciate your generosity and all, but like I said . . . We're good," I told Will's stuck ass before releasing the call and throwing Niecey's phone onto the bed.

"Wait a minute. What was all that about? And did he say anything about Aspen?"

"Naw, he wasn't worried about Aspen or anything else. All he wanted to do was to talk to you. I'm pretty sure he isn't going to drop her off anytime soon. Maybe in the morning sometime before the game, but not tonight. Only leverage he has for you to call him back, and he knows that."

Her eyes scanned my face, a small smile curling on her lips. "You think you know everything, huh?"

I shrugged my shoulders. "I know enough."

She squinted her eyes, curiosity all over her face. "You really got an account set up for me?"

I nodded my head as I kissed her neck, lips, and nose. "Set it up the day after I proposed to you."

"But-but how . . . Why would you do that? And why didn't you tell me?" Her small fist playfully hit my chin.

"Because it was supposed to be my gift to you on our first anniversary. But now that that's ruined, I have to think of something better."

"Something better than several million?" she asked sarcastically.

"Yep."

Our eyes beamed into each other's before she sighed and grabbed the sides of my face with her hands.

"Toby, you know I'm not with you for your money, right? I'd marry you tomorrow with only a dollar to our name and a pot to piss in."

"I know you would. That's why I work so hard to make sure that if you ever do need *our* money, it's there for you."

She kissed my lips. "You know I love you, right?"

"I do."

"And I'll never do anything to hurt you again."

"I believe you."

"Now come get this pussy and write your name all over it."

"My pleasure," I replied, sliding my dick into her moist folds. Those warm and gushy walls encased every inch I pushed inside her. Something about the way Niecey felt wrapped around me this time was different. Instead of being on a sexual high, it was more emotional. I could see our future and everything to come at that moment. My life started with her the day we met at my club and would end with her until I took my last breath.

We enjoyed each other until the wee hours of the next morning, making up for lost time. And just like I said, Will didn't bring Aspen back to the room until a couple of hours before he was scheduled to play. Of course, he continued to call all night long, but every time I answered, he'd have a little bitch fit and then hang up the phone. I was in the shower when he finally decided to drop his daughter off, but by the time I got out, he was gone. Aspen, Niecey, and I ate breakfast and did a little shopping before we all headed to the game.

Instead of using the tickets that Will gave them, I put a call in to my father who was personal friends with the owner of the team the Sabors were playing against. We were invited to watch the football game from the GM's sky box and were given access to anything we wanted from food, to drinks, to going down to the locker room and chatting with players before the coin toss. The smile on Aspen's face warmed my heart tremendously because it was a reflection of the one her aunt sported at the same time. Niecey's happiness would always be a priority to me, and if that meant her having to be around Will for Aspen's sake, we would figure something out eventually.

ShaNiece

"Niecey, I'm glad you and Toby finally got y'all shit together. I was worried there for a minute."

"Worried? Worried about what?" I asked my mother, looking back at a sleeping Aspen in her car seat and raising her head from the weird position that it was in. The half-empty sippy cup hung from her lips, and that damn unicorn was tucked at her side. She wore pink glitter tights underneath her cute little jean dress and some ballerina shoes to match.

"I was worried about y'all relationship and the wedding." She looked at me and then back at the road. "Well, mainly the wedding part. I was hoping I didn't have to take my mother-of-the-bride dress back before I got a chance to wear it."

I shook my head. "Believe me, Mom, you didn't have anything to worry about. Toby would marry me today if I told him let's go."

"I know Toby is ready to make you his wife, but are you sure you want him as your husband?" We stopped at a red light where she grabbed her small Diet Coke from the cup holder and took a sip. "Seems like you lost sight of that when you started talking to Will again. Had me, Toby, and Koi questioning if you were completely over him."

"Wait a minute." I turned to her, my arm resting on the door handle, playing with the button for the window. "You and Toby were discussing me?"

She nodded her head slowly and pressed her foot lightly on the gas when the light turned green.

We'd just come from a day of having fun at Chuck E. Cheese and were headed to her house. Will had a couple of away games this week, so my niece was staying with my mother. When Aspen called and requested that I join them for some pizza and a day of play with the big mouse, I happily accepted. Toby was at Lotus Bomb doing interviews for a new manager, and I had finished up on all of the paperwork I brought home for the weekend, so I was game. There was also the fact that my mother promised to make me one of her famous buttermilk pies if I came, and I was not about to let that offer pass me up.

"Toby and I actually talk a lot. Matter of fact, he called me the night he came to pick up your ass from jail. Told me everything that happened. Even told me how Will was at the bail bondsman trying to bail you out." Her eyes cut over to me. "Niecey, I'm only going to ask you this once . . . Did you and Will do anything the night you took Aspen home? Because if you did, you need to let Toby go so that he can find him a nice young lady who's going to love him the way he needs to be loved."

My mouth dropped at what she had just said. Where the hell was all this coming from? My mother had never really been one to pry in my relationships, but for some reason, she had her nose and two cents all up in this one. And when did she and Toby start talking? I knew they had a cool little relationship, especially with all the extravagant birthday and Mother's Day gifts that he gave her. But I didn't know that they were cool enough to the point that he talked to her on the phone and called her when we were having problems. In spite of me feeling some type of way about them having phone conversations, I was actually smiling on the inside. Leave it to Toby to make everyone who was important in my life fall in love with him too.

"You think long, you think wrong," my mother declared, our eyes connecting as she studied my face. "Did you or did you not sleep with Will? It's a yes-or-no question. Not a thinking one."

My eyebrows scrunched. "Mom, I would never cheat on Toby. He's the only man I want to be with." Visions of our makeup session in New York began to swirl around in my mind. If I ever thought about giving that man or his curved dick up, I'd shoot myself. There was no way in the world I could live on the same continent knowing that he'd be giving his heart and backbreaking sex to someone else and be okay with it.

I'd never admit this to him or anyone else, but I think that our time apart did open my eyes to a lot of things in regards to Toby. Although I never cheated on him, it was good to know that he wasn't going to tolerate me stomping all over his heart or feelings regardless of how much he loved me. When I first met Toby, I knew that he was different. His whole aura told me that from the first night he invited me to dinner at the loft and sang for me, to the day he got down on one knee and asked me to be his wife. It had been nothing but butterflies in my stomach and smiles on my face since he came into my life, and no one, including my ex, would come between that. Yeah, in the back of my mind, the question of "what-if" kept going off after Will and I kissed. But in my heart, I knew that Will and I would never be a couple again.

After talking over a few bridal shower details and stopping at the grocery store, my mother and I headed to her house to start on Sunday dinner and to meet up with this "mystery man" she'd been seeing for the last couple of months. Whoever he was, he had my mother flying on cloud nine and all giddy about love and shit. Their relationship was still kinda new, but I was happy for her and glad that she finally found love again.

We rode for about five more minutes before we turned the corner to my old street. Memories of my childhood came rolling through my mind. We used to spend hours upon hours running around this neighborhood, finding different things to get into. LaLa and her best friend JaNair would be playing hopscotch and ding dong ditch, while my ex-best friend Mya and I would be in the middle of the street playing football with the jocks and flirting with a few of the ones we liked. On those hot summer days, we'd all be gathered under one of the big oak trees that lined the street, shading ourselves from the sun, eating bomb pops, ufos, and soft serve cones, cracking jokes on each other and talking shit while picking teams for the water balloon fight we were about to have.

A few of the girls who lived on the other side of the bridge would come to our turf, trying to get the boys' attention, but that didn't last long after LaLa and her loudmouthed ass started jumping in people's faces. We'd be out in that street, rumbling back and forth with them, only to get our asses whipped by our mom as soon as we stepped into the house. Ms. Regina didn't necessarily push us to fight in the streets; however, she did make it clear that LaLa and I were always supposed to have each other's backs whenever someone brought the drama to us.

Just thinking about my sister and how different our lives were right now was crazy. Never in a million years did I think she and I would ever separate. We were twins. We talked the same, looked the same, and damn near did everything the same. We were each other's best friends and always had each other's backs. It broke my heart to know that she was out there drugged out and not giving a fuck about her daughter or anything else. When my mother picked up Aspen and me from the airport a couple of weeks ago, I asked her in a roundabout way if she'd spoken to LaLa. Asked her if she knew where she was or if she'd seen her recently. Instead of answering my questions, my mother changed the subject as if I never asked her anything about LaLa in the first place.

"Niecey . . . Did you hear what I just said?" my mother asked, breaking me from my trip down memory lane.

"No, I didn't. What did you say?" Turning around in my seat, I checked on Aspen, who was still asleep, a line of dried-up drool on her chin and a small round of spit bubbles at the corner of her mouth.

She sighed. "I said please stay in the car and let me handle this right quick."

"Handle what?" I asked, looking up at my mother, whose eyes were trained on her open front door. I was so lost in my thoughts a few seconds ago that I hadn't realized we were parked in the driveway of my childhood home.

"Let me go in the house real fast. You stay out here with Aspen and the groceries, and I'll wave you in once I'm done."

"Done with what?" I wanted to know. My eyes cast over to the front door again. A frail-looking figure was peeping out the window but shut the curtain back when my gaze connected to theirs.

"Mom, who is that in the house? And why is the front door open like that?" Reaching for my phone, I sent Toby a text, telling him to get to my mother's house ASAP. I had a feeling who was in there already. I just needed my mother to confirm it. "Is that LaLa in there?"

My mother scoffed and said something under her breath.

"Mom, is that LaLa in there?"

"Just stay in the car, Niecey."

Our eyes warred for a few moments. An awkward silence filled the air. When she rolled her eyes and looked at my niece through the rearview mirror, I was done with the games.

"You know what? Since you can't tell me who it is, I'm about to call the police. You're not about to walk up in there with your door wide open like that while I'm here." I pressed the emergency call button on my phone.

"Niecey," she snapped. "Hang up the phone and just wait here like I asked. I don't want the police or these nosy-ass neighbors all in my business and shit. They're already gossiping about me having Aspen all of the time. I don't want to give them anything else to talk about."

Grabbing the silver handle, she pushed the door open and got out, her brown leather purse and keys in hand. She started walking toward the garage, but stopped and came back to the open driver's-side window, the Burberry scarf Toby bought her last Christmas hanging low over the sleeveless shirt she had on. "ShaNiece, you're my child, so I know you. *Please* don't come in until I come back, okay?" Her eyes darted to Aspen and then back to me, a light mist forming on her bottom lid. "Let me just handle this real quick."

I pulled my bottom lip into my mouth and slowly nodded my head, my gaze still focused on the front door.

My mother patted the hood of the car with a light tap, satisfied with my response, and started her trek back to the house. The sound of her click-clacking heels faded the farther away she got from the car. With one last look and a head nod toward me, my mother closed the door to deal with the situation that was awaiting her on the inside.

"All right, Mom, you got five minutes to do whatever it is you're doing for LaLa—and then I'm coming in." Although I wasn't 100 percent sure that it was my sister who had peeped out of the window, I had a good feeling that it was. Call it twin intuition or whatever you wanted to, but when my eyes connected to hers, I got that same protective feeling I would get over my body whenever LaLa and I were out there fighting the girls from across the bridge. She didn't look like the LaLa I was used to seeing, but that twin connection we had would never fail, regardless of how mad I was at her.

I continued to watch the clock on the dashboard, waiting for those five minutes to wind down, when Aspen stirred in her sleep for a few seconds and then opened her eyes. Those big brown beauties locked on me as soon as I turned around to face her. I smiled at my niece and was rewarded with a sheepish grin before she dug her face into the unicorn's mane and giggled.

"Granny house?" she asked, her little voice just above a whisper.

"Yeah, we at Granny's house, baby. You wanna go inside?" She nodded her head and smiled. "You gotta help TeeTee with the groceries, though, okay?"

"Okay."

Removing my seat belt, I got out of the car and helped Aspen out of her booster seat next. The five minutes weren't up, but I didn't care. We grabbed the few grocery bags that were on the floor under her chair and headed into the house. At first, when I opened the door and walked into the living room, I didn't hear anything. But once we got closer to the kitchen, I could hear my mother pleading and on the verge of tears.

"If you don't want to get clean for me, LaNiece, at least do it for you daughter. She misses you and wants you around."

"She doesn't need me." *Sniff.* "From what I hear, she has Niecey to take my place."

"Take your place how? Niecey can and always will be her aunt—not her mother. That child came from you. She connected with you at the hospital the day she was born. You and ShaNiece may be identical, but that baby knows who her mother is."

"Whatever . . . Are you going to give me the money or what?" *Sniff, sniff.* "I have somewhere to go, and you holding me up."

"What happened to the money Will gives you? He told me that he deposits a few dollars in your account every month to make sure the bills at your house are paid."

LaLa snorted and laughed. "Is *that* what he told you? That he gives me money every month *to pay my bills?*"

"You are his child's mother, regardless if you're on drugs."

Aspen, who was standing behind me, wrapped her arms around my leg and began to squeeze, her little head resting against my hip. I looked down at my niece and gave her a sweet smile, trying to reassure her that everything was okay. I had a feeling that she recognized her mother's voice but could tell that something wasn't right by her tone.

"Will doesn't give a fuck about me being his baby mama. All he cares about is Niecey and if she'll leave the white boy for him."

"No, he doesn't," my mother replied softly.

"Yes, he does." The sound of glasses shattering on the floor caused Aspen's grip on my leg to get tighter and a small whimper to leave her lips. I grabbed my niece by the shoulders and knelt in front of her, a huge smile on my face.

"TeeTee needs you to go into Granny's room for a little bit, okay?" I whispered, and she nodded her head. I pulled my phone out of my pocket, unlocked it, and pointed to the YouTube Kids app. "Don't turn it on until you're in Granny's room, okay? Close the door, and TeeTee will come get you in a few minutes, okay?"

Her big brown eyes looked up at me, and she nodded her head. I smoothed my hand over her pigtails and then turned her around and gave her a little nudge toward my mother's room that was at the end of the hallway. Once she closed the door, I turned my attention back to the kitchen.

"LaLa—"

"Fuck, Mom. Just give me the fucking money so I can go. I already know Niecey's ass will be storming through that door any minute now. And if you don't want us to fuck up your house, I suggest you give me what I want so I can be on my way."

My mother's voice cracked. "Where . . . Where did I go wrong with you? What can I do to fix it, baby?"

"It's too late for me. Just continue to take care of my baby. Now, can I have the money so I can go?"

"I'm-I'm not going to give you any more money, LaLa. I'm not going to keep contributing to this nasty habit of yours."

There was silence for a minute. "Okay, then. I guess I'll just have to take it since you don't want to give it to me."

"LaLa—" ripped from my mother's mouth before I heard what sounded like them struggling with something and then a loud thump from someone falling to the ground.

When I heard my mother cry out in pain that was all it took for me to jump from behind the wall and make my presence known. My heart dropped to my stomach as I watched my mother trying to pull herself up from the ground, bloody handprints on the floor from the shards of broken glass embedded in her hand.

LaLa didn't even notice I was in the kitchen. She was too busy rummaging through my mother's purse, trying to find her wallet. Before she could even open the small black coin purse, I leapt over the center island and slapped the shit out of her. She grabbed her face and stumbled back, a look of pure shock when she finally realized what had just happened.

For the first time, I was able to get a good look at my twin, and she looked totally different. Her body was nothing but skin and bones. You could count a few of her ribs with the short top that she had on. Her once beautiful hair was in one of those hood rat ponytails, the edges damn near nonexistent. Her skin was pale and in dire need of some sun. The black liner that lined her mouth and her eyes was smeared, making her look like a raccoon. Flakes of cracked dry skin covered her ashy lips. She had this "geeked" look on her face, which told me that she was high and probably not in her right mind, but I didn't care. I was still about to whip her ass for putting her hands on my mother.

I hopped off of the island and grabbed her by her hair, swinging her across the kitchen and into the double stove. She howled out in pain, grabbing her side, but I wasn't finished. I ran over to where she was hunched over and just started letting go, connecting my fist to every part of her body. My mother was screaming my name, begging me to stop, but I was already in a zone and taking all of my anger out on her. I beat her ass for using my name when she got arrested. For abandoning her daughter and missing out on the important things in her life. I beat her ass for trying to steal from our mother a few minutes ago and for all of the times I didn't know about. By the time my arms started to tire out, LaLa had fallen to the ground and was curled up in a fetal position. Blood poured from her busted lip and nose. I reared my leg back to kick her one last time, but my mother grabbed my ankle and pulled it back.

"No more, Niecey. She's still your sister, regardless of what she's done. She's still your other half."

"She ain't shit to me but the bitch who gave birth to my niece."

LaLa started laughing after I said that, a slow, cryptic laugh that got louder and louder. She rolled over to her knees and braced herself for a second. Her head was probably still spinning from all of the times I knocked her upside it. Lifting one leg, she tried to stand up but lost her balance and fell back down. She grabbed her side and hissed, but continued to laugh after the pain subsided some.

I shook my head, disgusted. This couldn't be my sister, the same girl I shared a womb with for nine months. The same girl I was taught always to have her back whether right or wrong. My heart was hurting right now, but the anger I had for her easily overpowered that shit.

My mother moaned, causing me to take my attention off of LaLa and to help her up. Once she was standing up on her own, I walked over to the junk drawer and got the first aid kit. After cleaning my mother's hands and wrapping them up, I went back to where LaLa was now sitting and just stared at her, trying to figure out how she got to this point.

LaLa had always been good with fashion, but looking at her right now, you would never know it. The midriff shirt she had on was ripped in half, exposing the dirty white bra she wore. Her leggings, which were black at some point, were faded and barely hanging on her hips. The sky-blue flip-flops had seen better days, and her feet hadn't been done in what looked like months. My sister was a real-life crackhead, and I didn't know how I really felt about that.

"You don't have anything else you wanna get off of your chest, Niecey?" she asked, wiping the side of her mouth out with the back of her hand. "I think I deserve a few more rounds, don't you?"

I started walking toward her to give her what she was asking for, but my mother pulled me back. "Niecey, I already told you that was enough. Look at my damn kitchen."

Looking around, I saw that we did make quite a mess. The Italian chef decorations she had on her table, counters, and chairs were either broken in pieces on the floor or somewhere under the fruits and vegetables we knocked over in our tussle. Pots and pans were flipped over on the stove, while the lower cabinets were either pushed in or hanging off of their hinges. The glass front of the stove was cracked, and the bar stools that sat under the island were knocked over with their legs scattered all over the kitchen floor.

"I'm sorry, Mama."

"I am too," LaLa weakly added, now standing to her feet.

"You ain't sorry about shit, bitch."

"Niecey—"

"Naw, Mama," LaLa said. "Let her talk. I mean, she's the reason why I'm like this in the first place."

"*I'm* the reason? LaNiece, you crazy as hell saying some shit like that."

She wiped the little bit of blood falling from her busted lip and shrugged her shoulders. "You are. If you would've just listened to me about that whole Will situation, none of this would've ever happened."

"Well, *excuse* me for being mad at my twin sister for sleeping with my boyfriend and having a baby by him. I didn't only cut you out of my life; I cut him out too. So don't give me that *it's your fault I'm a crackhead* bullshit. Save that for someone who gives a fuck."

"You can't forgive me, but you can forgive Will?" She picked up one of the chairs from the table and sat down, wincing when her ass dropped into the seat. "Do you even *know* how I got started on drugs? I'll let you take one wild guess."

I waved her off and began to pick up some of the glass from the floor. "I don't have time for this shit. Let me clean up this mess and take my ass outside. Toby should be here any minute to pick me up, and I'm ready to go."

LaLa laughed. "You may not want to hear what I gotta say," *sniff,* "but I'ma tell you anyway."

She waited for me to acknowledge what she said. When I didn't, she continued talking. "You know Will and I have always been cool with each other. Always been friends. Hell, I'm the one who introduced y'all when he was too shy to speak up for himself. Anyways, I'd kick it with Will from time to time whenever y'all broke up. It wasn't nothing sexual or anything like that. We'd mainly talk about you and how he could get you back, or his failed football career while smoking weed and drinking.

"Well, one day, I went over to chill with him and a few of his buddies. I walked in on them doing cocaine. When they asked me if I wanted some, I declined at first, but sometime later that night, I ended up at the table snorting lines with them. At first, it was a small little habit that I would do before going out or fucking around with Jerome, but it became bigger the more I began to crave it.

"You and Will broke up one night, and he called me over to do some lines. You know . . . blow off a little steam from you and him breaking up again. We were high as fuck that night, and I don't know what happened. We started kissing and feeling on each other. Next thing I know, we're naked on his floor having sex." She chuckled. "The funny thing is, the whole time we were doing it, he kept calling me you, apologizing for hurting you and not being there for you. I was so out of my mind that I didn't even care that he was calling me Niecey.

"By the time we finished, my high had gone down a little bit, and I regretted everything that happened. I didn't speak to Will for a long time after that. I mean, I called him one time to get his connect on the coke, but that was it. A few months later, I found out I was pregnant. Never thought it was Will's because I had only fucked him that one time. Jerome and Li'l Ray were the only two niggas I thought were possibilities at being Aspen's father. It wasn't until I was almost due and Will stopped by the house looking for you when he asked if she belonged to him. I honestly didn't think she did and was shocked as hell when he demanded a DNA test. Thought the nigga was on some 'I might be the father shit' when in actuality, all he wanted to do was prove to you that the baby *wasn't* his. Funny how that turned out, huh?"

I swept the kitchen floor and picked up the island stools. "LaLa, I don't believe shit you're saying right now, and I really don't care. So, can you please stop talking to me? I thought you had somewhere to be. What? You need some money? Here." I went in my pants pocket and pulled out the eighty dollars I took from the ATM earlier and threw it at her. "Take that shit and get the fuck out of my mama's house. Isn't that what you came for? Not to see your daughter or spend any time with her, but to get some money so that you can get high, right?"

LaLa turned her head to the side, trying to hide the tears in her eyes. "Regardless of what you think, I love my daughter and tried to get clean for her."

"Yeah, but your dumb ass started getting high again. Will already told me. Told me how he spent all of that money on that rehab just for you to go back out there and use that shit."

"Did he tell you that he's also the one who supplies me with my little habit?"

My body froze at that statement.

"Nigga's lips loose about everything else except for how *he's* the one who gives me the money to fund the little habit that he introduced me to. The little habit he hopes will keep me out of the way so that you, him, and my daughter can be one big happy family."

"LaLa, what are you talking about?" My mother asked. "Will gives you that money to pay your bills so that you can have a house to go to when you finally get clean."

"Who told you that shit?" she laughed. "Mama, Li'l Ray still pays the bills for that house. Will doesn't pay shit. All he does is put enough money on my debit card so that I could get high for weeks at a time and stay out of the way. When the money runs out or gets low, I call or show up at his house, and he breaks me off with a little more. Him or that fake-ass-having-white-bitch-with-the-white-hair. I mean, it's enough to get me a motel room and binge for a few days, but not enough to pay my house note and everything else."

She laughed again. "Boy, does that nigga have you fooled. Thinking he's changed when he hasn't. Will is still the same ole trifling muthafucka from back in the day, humping on these bitches and trying to keep that shit on the low." Her eyes locked with mine. "Are you and Toby still together, or did you let Will run him away yet?"

I walked over to LaLa, eyes squinted, trying to make sure I heard her right. "What did you say about Toby?"

She licked her lips and scratched at her neck. "I said are y'all still together, or did you let Will run him off yet?"

"What are you talking about, LaLa? And don't lie to me. You know I don't play about Toby."

Still scratching at her neck, LaLa looked around the room and then down at the money that was still on the floor. "I-I-I need to go. I need my medicine." She stood up, but I pushed her back down into the chair.

"You're not going anywhere until you tell me what you meant by what you said."

I hated to do what I did next, but I wanted to know what she knew about Will and his little plan to break up Toby and me. Grabbing my mother's purse from off of the floor, I found her wallet and held up the couple of twenties she had in it. LaLa licked her lips as she looked from me to the money.

"Now, tell me everything you know."

By the time she was finished telling me how she had eavesdropped on Will planning to get rid of her, to get rid of Toby, and finally get me back to start a new family with him and Aspen, I almost lost it. Not only did this muthafucka almost cost me my relationship with Toby, but he was hurting his daughter and her relationship with her mother for some shit that would never happen again.

I couldn't believe I thought his ass had changed—that he had gotten his shit together. It was like he was worse now than he was before. Who thinks about killing their child's mother or keeping her on dope just to keep her out of the way? How could he ever think that I would want to be with someone like that?

By the time Toby showed up, I was so ready to go. After saying bye to my niece and apologizing to my mother for what happened again, I left. LaLa, who was walking out behind Toby and me, didn't say anything else to me as she made her way down the street to some beat-up-looking car and left. When I called my mom later that night to ask her if LaLa had taken any of the money that I threw on the floor, she told me that she didn't. Hopefully, her leaving that money there was the first step toward her cleaning up her shit. Until then, I was going to keep my distance from my sister. Everything she spilled out that night may have been the truth, but I still needed a little more time before we could go back to how we used to be.

William

"Fuuuuuuuuck!" I screamed out in frustration, kicking over the end table in my living room. The pricey lamp that sat on top of it shattered into a million pieces once it hit the ground. I didn't even care about the scratches I knew it would make on the hardwood floor. Wasn't like I would be living here for long anyway.

I walked over to my entertainment center and pressed the glass door, pulling out the tin box that I kept a few bundles of emergency cash in. The stress of being cut from the team after only being with them for a month was starting to get to me.

"Your performance on and off the field is unsatisfactory and doesn't fit the bill of a Sabor," was what the owner said to me before the team's lawyers gave me a mountain of paperwork to sign. All a load of bullshit if you ask me, but there was nothing I could do about it.

I reached out to a few of my friends on some other teams to see if they could put in a good word or two for me, but no one was getting back. Not even Armell and the rest of those assholes who used to party with me while I was up and sleep on my couch when they were having problems at home. Shit was all bad for me right now, and I needed something to get the edge off.

"You screaming and tearing up stuff isn't going to change anything. Maybe all of this was for the best."

I turned my heated glare toward Storm, who was sitting on my couch, smoking a primo and scrolling through her phone. The sheer kimono wrapped around her body left nothing to the imagination. For the last three days, she'd been cooped up at my house, trying to help me cope with the news of being cut, but suddenly, her presence was annoying me. The head and pussy no doubt was superb; however, her aura just wasn't cutting it for me anymore.

"Mind your own business, Raven, and worry about what the fuck you're going to do now since you're out of a job as well."

Dumping her ashes in an open beer can, she leaned back on the couch and crossed her legs. Taking another pull of her blunt, she smirked at me before blowing a thick cloud of smoke in the air.

"We both knew that was going to happen. Especially after that last failed attempt to get Toby to sleep with me."

After seeing that the picture message Storm sent to Toby of Niecey and me almost kissing in the airport didn't affect their relationship the way I thought it would, I called in a couple of reinforcements to work out this last phase of my plan. If us kissing wasn't a deal breaker for Toby, I knew him fucking someone else would be for Niecey. One of the new waitresses that worked at Toby's club was messing with my boy Armell, and just like any groupie-ass bitch, she was strapped for cash and always asking that nigga for some extra ends, so I seized the opportunity. I paid her a few stacks to slip something in Toby's drink the night of his brother's birthday party and had one of his bouncers waiting in the wings, ready to carry him out and record the whole thing if need be.

Everything was a go once Toby became light-headed and excused himself from the party for a few minutes. Storm caught up with him in the men's bathroom luckily and was able to convince him to let her walk him to his office. Once she got him there, she closed the door and set the recorder up. Had it directly facing the couch where Toby had passed out. She managed to get his pants pulled down his legs halfway before the office door swung open and Koi's ass walked in.

With her head buried in some paperwork, she didn't even notice what was going on at first. It wasn't until Toby's bitch ass moaned and turned over to throw up that she noticed the scene before her. It didn't take long for her to assess what was *really* going on, and instead of asking any questions, she dropped the papers in her hand and jumped right on Storm, pulling her hair and socking her all over her head. Now, for a white girl who grew up in College Park, Georgia, Storm also had hands, so she and Koi tussled for a minute before she lost her footing and gave Koi a chance to two-piece her.

Once she got knocked out, I knew my little plan was down the drain because the whole thing was caught on both Storm's phone and the office security camera. They were able to go back and see that it was all a setup from the start. The little ho waitress that was fucking with Armell even found a conscience and told the police the truth of what really happened. Of course, I denied the fact of knowing anything about what happened when the boys came knocking on my door, and with no real concrete evidence proving my involvement, I couldn't be charged with anything. However, that didn't stop the heads of the league from getting an anonymous phone call and hearing about everything that went down.

"Here," Raven cooed, bringing me back from my thoughts. She pushed the mirrored tray with six lines of that white girl toward me. "You need to take some of the edge off. Besides, I think you were a lot more fun when you used to get high."

She took another pull from her blunt and blew the smoke from her nose this time. Her platinum-blond hair pulled back in a low ponytail gave you a real good look at her makeup-free face. With high cheekbones, a slim jawline, and pink, pouty lips, I could see Raven gracing the cover of any high-scale magazine, but her thirst for dick, money, and drugs was too much to keep her focused on a real job.

"You know I've been clean for years, and you offer me the same shit that almost fucked up my career in the first place."

She sucked her teeth. "Career? Will, you're going to have to get over the fact that you don't play football anymore. Got your ass cut before your jersey even got a grass stain. You couldn't play on a professional field if you *paid* the league to take you back." She uncrossed her legs and recrossed them again, the small patch of blond hair on her pussy flashing quickly.

"Just accept that you're done, sweetheart, and move on. You lived out your little dream for a couple of years being on the practice squad and whatnot. Even got to play with the big boys for a few weeks, but now . . . You need to get over that shit and relax. Take the load off. Forget about your troubles today, forget about your problems tomorrow, and most definitely, forget about that bitch Niecey. Do a line or two if you don't want to do all six, and let's have a good time."

I thought about what she was saying for a second, and maybe I did need to escape my reality right now. Everything was closing in on me, and I didn't like the way things were panning out. I mean, Niecey wasn't fucking with me at all. Hadn't answered a phone call, text, or anything. We were back to communicating through Ms. Regina if she wanted to see or spend some time with Aspen, and I wasn't feeling that shit at all. How else could I try to talk myself out of my current situation if she wasn't at least willing to listen?

My phone vibrated on the table, and I picked it up. LaLa's ass was calling me for the one-thousandth time, and I wasn't trying to hear shit from her. She was one of the reasons why Niecey wasn't speaking to me anymore, opening her big-ass mouth and telling them everything about the drugs and shit.

Storm chucked her chin toward my ringing phone. "That's your baby mama again?"

I sat on the couch next to her and laid my head back. My phone continued to vibrate on my lap while I rubbed my sweaty hands over my thighs. My eyes wandered over to the lines of coke and then back down to my phone. Doing a few rows wouldn't hurt me that bad, and I was in desperate need of a quick fix. Pulling the tray toward me, I picked up the rolled dollar bill Storm had lying next to it and did the first line. Within seconds, the effects of the potent drug had my mind clear of the clouds, and my body relaxing farther into the couch.

"See? What I tell you? Do a couple of more lines and let's have a little fun," Storm whispered into my ear as she pushed the tray of coke back up to my face.

I bent my head down and vacuumed two more rows of blow, sniffing and tweaking the ends of my nose with my fingers after I was done. Storm's hand began to massage my bare chest and then made its way down to my dick, which was already rock hard and ready to dive into some pussy.

"Oh, wow. Glad to know I still have this kind of effect on you."

"Don't flatter yourself, Raven. You know my shit stay hard when I'm high. Now, either put this muthafucka in your mouth and suck away your apology for fucking up my plans, or call your homegirl Halo over here and let me finally fuck the shit out of her sexy ass."

She looked at me with a screw-face. "Fuck that bitch. She ain't my homegirl anymore. Ho ass forgot all about me after Toby hooked her up with some studio time and helped her write a few songs. The bitch head done got a little big, too, now that she's got a following on social media."

"You sound a little salty." I laughed as I guided her head and mouth down on my dick, my basketball shorts pulled down from underneath my ass and resting just above my knees. Thoughts of Niecey went through my mind. I closed my eyes and moaned. The way Storm's tongue swirled around the tip of my shit and the wetness of her mouth had me in heaven.

"Damn, Niecey. Suck that shit," I said, pulling her hair and pushing my dick farther down her throat.

"My name is not fucking Niecey, asshole."

"I know, but it's gonna be until I get this nut. Now shut the fuck up and get back to work."

Storm went back to handling her business, but this time, she moved from off of the couch and got down on her knees between my legs. I placed the tray of coke on the back of her head and snorted two more lines.

"Fuuuuuuuuck, Niecey. Get that shit, baby. Show me what you've been giving that white boy."

Storm mumbled something, but I couldn't understand a word she was saying. My dick was pushed so far down her throat that it felt like she had a thick-ass Adam's apple when I rubbed my hand across her neck.

"Get up, baby. I wanna look you in the face while I'm writing my name all over that pussy," I groaned. Lifting her from her knees, I straddled her thick thighs across my lap. When the head of my dick brushed against her wet fold, my body responded in a way that it had never responded before. My toes started to curl, and my back arched. The anticipation of what was to come already had me on the verge of exploding. With my hand on her soft hip, I guided her down on my shit and damn near had a heart attack. "Niecey" felt just the way I remembered her. Soft, tight, warm, and wet. Her pussy didn't fit the mold of my dick like it used to, but I was pretty sure a few more sessions like this would change that.

"Damn it, Niece. Don't rock your hips so fast. I want to feel you for a minute before you make me cum."

"I told you . . . *ummmm* . . . my name . . . *ooh* . . . is not . . . *shhhhhhh* . . . Niecey. So stop fucking calling me . . . *ummmm* . . . by that bitch'ssss name."

Whatever trance I was in at that moment disappeared at the comment Storm had just made. Her disrespecting Niecey and calling her out of her name for a second time made something snap inside of me. Grabbing her by the neck, I lifted her from my lap and slammed her back down on the hardwood floor, her head making a loud thumping noise as she cried out.

"What the fuck, Will! That hurt."

"Shut the fuck up and take this dick," I yelled, nudging my knee between her thighs and slamming my erection into her slick walls. "You should have just let me make love to you, thinking you were Niecey. Now I'm about to fuck you like the ho-ass bitch you are."

"Will," she cried. "Slow down, baby. You can have all this pussy. Just stop being so rough."

I tightened my grip around her neck, cutting off a little more of her air supply. Retracting my hips, I pulled my dick out of her warm coven and slammed it in again. The yelp that came from her whimpered cries did something to me and had the high I was already on taking me higher. My vision and my mind were starting to play crazy tricks on me.

"So, you been giving my pussy away to that bitch-ass muthafucka, Niecey!" I yelled as I pumped into her harder. "Is he fucking you like this? Does he make your pussy come like that?" I asked, feeling the first splash of her juices against my stomach. "You trying to leave me for that nigga, huh?"

She mumbled something, but I couldn't hear a thing she said. My hands were still wrapped around her throat.

"You still gonna marry him, Niecey?" My voice was now at a higher pitch, and I almost didn't recognize it. "Tell me you love me, Niecey. Tell me you're gonna forgive me for everything I've done and take me back."

"Will . . . please stop."

"I ain't stoppin' shit. Not until you give me what I want," I whispered into her ear before kissing the side of her face and attacking her neck, sucking on her skin until the purple-blackish hue of a monkey bite could be seen. "I'ma send you back to that muthafucka with evidence of me being inside you all over your body. Bet he will kick your ass to the curb then."

"Will, I can't . . . I can't bre—"

"You think I'ma let you go, Niecey? After all of the changes I made for you? Yeah, I know I fucked up with LaLa, and I know I fucked up with the drugs and not being there for you back in the day, but can't you see that I've changed? Huh? Can't you feel it in the way our bodies move together? In the way your body responds to me?" I asked, pulling her leg over my shoulder, diving deeper into her wetness, my hand still using her neck like an anchor.

"You and me are going to be together from this day forward, Niecey. You and me. Just like old times. And when I give you this baby, I don't want to hear shit else about that asshole Toby, you hear me?"

I took her silence as an okay and continued to fuck the shit out of her. When I felt that familiar tingle in my toes and the drawing up of my balls, I knew I was about to explode.

"Cum with me, Niecey. Cum with me, baby," I screamed out before releasing every last drop of nut I had inside of her, decorating every last part of her insides with my seeds. There was no way in hell that she wouldn't be pregnant after this. Her carrying my baby would have to be a definite dealbreaker for Toby.

Once my body stopped shaking and the swirling in my head subsided, I rolled over to the side of Niecey's stiff body and looked up at the ceiling. The coldness of the wooden floor instantly cooled down the high tempera-ture in my body. I grabbed Niecey's hand and brought it up to my lips to kiss but stopped when I noticed it wasn't Niecey's hand I was holding. I peered down at the beige-toned fingers with the hot-pink fingernail polish. A two-carat emerald ring sat on her pinky finger, and a tattoo of a scorpion was between her thumb and index finger. I shot up from the floor, trying to remember everything that had just happened in the last ten minutes but was coming up with blanks. Taking my foot, I nudged a sleeping Storm in the side, but she didn't wake up.

"Raven, get up." I looked around the room for my phone and found it underneath a pillow on the couch. My mom was due to pick up Aspen in about an hour from Ms. Regina's house, and I needed Storm to be gone before they came back.

My eyes wandered across the room to the coffee table. Remnants of the coke I'd done was still there. I looked over at Storm and got mad all over again, angry at myself for becoming so weak.

"Raven . . ." I nudged her with my foot a little harder this time. "Get your ass up. You have to go. And take this coke and everything else with you. I can't believe I let you make me relapse. I was doing so fucking good." Swinging in the air, I shadow-boxed with myself until a little of the anger inside of me was gone.

"Get the fuck up!" expelled from the top of my lungs at Storm, who was still lying unmoved on the ground. I went to pick her up and help stand her on her feet, slapping her cheek to try to get her awake. When her head rolled to the back and her neck came into my view, I removed my hands from her body and let her fall to the ground.

"Raven?" I kneeled over her lifeless body and pressed my fingers against the soft flesh underneath her chin. I found no pulse, which caused my mind to start racing.

"Raven, get up." Grabbing her shoulders, I shook her body, only to get the same response—nothing.

I rose back up to my feet, my mouth open and head shaking in disbelief. My hands laced on top of my head, and my breathing became harder and harder to control.

"I killed her . . . But I didn't . . . We were just . . . Fuck! What am I going to do?"

I started walking around the room, cleaning up the mess we'd made and wondering what I could do with her things. I didn't have anyone I could call without this getting in the news and the police possibly ruling this a homicide instead of understanding that we were just having a little passionate sex—passionate sex where I obviously went a little too far after wrapping my hands around her throat.

"Shit, shit, shit," I cursed, trying to figure out what my next move would be.

So much shit had happened to me in the last month, and now this. I was for sure finished in the football world, and Niecey probably would testify against me if it meant she wouldn't have to see me again ever. What about Aspen? LaLa would probably go to rehab and actually get clean so that she could start to take care of our daughter again . . . the right way.

"Fuck! I fucked up." My nerves were going crazy by now. My hands and body shook as I looked down at Storm's body again. "I need to calm down and think. I need to get my shit together, so I can get rid of her body and get ready for my baby to come home. But fuuuuuuuuuck!" I threw my phone against the wall, and it shattered on impact. "How can I calm down? I need something that will instantly calm me down so that I can think."

My eyes somehow landed on the mirror tray with the one line of coke left. Pulling a bill from the stack of money I got from my emergency stash, I sniffed the last line and waited for the drug to take effect. When that didn't happen after ten minutes, I went to the kitchen and got Storm's purse, dumping it and its contents on the couch. I knew she had to have some more of the drugs somewhere in her shit. She always had a good amount of the pure cut on her.

"Bingo," ripped from my lips when I noticed a small, clear bag underneath a pack of her cigarettes. I hurriedly opened the baggie and dumped the white powder in my hand. Bringing it up to my nose, I sniffed the blow up until there was nothing left but residue. Even then, I brushed my finger against my open palm and rubbed the last of the coke over my teeth and gums.

With my eyes stapled on Storm's naked body, I sat on the floor next to my entertainment center, allowing the drugs to take control of my nerves. Visions of the news outlets, my old teammates, Niecey, and my family disgraced by my actions clouded my brain. Who would believe that this was an accident? Better yet, who would understand that this was only an accident? An accident that occurred because I thought that I was fucking my ex and trying to teach her a lesson about leaving me. Who would believe that I didn't know what I was doing, even while high out of my mind? The police already had their suspicions about me behind the whole Toby thing, and now with proof that I had access to drugs, there was motive to start looking into my background for evidence that could link me to what happened.

I couldn't go to jail for this. I couldn't go to jail for what happened with Toby. I would be facing some serious time and would probably never be eligible for parole. Nah, I couldn't go to jail. I wouldn't be okay with my baby coming to see me while I was behind bars.

Tears began to fall from my eyes. How the fuck could I get myself out of this? Walking down the hall to my room, I stopped in the kitchen and grabbed the notepad sitting on the counter and snatched a pen out of one of the drawers. I sat at the vanity in my bathroom and wrote a letter to the only person I knew it would mean something to. Once I stuffed the note in an envelope and placed it on my nightstand, I went to my closet and removed the shoe box that held my .38 from the top shelf.

There was no way I could get out of this without upsetting everyone who ever believed in me. My mama, my AA coach, my therapist . . . Niecey. All of my failures and lies had finally caught up to me, and I could honestly say that I didn't like the person I still was. I thought I had changed, but in actuality, I was still the same selfish, coldhearted, drug-using, lying, and now murdering asshole that I'd always been. I may have fooled myself into thinking that I had changed for Niecey, and for a minute, I had her fooled, too. But now that it was clear to her and me that I wasn't about shit, there was no use for me to be here anymore.

Sitting on my bed, I chuckled, thinking about how ironic it was that I was sitting in the last place that I was able to feel the softness of Niecey's lips. With The Dramatics' song "In the Rain" playing softly in the background, I looked up to the sky with tears in my eyes and said a little prayer.

"Lord, please forgive me for all of my sins. Please let the people I've hurt in my life find it in their heart to forgive me for any pain I may have caused them. Watch over my baby girl and please keep her clear of any man that is remotely close to being like me. Please right all of my wrongs. Hopefully, I'll see you on the other side. If not, I hope you heard this prayer before I go. Amen"

Placing the cool metal in my mouth, I closed my eyes and let the last few tears fall down my cheek before applying pressure to the trigger and departing this earth for good.

I'd made some good choices in my life, and I'd made some bad ones. Some I regretted, and some I didn't. Hopefully, if my spirit was given a chance to grace this earth again, I would be the type of man Niecey always wanted me to be. You can have the girl and give her everything in the world, but if your love isn't the right kind of love, she'll never truly be yours.

Epilogue

"Wait a minute. Wait a minute. Wait one damn minute, Niecey. You said my brother-in-law did *what* again?" Audri asked, scooping a spoonful of curried shrimp and rice into her mouth. After chewing her food a few times, she picked up the white linen napkin lying next to her plate and dabbed it across her lips.

"Damn, Audri, you nosy as hell. Why are we even talking about this anyway?" her sister Ariana interrupted. "We're supposed to be celebrating her getting married, not talking about the shit that almost got her left at the altar."

"Ari," Audri hissed through her teeth.

"What? I'm only telling the truth." She turned her attention to me. "Niecey, do you want to talk about what almost ended your relationship with Toby, or do you want to continue to enjoy the fact that you will be Mrs. Tobias Wright in one more month?"

I picked up one of the mini fried dumplings I couldn't get enough of and popped it into my mouth. "I don't mind. This is the first time we've all been in the same room since it happened, so I knew you guys would have some questions."

"Well, there's a difference between having questions and just being plain nosy."

"How am I being nosy because I asked her to repeat what *she* said about Toby?" Audri asked, biting into the flaky crust of the spicy beef patty in her hand.

"Instead of worrying about what's going on in her love life, you need to worry about all that food you've been stuffing in your face since we got here. I know you're eating for three again, but damn, leave some food for us," Ari playfully snapped.

Audri's cheeks turned red. "Says the person who's been scarfing down those banana fritters since the waitress placed them on the table. I don't think any of us have had a chance to taste one of them yet, have we, ladies?" She looked around the table for our responses, and when everyone just laughed, she turned her attention back to her sister. "So, I guess your eating for two has you devouring all of this delicious food as well, right?"

Ari waved Audri off and picked up another fritter.

"Okay, you two. I know hormones are raging out of control with you both being pregnant right now, but I need y'all to check those attitudes and let my baby enjoy her day," my mother said, placing her hand on my bare shoulder and giving it a light squeeze. The blush pink chiffon dress she had on fell down her body length as she stood up next to me. "Oh, and before I forget, I wanna thank you all for coming to ShaNiece's bridal shower. It means a lot to her and me that you were able to attend on such short notice."

The group of fifteen women sitting at the table smiled and nodded their heads, silently acknowledging my mother's appreciation. Everyone was dressed in some flowy material with different hues of pink to match the cherry blossom and white color theme.

"Now that that's all squared away, let's continue to enjoy all of this tasty Jamaican food so we can get to the fun stuff."

A chorus of "okay," "all right," and "yes" echoed throughout the room, before the sound of silverware hitting the bottom of plates, light conversations, and glasses clinking together was the only thing you could hear.

My phone, which was nestled securely between my boobs, started to vibrate. I rolled my eyes playfully and blushed, already knowing who it was. Toby had been texting me for the last few hours, trying to get me to ditch my bridal shower and meet him at the loft. I made the mistake of sending him a few pictures of me in my body-hugging dress, and he couldn't wait to pull it off of me.

My Baby: You need to come home right now. If not, you know I don't have a problem with coming to get you.

"Only one person can have you smiling like that," Koi sassed as she pointed her fork at me, jaws chomping down on whatever she was eating. "Your ass gon' be stuffing your face like Audrielle and Ariana if you and Toby don't slow all that humping shit down."

My Baby: All I need is twenty minutes. They won't even notice you're gone. Meet me out front and come sit on my dick and face, but not in that order.

"Oh, girl, y'all better get used to it now because if Toby is anything like Cai, and I'm assuming he is because they're *twins,* Niecey gon' be pregnant before the night is over and on baby number four in two years. Mark my word the way her titties and booty is sitting up in that dress. I know that's Toby's ass calling you back-to-back. Phone been going off since we got here. I told you sending him those pictures was a bad idea." Audri laughed.

"Says the woman who was late opening up the restaurant. What were you and Cai doing back there in that office when we got here?" Ari questioned.

"What married folks do. I ain't ashamed to admit that I'm a freak for my man. Have you seen how fine he is? Aaaand Mama Faye just retwisted his dreads. Bitch, please. My legs opened the second he walked through that door and looked at me. I'm pretty sure Niecey would be the same way if Toby waltzed his fine ass in here too."

I drew my bottom lip into my mouth and bit it as all eyes focused on me waiting for a response. Instead of verbally giving them one, though, I slowly nodded my head and started to Dutty Wine in my chair to the dancehall music playing, telling them everything they needed to know. The whole table went crazy with yelps and laughter, ways of sexually pleasing their men now the topic of discussion. I felt my mother's body shift next to me, but I didn't look her way. Me talking about sex and riding my man's dick in front of her was definitely not the norm, but she knew I lost my virginity a long time ago.

After responding to Toby's messages and putting my phone back in its safe place, I piled my plate high with a few of the goodies on the table and began to dig in. Ackee and saltfish, boiled and fried dumplings, curried shrimp, jerk chicken, breadfruit, and fried plantains were just a few of the family-style dishes we had in rotation on the Lazy Susans.

Instead of a traditional bridal shower, I opted to have a bridal brunch at Cairo and Audri's new Caribbean restaurant, Faye's. The doors to the place weren't scheduled to open until sometime later in the fall, but my friendship and family ties with the owners allowed me use of the spot before the doors actually opened. I looked around the beautifully decorated private section we occupied in awe. Warm, Caribbean colors were placed throughout. Audri told me that she wanted to give the patrons a feel of actually being in the Caribbean with the color scheme, and it's safe to say that she pulled it off. Light turquoise, sandy browns, and coral pinks did add to the aura, but in my opinion, the bamboo tables, cushioned wicker chairs, antique artwork, banana leaf placemats, and down home cooking style was what really gave you that island feel.

"Okay, ladies. Now that everyone is pretty much done with the delicious spread provided for us today, I think it's time to play a few games. First one up is . . . Who knows the bride best?" Koi announced, passing out pencils and a small decorative stock card that had the numbers one through ten on it. "The card I'm passing out now is for the game after this one, so please don't write anything on it yet."

"Ms. ShaNiece," one of the young waiters whispered in my ear, his thick Jamaican accent proud and strong. I looked up at him. "Someone is requesting tuh see you in da back."

I raised my eyebrow. "Here to see me?"

He nodded his head as his dark eyes scanned the table full of my family, friends, and closest coworkers. "Yeah, mon. They not want to come inside."

"What's wrong?" Audri asked as she watched me gather up the bottom of the white silk halter dress that I had on with beautiful beading underneath my breasts and circling my waist.

I shook my head. "Nothing's wrong. The waiter just said that there's someone here to see me."

"Someone here to see you where?" She looked around.

"He said in the back."

"In the back? Awww, shit, Toby came to get his pus—"

"Ari!" Koi and I both yelled. My mother cleared her throat, and Ari shrugged her shoulders.

"My bad, Ms. Regina. You know how I can get sometimes."

"No problem, Ariana. I know my baby isn't a virgin. But that doesn't mean I wanna hear about her sexual encounters—engaged or not," my mother said, fanning her face with her napkin. Her pearl necklace was snug around her neck, and her bouffant hairstyle gave her that regal, sophisticated look.

"Well, are you going to go see who's back there? I bet you it's Toby. You know them Wright brothers ain't got no problem coming to get what they love." Audri laughed.

"Well, I just hope it isn't LaLa trying to ruin your day," I heard Koi mumble under her breath as she walked past me, still passing out game stuff.

I ignored her comment and turned in the direction where I saw the waiter go, his strong frame still in sight but quickly fading out the farther he walked into the back of the restaurant. Giving my mother and the rest of the table a soft nod and excusing myself, I headed on back to see who was waiting outside to see me. From the tour that Audri gave us when we arrived earlier, the only thing I remembered being in the back of the restaurant was a closed-off section that she said was still under construction and an exit door that led out to the small employee parking lot.

My mind immediately went to Toby's ass possibly being the person outside waiting for me. He did text that he would come to get me, but then again, he said to meet him in front of the restaurant. The small smile I had on my face immediately dropped when Koi's comment began to stir around in my head. What if it *was* LaLa outside trying to ruin what I wanted to classify as one of the most important days of my life? I mean, I hadn't heard from her since Will killed himself. When my mother called to tell her the news, I thought LaLa would've thought about sobering up so that she could be there for her daughter in the wake of her father's death, but leave it to my twin's selfish ass to choose drugs yet again over the needs of her daughter.

Since the suicide happened, Aspen had been staying with Toby and me during the week and with my mother on the weekend. At the end of every month, though, Will's mom would get her and keep her at her house for a few days. If I were honestly speaking, I felt sorry for Will's mom. Every time she came to pick Aspen up, you could see the sorrow in her eyes. I mean, my niece was the spitting image of her daddy, so I knew it was hard for her to look into her granddaughter's face without feeling some type of way.

I smiled thinking about my future husband and how supportive he'd been through the whole ordeal. When I got the call that Will had killed himself after killing that stripper chick Storm, I didn't know how I felt about the whole situation. No, I wasn't happy that two people lost their lives, but at the time, I hated Will for everything he did to me, my sister, and his daughter. The lies, the manipulation, the drugs . . . All of that shit was still fresh on my mind. So, like any sane person who didn't want to deal with something, I forced myself not to feel anything.

Besides, I had to be strong for my niece, to show her that regardless of how her parents left her, she still had somebody who loved her like she was their own. I lay in bed with Aspen many nights, trying to answer her questions about her mom and dad's whereabouts as best as I could. I even reached out to LaLa a couple of times just so that she could hear her voice, but the calls never were answered or returned.

You know, it's weird how fast things can change in people's lives. One minute someone you love is here, the next minute, they're gone, never to be seen again. If Will were still here, would I have ever forgiven him? Eventually, I think I would have. The same way I'd forgiven my sister for doing what she'd done to me. But would I have ever forgotten it? Naw, but I'm pretty sure Toby would be there by my side with a shoulder to cry on or a hand to hold, just like he was when Will's mother gave me the suicide letter he'd written to me before he took his life. I didn't want to read it at all, but it was Toby who told me that even though I felt nothing toward Will, I still needed that closure, and this letter would give me just that. A lone tear fell from my eye as I remembered the words Will wrote.

Dear Niecey,
I know I'm probably the last person you want to

be receiving this letter from, but I need you to know that I am sorry. I'm sorry for introducing LaLa to drugs. I'm sorry for having sex with her and getting her pregnant, and I'm sorry for causing you all of the hurt and the pain that my mistakes have contributed to. When I first met you, your smile lit up my life. It was that same smile that got me through those grueling football practices and that long healing process when I got injured on the field. It was that same smile that stayed on your face regardless of how many times I fucked up, and you took me back after I swore that I would never do it again. The same smile that would make me feel like everything would be all right in a world that was full of darkness and pain for me.

If I'm honest with myself, somewhere along the line, that smile that lit up my life became a frown, and I had no one to blame but William. I hurt . . . I broke . . . and I lost the most important thing to me, and I have regretted it since the day you walked out of my life.

It's funny how another man can take that frown, turn it upside down, and make that same smile ten times brighter for him. Looking back, I wish I could have changed some things, but I now understand that your smile was never meant to be kept by me. Toby found him a winner. He's the rightful owner of your smile. And I hope he cherishes your heart way better than I did.

In closing, take care of my daughter for me and let her know that her daddy was not always a bad man. I just had some demons that were able to get the best of me when I should've been giving my best to her. I love both of you and always will. Take care.

~William

After Toby read that letter to me while we lay in bed that night, and I read it to myself the next morning, I finally shed a few tears for my friend who was once my lover, and once the person I thought I would spend the rest of my life with when we were younger. I tried to hide in the bathroom while I was doing all of this crying, but Toby found me, like he always did, and kissed my tears away. No judgment . . . no worries . . . no questions. My happiness was his only focus, and I could gladly say that I was happy as hell.

The sound of pots and pans hitting the stove and the chef screaming out orders in Patois brought me back from my thoughts. I was just about to walk past the kitchen and out of the exit doors when the waiter who came and got me grabbed me gently on my arm.

"Tis way." He pointed with a tilt of his head. I looked over his shoulder and then back to him.

"I thought that room was under construction."

"It twas. But now it isn't," he answered with a broad smile on his face. Stepping to his left, he bowed his head and swept his arm to the side. "After you."

I hesitantly walked toward the once roped-off area, my eyes still curiously connected to his. I looked over my shoulder and glanced to the front of the restaurant where my mother and everyone else was sitting. All eyes were focused in my direction and on me. The music that was playing earlier now was cut down. Placing my hand on the heavy wooden door, I prayed that whoever was on the other side of it didn't turn out to be LaLa and pushed it open.

The sound of piano keys softly began to play as soon as I stepped into the dimly lit room. The sweet smell of the tropical flowers stationed throughout the small, intimate space filled my nose. Candles were lit in all four corners of the room. Its illuminating light danced off of the walls. I swallowed the lump that was stuck in my throat and finally took in the breath that I desperately needed. I turned back around to the door I had just walked through and lowered my head, willing myself not to cry, but it was too late. The first tear that rolled down my cheek was followed by another, and I couldn't hold it in anymore.

"The first night I took you out, do you remember what song I played and sang for you?" Toby asked, his voice a little above a whisper but loud enough for me to hear him over the piano he sat behind playing.

I shut my eyes and let the last few tears fall before wiping my face with the back of my hand and turning back around to him. Dressed in a black-on-black fitted tux, my baby looked sexy as hell right now. His shoulder-length hair was gone and cut into the short style he had when we first met. The caramel-blond color in his hair shined under the glowing light. His facial hair was also cut and neatly trimmed low. He had that sexy five o'clock shadow thing going on, and I could feel my pussy juicing up every time I looked at his face. When those greenish-blue irises that I loved so much finally connected to mine, I lost it again.

"What are you doing here?" I asked between cries. "You're supposed to be waiting for me out front."

He smiled. "Didn't I tell you that I was going to get you if you didn't meet me outside?"

I laughed. "But that was like ten minutes ago." I looked around the room again. "There ain't no way you could've set all of this up in that amount of time without anyone seeing you." A thought crossed my mind. "Freaking Audri. Her ass knew about this the whole time, didn't she? That's why she lied and said that this room was still under construction." When she first told us that, I thought it was kind of odd that the whole restaurant was finished except for this one room. But I figured she was trying to make up her mind on what she and Cai wanted to do with it.

Toby didn't answer my question. Instead, he played a few notes on the piano and asked me once more, "Do you remember the song I played and sang for you on our first date?"

I slowly nodded my head, remembering the Jon B. song he performed. I walked farther into the room and closer to the piano. A beautiful arch decorated with pink roses and crystals served as the backdrop. At first, I hadn't noticed the white chiffon draping covering each wall and hanging from the ceiling, but now that my vision was a little clearer, I could see everything.

"Toby—" I started, but he cut me off.

"Don't talk. Just listen. Can you do that for me?"

"But, babe—"

"Can you do that for me?"

After pausing for what seemed like five minutes, I finally croaked out, "Yes."

Toby patted the space on the piano bench beside him, and I sat down. He cleared his throat and began to speak.

"I sang that Jon B. song for you that night because I felt that you needed to hear it with everything you were going through with Will and shit. Originally, I wanted to sing you something else, but the conversation we had over dinner about your previous relationship caused me to change my mind."

"What song did you want to sing at first?"

He looked into my eyes and smiled. "You promise not to laugh if I sing it for you now?"

I shook my head, and he kissed my forehead. "Okay."

Toby began to play a melody that I think I'd heard before, but I couldn't quite place the song yet.

"Why do birds suddenly appear every time you are near? Just like me, they long to be close to you."

He looked at me and smiled and then nodded his head
to someone in the corner. Halo came from behind a huge
floral arrangement and began to sing as well.

"*Why do stars fall down from the sky every time you
walk by?*"

Her voice was beautiful, and she looked beautiful too.
Dressed in a satin salmon pink cocktail dress that stopped
just above her knees, she walked closer to the piano in her
gold Giuseppe heels and stood next to the curve in the
baby grand. Her eyes trained on mine as she continued to
serenade me with Tamia's part of the song "Close to You."

Halo and I weren't the best of friends, but after getting to know her during the studio sessions she had with
Toby and talking to her while she and I would have dinner with our men, I was becoming pretty fond of the girl.
Especially after she finally kicked Storm out of the picture. After finding out how her former best friend used
her phone to send Toby the photo of Will and me at
the airport, she'd had enough. It also helped that Toby
threatened not to work with her if she did keep Storm
around. Crazy how when you get rid of the negative shit
in your life, good things start to happen for you.

Speaking of good things . . . My attention turned back
to my handsome fiancé, who was now standing up from
his seat next to me and allowing another man who took
over playing the piano to sit in his place. While the new
dude and Halo continued with the song, Toby took my
hand in his and pulled me into his arms. My body melted
into his as we swayed back and forth under the beautiful
arch. Closing my eyes, I laid my head on Toby's chest and
just relished this moment. Our moment.

"*If only for a minute, I'd settle for an hour. And if you
could stay . . . Just for one day . . . That would make me
so . . .*"

Toby sang in my ear, causing a shiver down my spine.
Placing his hand under my chin, he lifted my face to his

and kissed my lips. "Do you remember that night we were in New York, and you told me that you would marry me anytime and anywhere?"

I nodded my head, remembering the conversation we had after we woke up during the middle of the night and had another round of sex. It was after Toby told me about the money he was saving up to give me as a gift for our first anniversary. After expressing to him that I would marry him with only a dollar to our name and one pot to piss in, I hoped he understood that I meant that. When Toby and I got together, I was at a very low point in my life. I had given up on finding true love in a sense, but he changed all of that for me by just being him—by just being there for me. So, hell yeah, I would marry Toby today, even if he lost every penny he had in the bank. He would still have me.

"I remember. Now, what about it?" I asked as Halo and the guy who I now know as Brandon continued to sing their duet.

"What about right now? In front of your family and all of your friends?"

"But all of my fam—" I started to say but got cut off when the door to the small, intimate room opened and everyone who was at my bridal brunch walked in, followed by a few faces that I knew and was just as happy to see. Aspen and her grandmother were dressed in their beautiful pink dresses. Cairo, Finesse, Beano, and several more fellas just as handsome as them rounded out the small group that stood around Toby and me . . . Smiles on everyone's faces.

My mother, who was in the back, slowly walked to the front when the crowd divided, a more sober-looking LaLa holding her hand.

"Toby—"

"Shhhhhhh . . ." He kissed my lips, covering my cry. "I know that you and your sister are still working on your relationship, but you would regret her not being able to share this day with you in the future. For the last month, she's been in a strict rehab. One where they can't have any outside communication with anyone until they've passed certain milestones in their recovery."

At that moment, LaLa made her way to me. Her eyes were downcast at first, but once she was within arm's length, she brought her hands to mine and placed a one-step stone in my hand. I looked into the eyes identical to mine and let the tears fall at the same time hers did. I pressed my forehead against hers, silently apologizing for not being there for her when she needed me the most. There were still a lot of things that we needed to work on like Toby said, but I couldn't deny that I was happy she was there.

Sniffling could be heard throughout the room as everyone reacted to my and LaLa's touching moment. After one last squeeze to my hand, she walked back over to the rest of the family, pulling Aspen against her body and giving her a light hug.

I looked up into Toby's eyes, my heart fluttering like crazy, my soul emotionally connecting to his. This man was amazing, and I was so happy that he was mine.

After agreeing to marry him at that moment, we exchanged vows, exchanged rings, and consummated our union with a kiss that I'm sure gave everyone in that room a show. I had walked into Cai and Audri's restaurant a couple of hours ago as an engaged woman and was now celebrating with my closest family and friends as a married one.

"So, did I do good with this surprise wedding, Mrs. Wright?" Toby asked as he twirled me around and pulled me back into his arms, his hands circling my waist and cupping my ass.

"You did. And I'm so happy to be your wife finally."

"Oh, yeah?"

I nodded my head and kissed his lips.

"And how do you know what we have will last?"

My cheeks rose as a small smile curved on my lips. "Because *we* have the right kind of love."

"That we do. Just me . . . you."

I grabbed his hands from around my waist, placing his open palms on my belly. "And them."

Toby stopped dancing. His eyebrow dipped low, and his gaze went from my stomach to my face. "*Them?* Niecey . . . Are you telling me . . . Are you trying to tell me . . ."

"That I'm pregnant with twins." I finished his sentence and held up a couple of fingers. "Two months to be exact."

His eyes became misty as he pulled me into his arms and squeezed my body tight. "Thank you, baby. You just made me the happiest man in the world right now." I wiped the tear from his cheek, and he kissed the back of my hand. "I love you, Mrs. Wright."

"And I love you too, Mr. *Right*."

The End

Finally, right . . . LOL!

I hope you enjoyed this little story. Niecey and Toby can now be put to rest.

Anyhoo . . . I wanna THANK YOU for still rocking with your girl after putting out my first book. I think I'm getting a little better with this storytelling thing now.

Before I go, I wanna give some shout-outs to a few people:

Blake Karrington
Shantaé Montgomery-Knox
Nickey Mallory
Sylvia Campbell

Vhanessa Hanzy
Desiree Granger
Candace Mumford
JM Hart
These people have been a driving force for me. Y'all don't know how many times I wanted to give up and get over this writing thing. It was their words of inspiration and belief in my talent that I am still doing something I "sometimes" (LOL) love to do. Thank you, guys, from the bottom of my heart.

And to all of my Sister Wives, Thotties, and Book Baes (LOL) . . . I love y'all too.

Wanna keep in touch? Hit me anytime on any one of these social media platforms. I always respond:

Facebook
Reading Group: The Literary Rejects
Author Page: Genesis "She Writes" Woods
Personal Page: Genesys Woods
IG/Twitter/Website/Email
@iamgenesiswoods
www.genesiswoods.com
thebeginning616@gmail.com
YOU GUYS ROCK!

#ExpandYourMind #ReadABook
~Gen